What Comes of Eating Doughnuts With a Boy Who Plays Guitar

What Comes of Eating Doughnuts With a Boy Who Plays Guitar

Gem City Book One

Nicole Campbell

Copyright (C) 2015 Nicole Campbell
Layout design and Copyright (C) 2018 Creativia
Published 2018 by Creativia
Cover art by Taylor Cross
This book is a work of fiction. Names, characters, places, and incidents are the product of the author's imagination or are used fictitiously. Any resemblance to actual events, locales, or persons, living or dead, is purely coincidental.
All rights reserved. No part of this book may be reproduced or transmitted in any form or by any means, electronic or mechanical, including photocopying, recording, or by any information storage and retrieval system, without the author's permission.

For Melissa, the architect of the greatest summer adventures, and without whom the inspiration for this novel would not exist. Thanks for some of the best memories of my life.

Please visit NicoleCampbellBooks.com for a suggested playlist if you like to listen while you read. You may also search the book title on YouTube or Spotify.

♪ *"You Gotta Be" – Des'ree*

Prologue

After hitting the snooze button for the fourth time, Courtney heard her mom coming down the hallway. Her brain quickly assessed the room situation, and she knew that there was not enough time to shove all of the clothes from the floor into her closet before her mom would open the door and give her signature "frustrated sigh." She snapped her eyelids back together as the door creaked open softly.

"Courtney, do you know what time-" *sigh... yep, there it was.* "This room is disgusting! You're going to come home one day and find all of your clothes in the trash," her mother threatened. She opened one eye to see her mom, already dressed and with make-up on, looking annoyed. People loved to tell her they looked more like sisters. This pleased Mrs. Ross endlessly, but was more of an outright annoyance to Courtney.

Courtney brought her thoughts back to reality and did her best to put on an apologetic face.

"I'm sorry, Mom, I know. I got home late from work, and practice was killer yesterday. I swear I'll clean all of it up this weekend." Her arms protested as she stretched them over her head; she hadn't been lying about a rough practice. She was fairly certain she'd have tiny blue fibers from their tumbling mats embedded into her knees for the rest of her life. The fact that she could land her standing tuck no problem

What Comes of Eating Doughnuts With a Boy Who Plays Guitar

in her back yard and not at practice was a rapidly growing source of frustration.

"Yeah, yeah, I'll believe it when I see it," her mother replied, but Courtney knew by the half smile that she wasn't really mad anymore. "You really do need to get up though, you told me to remind you about your AB study thing this morning." Courtney's eyes now flew open and she leaped out of bed.

"A-P Mom, AP, not AB," she scolded. She frantically searched her room for the assigned uniform for the day. "Mom, where is my calendar? I don't remember which skirt I'm supposed to wear for tonight's game, and now I'm going to be late to study with Ben!" She took one look at her appearance in the mirror and gasped. It really didn't matter how many people told her she was lucky to have curly hair; on days like today, she knew it was a curse. Furiously, she attempted to tame it into a ponytail with her green ribbon. Looking up, she found her mom holding the aforementioned calendar, in addition to the correct white skirt for that night's basketball game.

"Have I mentioned to you lately that you're the best, coolest, youngest-looking mom in all the world?" Courtney gave an overly sheepish grin before grabbing the skirt and throwing on her uniform. Her socks may not have matched, and she may have had to eat her breakfast while doing her makeup in the car on the way to school, but she hoped she looked plenty cheery upon her arrival to campus. Glitter eye shadow could do that for a girl. One final appearance check against the reflection of her silver Mustang revealed that there was nothing stuck in her teeth. *Thank you*, she thought gratefully as she realized she appeared almost put-together.

She tried to remain calm and collected as she quickly flitted across campus to the library. Though she would never admit it for the fear of sounding nerdy, she liked that her cheer uniform matched the school décor as she hurried under the giant green and gold "Horizon Huskies" sign above the main entrance. It gave her a much-needed sense of belonging.

Ben already sat at a table in the media center, and it struck her that there was hardly a trace of the scrawny kid with the too-short pants after a mid-year growth spurt. She remembered being partnered with him for her first school project after she had moved to Scottsdale six years ago. She'd been pleasantly surprised at how well they worked together. They had nailed their presentation on Spain that year and had been electing to work together ever since.

"Hey, sorry I'm late. It seems like I can't catch up lately," she explained to him.

"No problem, beauty takes time, right? Or so I hear," Ben responded with a crooked smile. Courtney never knew how to take comments like that. She wavered back and forth between thinking he was complimenting her and being convinced that it was sarcasm. She decided on a light laugh before plopping down next to him.

"Here are my notes from the first half of the study guide Mrs. Wells gave us. I didn't think it was too bad, but I just want the AP tests to be over. Studying for this, plus Chem and Econ, is sucking the life out me." Courtney handed him the papers and tried to relax and determine where to rest her gaze. Looking people in the eye was a bit much for her, so she usually settled for the middle of their noses instead. She couldn't tell if she was anxious because she was around Ben, or if she was anxious because she was *her*. Fidgeting, she reached up to smooth her ponytail and tighten her bow.

"Yeah, I hear ya. After basketball is over, I'll feel better. Too much pressure." He shared this with a barely perceptible sigh. She was surprised he was being even this open with her. They had been in classes together since their introduction in the sixth grade, but they usually just kept things academic. She had always thought he was cute in a nice-guy sort of way, but that was even truer now that he had hit six foot something and filled out. She admired his unkempt auburn hair and warm brown eyes. *He has, like, actual arm definition now. When did that even happen? He looks like-* "When are you done with your season?" he asked as he interrupted the very important conversation she was having with herself.

What Comes of Eating Doughnuts With a Boy Who Plays Guitar

"Oh, um, well, we have nationals after basketball ends, and then cheer camp in June. We'll vote for captains then." Her mind wandered. She knew she would be the best choice for captain, but it would probably come down to who garnered the most attention, which wasn't always her- the struggle of social anxiety was real. Shaking herself out of her worry, she continued, "It's weird that we'll be seniors next year, right? It's like the last time for everything." Her finger found a purpose in pulling on a stray curl that was trying to escape. "I don't know. It's crazy how fast the last five years went by. It seems like we just met in Mrs. Vasquez's class- and you were still rocking the bowl cut," she teased him hesitantly.

"Way to go deep there, Ross," Ben said with a laugh. "You had to bring up the bowl cut, huh? You know it was cool then. We all had to be Bieber." He waved off the memory like it was painful. "Maybe we should actually go over our study guides before you take us too far down memory lane. I'm worried about what else you have stored up there." He playfully knocked on her head. Courtney resisted the urge to blush. Why did she always have to say the stupid things that were in her brain? *Develop a filter already,* she chided herself. She wished she could just laugh it off, but she knew this scene would be replaying in her head later like a movie reel. *Just let it go. Forget it, he didn't even mean anything by it. Be like Vanessa,* she thought. Her best friend always seemed to be so effortlessly confident, no matter who was around. She imagined that cute boys never called her by her last name like she was "one of the guys." *You need to take notes or something this summer.*

"I'll try to stay focused, sir." She saluted him with a sarcastic air. No need for him to know she was halfway down the rabbit hole of self-doubt. Throughout the rest of the study session, she just kept thinking that there were only nine more weeks until she could get out of town and attempt to do... something. Meet people? Have fun? *Don't set the bar too high now, Courtney. Great. Now you're talking to yourself in the third person and not even employing decent sarcasm. It's going to be a long day.*

♪ *"Back Home" – Andy Grammer*

One

The churning ball of dread in Courtney's stomach was finally *gone*. Finals were over, and she could actually inhale deeply. She took a few breaths just for good measure. She actually got up and put all of her clothes away willingly without waiting for her mom to call her on it. She felt like a bouncy ball in her excitement for her trip the next day.

"Hey, Court," she could hear her mom down the hall, "please don't forget, you need to call Vanessa to confirm your flight-" Her mom stood in her doorway, wide-eyed, breaking into a grin. "I can see the carpet!" she exclaimed. "Oh, my lovely Berber. I've missed you." This statement was followed by some god-awful dance from the seventies.

"Okay, okay, okay, Mom, I get it. No need to break into a disco. It's clean. Amazing what I can do when I'm not at school, practice, and work all day, huh?" Courtney asked simply.

"You're right. You deserve this summer off. I can't believe you're going to be a senior. I'm going to have to start telling people I had you when I was fourteen," she joked.

"Ha. Ha. Ha," Courtney replied dryly.

"So what would the future Husky Cheer Captain like for breakfast this morning? Don't get the wrong idea, I'm not going to cook, but anywhere you wanna go can be arranged. Far be it for me to deny the cheer queen her last breakfast before her departure." Her mom's eyes sparkled with all of the vicarious thrill she got out of her daughter's cheerleading accomplishments.

"Oh my god, give it a rest, woman!" Courtney said in a half-serious tone. "I still can't believe they voted for me. I keep thinking they'll replace me while I'm on vacation or something."

"*You* give it a rest. You've earned everything that you've gotten, so just relax already. Your dad and I are so proud of you. Let's go eat something ridiculous and then you can pack for your trip."

"Well, when you put it that way, I guess I can't say no."

While sitting at breakfast, waiting for the coma-inducing pastry, Courtney's phone rang. She saw the picture of her too-adorable best friend pop up on the screen.

"Mom, it's Vanessa, I gotta take this." She headed outside of the restaurant. "Girl! What are you doing?" she practically squealed as she picked up the phone.

"Only planning your party for tomorrow night, you know, nothing too exciting." Vanessa was known for keeping a rather jam-packed social calendar in her small-town world of Gem City, Ohio.

"I'm sorry, my *what* now?" Courtney said.

"Whatever. You have been stressed and negative and BLAH for too long. Time is up, girl, and we're gonna get a little crazy. We are having a party, and I have invited everyone, well, everyone good, anyway. Some people you'll remember from before you moved, but we've gotten some new lovelies in town lately. Plus, Luke is inviting a bunch of guys from the basketball team. There will be no shortage of selection," Vanessa insisted. Courtney's heart rate jumped which annoyed her. This was what she was hoping for- a summer to relax and be herself. It was so stupid that her stomach turned in knots thinking of all of those people showing up to see *her*. "Helloooooooo? Are you alive over there? I know you too well- quit with your 'social anxiety' bullshit and get excited."

Courtney laughed, her stress easing. "Ah, you do know me. Okay," she breathed, "I'm just going to be excited, you're right. I look forward to the plethora of 'pretties' that you speak of."

"While we're at it, stop speaking like Abe Lincoln, it's bringing me down from my summer high. No SAT vocab allowed. We will talk like cavemen if we have to. Got it?" Vanessa demanded.

"Really? Abe Lincoln?" Courtney couldn't help but grin when talking to her best friend. "Well, you're the boss, so yes, ma'am. Or should I just grunt at you as a response from now on?"

"That's better, thank you! Hey, Luke is calling me obsessively on the other line, so I'm gonna go, but text me your flight info again and I will see you tomorrow!" Vanessa practically sang into the phone.

"You got it, tell Luke I said 'hi,' and that I can't wait to meet him." Courtney had missed this. Vanessa was the one she could always count on to bring her out of her shell and really *get* her. She couldn't believe she was going to spend an entire month in her old hometown. It had been several years since she'd been back- not since she'd gotten rid of the braces and learned how to -sort of- control her curly tresses. There was a cautious optimism in the air about the prospect of a summer adventure. She walked back into the restaurant and sat down in front of the largest cinnamon roll she had ever seen and laughed. She and her mom clinked their forks together. "Cheers!" they cried before devouring a week's worth of calories.

She took advantage of the sugar high to pack her bags, snacks, and books for the plane and to pick out an outfit for the party being thrown in her honor. *In my honor,* she thought, *like I'm the Queen of freaking England.* At which point she curtseyed in the mirror and practiced her British accent. *And you seriously have to wonder why the boys are not knocking down your door for a date? You. Are. A. Nerd.*

It took everything she had to get through dinner and make herself go to sleep. It was as though it were Christmas Eve and she was a five year old waiting for Santa. *Vanessa would not be pleased to be likened to an old fat man.* Finally, she nodded off with thoughts of going back to the one place that she could call home.

♪ *"This Is How We Roll" – Florida Georgia Line*
"Famous In a Small Town" – Miranda Lambert

Two

Courtney was quite literally sitting on the edge of her seat, waiting for the plane to touch down. The flight had seemed endless, and she was tired of lemon-lime soda and peanuts. She just wanted to see Vanessa and have fun without worrying about school or work or cheerleading or anything. In an attempt to calm down, she visualized herself leaving the worried, anxious, self-conscious version of Courtney Ross on the plane and walking into the airport a more relaxed and confident copy. *Nice deep breaths, you can do this*, she coached inwardly. *Although, I'm guessing most teenagers don't have to meditate to convince themselves to have fun.* Her mouth inadvertently turned into a frown at the thought.

Finally, the plane touched down and the seatbelt sign went off. She practically tackled the woman sitting next to her, albeit apologetically, to get her bag and run off of the aircraft. Dodging people and suitcases, she hurried down to baggage claim. She breathed in deep as she saw a head of shiny blonde hair atop a girl with golden tanned skin and legs for days in her cut-off shorts. "V!" she shouted.

"Court!" Vanessa responded, whipping her hair around to take in the sight of her best friend. "Shut UP! You look freaking amazing," she exclaimed as she looked Courtney up and down.

"Stop it, I do not. You look like a hot girl out of a country song in those shorts."

"Oh yeah, baby, this is how I roll." Vanessa wiggled her butt, making several of the grown men standing nearby glance over. "Speaking of which, let's grab your bag and I can show you my new ride." She had a sparkle in her blue eyes. Courtney couldn't believe what she was seeing when they finally got to the parking garage, but it was a brand spanking new red Camaro. She looked at Vanessa, who chivalrously opened the passenger door for her. "Our chariot awaits." Courtney slid across the soft tan leather seat and inhaled the new car smell.

"*This* is what we will be driving around in all summer? This car is hella cool!" Courtney was gushing, though she secretly felt guilty, like she was cheating on her little Mustang. "You must be cruising around like small-town royalty in this thing."

"Oh, you have no idea. All the guys are so jealous; it has become hard for me to tell if they are hitting on me or just trying to get into my car." Vanessa laughed, swept her long sun-kissed hair into a high ponytail, and plopped her sunglasses onto her face. "Ready to ride?" Courtney just smiled, put on her own shades, and felt more at ease than she had in a long time. As she let the heavy summer air fill her lungs, she realized this was exactly what she had been waiting for.

* * *

Courtney made Vanessa drive her the long way through town so she could reacquaint herself with the place she had called home for so long. They drove past the park, their elementary school, and then finally Courtney's old house. It was a little yellow Victorian in the middle of "downtown," which was a hilarious term now that she lived outside of Phoenix. She missed its creaking hardwood, wide front porch, and the little balcony off of her room. She knew that moving to Scottsdale wasn't the worst thing in the world, and that her dad really liked his job there despite the constant traveling, but it was hard not to wish that things hadn't changed. Vanessa pulled her quickly off of memory lane, and insisted they shop for party supplies. Courtney naively envisioned streamers and balloons for a moment, until she remembered whom she was dealing with. Courtney never drank much at any of the parties she actually dragged herself to back at home, but she was existing in Vanessa's world now. She imagined some sort of brightly colored beverages with cheesy names would be in her near future. They ran quickly through the tiny store and headed to Vanessa's to set up.

"Luke is coming over early to help, so you will get to meet him then," Vanessa bubbled excitedly as they walked into her house. The main floor looked the same as it always had. There were a lot of roosters. Like, a *lot* of roosters. Mrs. Roberts' obsession made Courtney's lips stretch out in a smile.

"So tell me more about him. I need to satisfy my protective instinct and make sure he's good enough for you."

"Hmmmm, well, when he gets here you'll see that he's freaking hot, though he knows it, so I try not to remind him too often," Vanessa said as she winked at her. "And he can actually hold a decent conversation, so bonus points for that, and most of the time he likes me slightly more than I like him, so I win. Usually," she finished, smiling.

"Oh my god, you *love* him! You talk a good game, friend, but you can drop the act." Courtney laughed knowingly.

"Eh, stick it." Vanessa's words held a bite as usual, but Courtney could see her smiling as she unpacked their purchases. Vanessa's house was somewhat of an anomaly. It was a newly built tri-level, but had a typical country feel to the main floor. Vanessa was appalled by the roosters that Courtney found so endearing. Her parents had allowed her the entire walkout basement to herself for a "hang out space," as they called it, and had given her quite a generous budget to furnish it how she wanted. It was like entering a different universe down there. Courtney wanted to buy a sign for it that said "We're Not In Kansas Anymore." Vanessa had gone for a very boho feel (save for the giant flat screen on the wall). It was inviting, with low lying couches in varying degrees of white, completed with a seemingly endless array of colored beaded pillows. It made Courtney want to sink into one and never get out. The low light emanating from the collection of Moroccan lanterns gave a sense of relaxation she hadn't managed in a while. She made a mental note to re-think her very contemporary room design when she returned home.

"V... you surprise me sometimes," Courtney said, slowly taking it all in.

"Why? Because I'm so awesome?" Vanessa answered, midway through creating a playlist for that night's festivities.

"This is just not the party pad of a girl living in small-town Ohio. It's amazing. Breathtaking, even."

Vanessa looked at her seriously, which was rare, for a moment. "Do you really like it? Luke makes fun of me for being so particular, but I don't know. I just…"

"It's perfect, and it's you. I want you to help me decorate my room."

"Well, for a small fee, of course." *Moment over.* Vanessa was back to her old self. Courtney threw one of the beaded pillows at her head and giggled. Her brain kept trying to remind her to be nervous about the party, but she forced it to be quiet by vacuuming the room and thinking about her outfit. She made her friend help lug two suitcases up the stairs to the bedroom on the second story. It was covered in photos, clothing, and pieces of cheer uniforms, much like Courtney's own room.

"I'll get around to cleaning this up. I never come in here except to sleep. I wish my parents would just let me move into one of the guest bedrooms in the basement," Vanessa complained.

"Yeah, they're not that dumb. You already sneak out enough as it is from up here. If they gave you the basement, you might as well have your own apartment."

"Now there's an idea." Vanessa smiled as she started throwing clothes into her hamper and making her bed.

"Hey, V?" Courtney asked seriously. "Can you look at the outfit I have for tonight and be brutally honest about it?"

"Have I ever been anything but?" she replied as she bounced over. "Oh, no, no, no, NO, no. And then also no."

"What? What could possibly be that wrong with a denim skirt and white t-shirt? I thought that's what you small-town folk wore to your tailgate parties and what not," Courtney replied, slightly hurt by Vanessa's reaction.

"Girl- You are freaking hot. And look at this skirt; it's down to your *knees*? Are you a nun? Get me some scissors, STAT. I am making this over. And the t-shirt? No. You will wear…" she faded out as she went into the laundry room down the hall and rummaged through her clean clothes, "this!" she shouted and held up a red and white striped halter so small it looked like it came from the toddler section. Courtney's stomach tightened. The thought of wearing something that skimpy made her want to hyperventilate. She instinctively reached for the safe white t-shirt.

"Nope." Vanessa snatched it out of her hands. "You are going to rock this party if it kills me. Honestly, Court, a knee-length skirt? Do you even know who I am?" she continued, laughing as she cut an alarming amount of fabric off of the jean skirt. Courtney had to practice some deep breathing to accept that this was happening. She took her scissor-fashioned skirt and halter-top into the bathroom to get dressed and have a heart attack in peace. *You can do this,* she thought, *you can be confident and flirty and wear this incredibly small outfit and not worry what anyone is thinking. Just think of it as a cheer uniform.* Except when she was in uniform, there were twenty other girls dressed exactly the same. Pushing that thought out of her head, she repeated the affirmations until at least part of her believed them. Finishing her make-up, she heard a male voice downstairs calling for Vanessa. She took one last look in the mirror, fluffed her long curly mane, and went to meet the famous Luke.

♪ *"Summer Girls"* – LFO
"Raise Your Glass" – Pink
"Call Me Maybe" – Carly Rae Jepsen
"Geronimo" – Sheppard
"Everything to Everyone" – Everclear

Three

Courtney ran quickly down the stairs, but pulled back as she looked up and realized she'd just walked in on Vanessa and Luke in a rather tangled-up moment. Seeing them revived a familiar twisting sensation in her stomach that appeared whenever she thought about the lack of romantic interests in her life.

"Inappropriate!" Courtney yelled as she lightheartedly covered her face with her hands. *I would even take interests of a non-romantic nature. Nerdy mathlete interests.* She tried to picture the guys on the academic decathlon team, but it wasn't helping. The two broke apart slowly, and Courtney reached out her hand. "Luke, I presume?" Unexpectedly, Luke bypassed her hand and picked her up in a bear hug.

"Save your handshake for somebody else," Luke said as he put her down, grinning. "I listen to Vanessa go on about you all the time, so we are already friends. And we hug."

Courtney laughed. "Well, aren't you friendly?" She finally had a second to take in the sight of him, and was in awe of her best friend's taste. Tall, with a body out of an Abercrombie ad, but a sweet face with an easy smile that made her immediately feel comfortable. He had soft brown hair that curled just right at the ends to make him look like he did it on purpose, with striking green eyes and impossibly perfect teeth. She suddenly realized she'd probably been staring at him and tried to cover by looking around the room.

"Yeah, I know I'm a catch, stare all you want," Luke declared, totally calling her out and playfully showing off his six pack in lifting up his shirt. Courtney immediately turned red and looked to Vanessa for help, but Luke cut her off. "Dude, you gotta lighten up, I'm just messing with you. Come, eat, be merry. It's almost party time." He busted out a surprisingly good interpretation of the Roger Rabbit, at which point Vanessa joined in.

"Nice moves," Courtney complimented, feeling relieved. "I will take you up on the 'eat' part, though. All I've had today is plane food." The three went upstairs to grab some snacks before anyone else arrived. Courtney felt Luke's eyes on her while she was eating some goldfish and glanced up. "Yes?"

Luke just smiled and looked at Vanessa. "You're totally right, Fisher is gonna flip over her." Vanessa immediately shot daggers at him with her eyes. "Umm, I mean, what? Like, these crackers are amazing, agreed? Who would have thought to make crackers look like fish? Am I right?" His eyes were looking anywhere but at Courtney or Vanessa now.

"Ummmm, say what? What is a Fisher?" Her heart started pounding in its usual anxious way.

"Okay, girl, chill. I know where your head's at, and it doesn't need to be. His name is Ethan Fisher, and I just *casually* mentioned how awesome you are. He seemed interested. That's it. It is not the crisis you are imagining in your warped little mind right now. You do not need to access the nuclear codes. Breathe," Vanessa explained, "and try to tell me you don't feel just a little bit excited about our boy Ethan. And his washboard abs. In case I didn't mention that part before." She finished that sentence with a gleam in her eye.

"Yeah, V, I'm standing right here," Luke responded.

"Oh shut up, you know I like yours better," she chastised, lovingly patting his midsection.

Courtney glared at Vanessa suspiciously. " 'Casually,' huh?" she asked in an unbelieving tone. There was a moment where Courtney contemplated whether there was any possible scenario in which she would not give in to Vanessa in the end. There wasn't. "Whatever, you win. I will wear this crazy outfit, and I will be cool about this 'Fisher' situation." She knew there was no use in arguing with Vanessa anyway. Courtney was determined to at least fake the confidence she wanted to portray until it actually showed up.

"Who are you and what have you done with my best friend?" Vanessa replied with a deadpan expression. Courtney stuck her tongue out and Vanessa winked at her. "Very mature," she said as they busied themselves with last minute party preparations.

"Okay, Courtney. Can't I call you Court? Maybe Little C?" Courtney narrowed her eyes at him slightly. *No one will be calling me 'Little C.'* "Okay, then, Courtney it is. I know that we just met and all, but I am telling you, as your newfound friend, you need to have one Jell-O-shot before everyone gets here. If you don't want one, it's fine, this isn't like an after-school-special on peer pressure, but I am telling you that you need to chillax," Luke said as if he were giving her a pep talk before the big game. Were her nerves that obvious? She had thought she was playing it cool. *Dammit.*

"Chillax is not a word. But all right, one, let's go." He didn't hesitate and put the small cup in her hand. "Bottoms up," she toasted more confidently than she felt and downed the jiggly green elixir.

"Woot!" Luke shouted. "Now we're gonna have ourselves a good time!" As if on cue, the doorbell rang, and Courtney suddenly felt glad she had listened to him.

Over the next half hour or so, she felt surrounded by a blur of faces and names. She was happy to see a few familiar ones, but truth be told, Vanessa was the only person she had stayed close to after having left Gem. She said a lot of "hellos" and maybe snuck another Jell-O shooter. Or three.

What Comes of Eating Doughnuts With a Boy Who Plays Guitar

Finally feeling okay walking around in her best-friend-approved outfit, she saw V across the room talking to someone. When Vanessa caught her eye and smiled knowingly, Courtney knew she was chatting with this Ethan character. She was out of his eye-line for the moment, so she took advantage of the opportunity to size him up. Tall, dark, and freaking hot? Yes. He had perfectly messy dark hair and sun-kissed skin. *What is with all of these Ohioans being darker than me? I live in an actual desert,* she thought. The fitted off-white shirt made his dark good looks that much more inviting. *So far, so good.* She noticed a wide silver ring on his finger, which drew her attention to his hands, which happened to be holding a guitar. *Oh, I. Am. In. Trouble,* she knew instantly. She was feeling some liquid courage, so her stomach only did a small flip when Vanessa motioned for her to come over.

As she paraded up, Ethan turned to make room for her. Courtney's eyes glanced up at him. *Be cool, be cool, be cool,* she repeated the mantra in her head.

"Ethan Fisher, this is my very best friend Courtney Ross. Court, this is Ethan. He just moved to Gem last year," Vanessa said, introducing them.

"Hey!" Courtney said, maybe just a tad too loudly. "Nice to meet you. I've heard a lot about you. Well, you and your abs," she blurted out. *OHMYGOD, did I just say that!?* She mentally upbraided herself. Ethan looked unsure for just a moment, but broke out into a smirk, the kind that made him look like he knew something he shouldn't, and let out a genuine laugh.

"My abs, huh? Well, glad to know I'm appreciated for something," he joked as he patted his stomach. He looked at Courtney as if he was trying to make up his mind about her. "Speaking of my stomach- V, can I stash my guitar somewhere until later? I'm starving. Courtney, you wanna show me where the good food is?" He smiled effortlessly, and she started to swim in his deep brown eyes, forgetting to only look at the middle of his nose. Vanessa answered for her, thankfully saving her from another staring incident.

"She would be happy to. I'll take your guitar in the other room, love, thanks for bringing it." Vanessa was then pushing Courtney along. She followed after Ethan, but turned around to Vanessa and mouthed "OH MY GOD" before resuming her composure. She thought she heard Vanessa murmur something to the effect of "told you so," but the party was too loud to be sure.

They made it to the food set-up outside, and Courtney looked around. It appeared that Luke and Vanessa were quite adept at stocking beverages, but the food situation was lacking. A couple of sad-looking bowls of chips and veggie trays weren't super appetizing. "So, Courtney Ross, are you going to tell me where she keeps the real refreshments around here? Or are we going to dine on Doritos?" He gave her that dangerous smile again.

"I, um, yeah. Let's explore the kitchen, shall we?" Slowly regaining her focus, she led him upstairs. She was acutely aware of how short her skirt was with him walking behind her on the steps, but forgot all about her worries as she felt his hand on the small of her back when they came to the main floor.

"Lead the way." He glanced around the kitchen for a moment. "Where are V's parents tonight, anyhow? Don't they usually put the kibosh on this type of thing?"

"Ah, yeah. They had a weekend planned in Historical Gatlinburg, but I kind of ruined the family trip. I couldn't get a flight in later this week for the same price, so they let V stay home to play hostess to me," she answered. "You're welcome." She liked the way he looked at her when she teased him. Even if it made her feel like vomiting. *Do not throw up, or so help me I will... do nothing. Be humiliated. Stop talking to yourself already.* "So, tell me something," she said as she hopped up on the counter to reach the high cabinet, "how do you feel about chocolate chip cookies and pizza rolls? That's totally classy, right?" Amidst her self-congratulations about her nonchalant and witty banter, she had forgotten about the hastily taken shots and lack of real food. And she almost fell off the counter. She attempted to catch her balance, but felt Ethan's hands at her hips, steadying her.

What Comes of Eating Doughnuts With a Boy Who Plays Guitar

"Okay, girly, maybe we let me handle the high shelves, all right?" He helped her down and she landed lightly on the floor. "You're like a hobbit," he said, marveling at her five-foot frame. She forgot to be nervous about her short skirt and if her top looked acceptable after almost falling. Her skin tingled where his hands had touched her.

"I think that's a fairly decent idea," she answered, breathing heavier than the circumstances called for. And then what he had just said dawned on her. "Waaaaiiiiit a minute. Did you seriously just refer to me as a hobbit? Like a small hairy-footed creature from the Shire? That's the first tiny fantastical being to come to mind... you couldn't have gone with, like, a fairy or a pixie or something else that sparkles?!" she demanded.

Surprisingly, he held his position. "No way. One, I think girl hobbits are sexy, personally. I mean, what's not to like? Short, cute, and they are probably awesome cooks too with all of those breakfasts and second dinners. Pixies and fairies are dainty. I get the feeling that you're way too kick-ass for that. Look at your arms, woman. I think you could probably take me in a fight. So yeah, hobbit it is. Or maybe I could call you like, 'bear claw'. Because, you know, roar, or girl power, or something. I don't know, now you're glaring at me and it's making me nervous," he finished, laughing.

Courtney paused to decide if she was offended or not. The word "sexy" threw her off. She replied, "I can assure you that you will not be calling me a bear claw. That makes me sound like a doughnut. But I think on your way to digging a hole, you sort of complimented me, so I'll let it slide. Watch yourself, though, because I probably could take you in a fight." She was *flirting* with him. Like actual flirting. She had no idea if it was the alcohol or what had gotten into her, but she was enjoying whomever this person was who had taken over her brain.

Soon he handed her a plate of pizza rolls and cookies as planned, though she was no longer hungry. He sat down on a barstool, and she hopped up to sit on the counter. She couldn't take her eyes off him, or forget how it felt when he touched her. They chatted easily about school, and about Luke and Vanessa, and about his band. Ethan was the lead guitarist and singer for a band called Tin Roof.

"Well, I wanna hear you play. You brought your guitar tonight, right?" Courtney asked him.

"I did," he answered confidently. "I'm sure once they have the bonfire going out back I'll get around to playing some acoustic stuff. You have any requests?"

"Ummm, well, that's a difficult question."

"Why, what kind of music do you like?"

"Would you prefer the list by genre or decade?"

"Okay, I'll bite. Let's go by decade." The way his eyebrows moved together made him actually seem interested. There was a distinct possibility she was about to forget the name of every band she'd ever listened to.

"Well, my dad is all about the 70s, so even though it's not my favorite decade, I've gotta have love for, like, Eric Clapton, Queen, The Eagles, The Doobie Brothers, some Fleetwood Mac, and a little Skynyrd. I'm not a huge Beatles fan, though." She looked up to see if he was following.

"I'm listening." A surprised expression crossed his face.

"You asked for it. My mom is an 80s super-freak, so from that I have an attachment to really any hair band ballads, The Bangles, old school Whitney and Mariah, pretty much anything early Jackson- Michael or Janet, Wilson and Phillips, some Duran Duran, and well, Salt-N-Pepa, because who doesn't love 'Shoop'?" she insisted.

"Who indeed," Ethan agreed, his eyes sparkling. "I think I can rock a hair band ballad or two. But first, I gotta hear your list for the 90s." He said it almost as a challenge, but she was ready.

"Ok, I confess that I'm sort of a 90s junkie. Well, and into the early 2000s, I guess. In what other decade could you listen to The Fresh Prince and Jazzy Jeff, Nirvana, Blink 182, Oasis, and The Spice Girls and still be current? The 90s are like my musical holy-land. I know that sounds lame, but I'll try to narrow it down for you. So, you've got Radiohead, Everclear, Sublime, Matchbox Twenty, The Wallflowers,

What Comes of Eating Doughnuts With a Boy Who Plays Guitar

Train- for sure- Fiona Apple, Bush, and by proxy No Doubt, Third Eye Blind, Counting Crows, John Mayer, and then also some more John Mayer, because well, I love him… I could really go on for a while."

"You're a fan of that 'Wonderland' song of his then? That's definitely a fun track," he grinned. She ran her tongue over the backs of her teeth, knowing exactly what he was doing. She had to take a breath, not used to anyone hitting on her quite that overtly. Or really at all. Certain her face was betraying her with an unmistakable shade of red across her cheeks, she resolved to move on without letting him know his effect. "It's a good song," was all she gave him back. "I also loved Britney's first album; it was beautiful bubblegum pop. Destiny's Child, without a doubt. I love me some Hanson, 98 Degrees, The Backstreet Boys, really, any member of the boy band phenomenon. However, you will also find on my perfect playlist a little Limp Bizkit, Chili Peppers, Something Corporate, Taking Back Sunday, and the Phunk Junkeez." She finally stopped, now all too aware that her buzz had made her let out even more words than usual, and she hadn't even been watching his expressions to see if she should shut up. *Well… just be prepared for him to suddenly have somewhere else to be.* She swallowed and waited.

"Ok, so you're a fan of the 90s, then," he laughed. "I gotta say there were a couple in there that I'd forgotten about. And some I wish I had. I'm not a big fan of the emo-pop-punk invasion. Mediocre vocals and not enough bass, but maybe that's just me."

"Aww, but you'd make such a cute emo boy with your long hair," she teased him, ruffling his mane. He playfully swatted her away and restored it back to its previous state. "And I get that, but I have to appreciate the genre for all those hot boys putting their feelings out there." He was still hanging around, and that was enough to allow herself one deep breath.

"Fair enough," he let up, shaking his head. "I see myself as casting a pretty wide musical net too, but you may give me a run for my money. I do feel like you left out a few. I mean, we're talking Pearl Jam, Smashing Pumpkins, Stone Temple Pilots, old school Green Day, the Gin Blossoms-"

"Yes! The Gin Blossoms, absolutely."

"And, I know it may be uncool to say, but John Mayer's Continuum album was pretty sweet, I'll give you that."

"Well, your secret's safe with me, but yeah, the guitar on that album was freaking awesome."

Ethan cocked his head at her.

"What?" she asked.

"I just am having a really hard time believing that I'm having this conversation with a miniature cheerleader from Phoenix, that's all. Do I even want to ask you about more recent stuff?"

She narrowed her eyes at him because of the "miniature" comment. "Ay, well, it changes almost daily, but right now I'm very into anything Mumford and Sons puts out, The Avett Brothers, Ed Sheeran. I'm always down for a little Top 40 just to stay current," she continued. "Also, because I'm a cheerleader, in a perfectly normal size, I might add, it's mandated that I love Taylor Swift. And I do. Like, I love her. I think she's a goddess who walks among us."

Ethan cracked a smile as well. "You have very, ah, unique taste."

"Is that your way of telling me I'm weird and judging my musical selections while trying to sound nice?"

"Not at all. I will say that I didn't expect such a variety upon my first impression of you- I was kind of thinking you would spout off a list of American Idol winners, but I am pleasantly surprised to be wrong," he admitted.

"Amateur," she teased him, swinging her legs slightly as she sat on the counter. She was getting a kick out of talking to him about music. There weren't many people who shared her interest in the older stuff she'd named.

"Well, I suppose I deserve that. So is that it, then?" he asked.

"Well, that and country," she explained, feeling nervous that he would be internally criticizing her confession. Ethan raised one eyebrow. "Don't judge me! It takes me back to my small town roots. Girls in cut-off jeans and dirt roads and all that," she said as she gestured to her own ensemble.

"Well, I can't say I hate the cut-off jeans. I'll see what I can do to fulfill at least one of those requests," he answered with a telling smile. She was learning that this look made her forget to breathe normally. "Come on then, new girl, let's go see if you approve of my musical talents. I can't disappoint the bear claw." He stood up and held out his hand for her. She grabbed it and hopped off of the counter, feeling flustered again at his skin on her skin.

She regained her self-control enough to form words. "Sounds good, however, I technically lived in this town before you did, so if anything, you're the new boy." She looked down briefly to smooth her skirt.

Ethan quickly pulled her toward him, making her suck in a breath, and his hands were suddenly very low on her back. She looked up to find him smiling, eyebrows raised. "Um, the new *boy?*" he questioned.

His face with that jawline, and that hair, and those lips, was just so close that Courtney had a difficult time even remembering the English language. "Um, well, figure of speech and all that," she stammered back.

"Well." He smiled as he pulled her even closer. Her hands landed on his biceps and she risked a glance up at him. He bent down even further to say slowly in her ear, "I prefer to think of myself as more of a man than a boy, you know?" She could smell his soap, his spearmint gum, and a hint of cologne. Oxygen was overrated anyway. Who needed to breathe? All she could think about were Ethan's lips finding hers.

"I think I could get on board with that train of thought." Her hands found their way up his arms to the back of his neck, and her fingers tangled in with his hair. *His hair is so much shinier than mine. I wonder what kind of product he uses. This is not important right now, Courtney.*

"Good," he said as his nose grazed hers. She closed her eyes, her entire body tingling with anticipation. Her toes pointed as she leaned in to meet him.

"Dude, Ethan! Where the hell have youuuuuu-oops!" Luke nearly shouted when he got to the top of the stairs and walked right into their moment, breaking the spell. Ethan stepped back, but wove his fingers together with Courtney's as if to acknowledge their closeness from only seconds ago.

"Luke! Do you have, like, special spidey-senses for when the worst possible time is to do something?" Ethan asked with a hint of real frustration. Luke looked sheepish but recovered quickly.

"Why yes, yes, I do. I was bitten by a radioactive clock when I was younger, and now I bear the curse of bad timing. I'm very self-conscious about it, so maybe you just don't bring it up in front of my new friend here. Thankfully I don't have to mess with the webs like that Peter Parker dude." It was clear from his laughter he was very proud of his joke. Courtney and Ethan couldn't help but laugh along with their eye-rolls. "Now come on, the party-goers are getting restless down there. They want some rock star action, man. Vanessa is already getting the bonfire started, so grab your guitar."

Courtney tried to let her disappointment go about the hottest lack-of-kiss that ever existed. Ethan looked at her as if for approval. She inhaled. "Well, if there is a promise of s'mores, then I'm not sure what we're doing still standing here." Luke looked happy about her unspoken forgiveness, and Ethan squeezed her hand and led her towards the stairs.

Courtney sought out Vanessa while Luke and Ethan went to get his guitar. She needed a minute to fill her in on what had just happened, and perhaps bow at her feet for *casually* setting things in motion with Ethan.

"Hey, V, need some help?" she asked as she came across her friend trying to light the collection of sticks and grasses. She was thankful not many people were outside yet.

"Nah, I'm good," Vanessa said, turning around to greet her. "Annnnd apparently so are you!" she commented, looking at Courtney's smile and flushed appearance. "You've been upstairs a while, girl, so spill. Now. Please tell me there was heavy breathing involved."

Courtney flushed even more. "Well, I might have been the only one with a breathing problem, but for the love of all that is holy, he is beautiful. You could have given me a warning!"

"And have you flipping out before he even got here? No way. He is super hot, though, right? I did good," Vanessa said, literally patting herself on the back. "So tell me what happened already."

"Well, there's not a whole lot to tell due to Luke's most untimely appearance," Courtney replied with a sour look, "but the flirting was intense."

"Damn it! I told Luke to leave you guys alone! I will kill him for you if you want." Vanessa looked positively annoyed, and Courtney almost felt bad for Luke, despite her own disappointment.

"I don't think the situation calls for murder just yet, but I appreciate your solidarity, sister." Courtney grinned. "Am I all red and splotchy? I feel red and splotchy. I need to, like, meditate or strike a downward facing dog pose or whatever that yoga thing is that famous people do."

Vanessa burst out laughing. "Why don't you just go mention wanting to do a 'downward facing dog' to Fisher? I think his eyes might pop out, and I wanna watch." Courtney realized the implication and cracked up along with her. After the giggles subsided, Vanessa looked at Courtney with her 'stern best friend' face. "Courtney Ross, you need to listen to me, seriously. You are freaking adorable, you're going to be a varsity cheer captain, you're hella smart, and you have a whole 'city girl' thing going for you in this town. Ethan is awesome, but so are you, so go over there and make him work for it," she said, as she glanced towards the basement door. Luke, Ethan, and several other people were making their way outside for the bonfire.

"Good talk, coach," Courtney said, feeling grateful for her friend, even if she had no idea how to follow through with her advice. She tried repeating what Vanessa had said in her mind as she walked towards the boys to grab a seat. As she moved past Ethan, she felt him grab her hand and pull her back. "You are sitting next to me, bear claw," he teased. "You might need to use your strength to protect Luke from me when I realize the full extent of my anger for his shitty timing." Ethan shot Luke a definite look. Courtney's pulse quickened at his casual reference to their almost-moment. She also became curious as to what the conversation had sounded like when he and Luke had gone to look for his guitar. She made a mental note to attempt to pump Luke for information later.

"Try me, bro. I could take both of you and not even spill my drink," Luke bragged, flexing his admittedly impressive biceps. He opened a beer and put one in Courtney's hand as well. She debated opening it, but decided to 'do as the Romans do', and all that. She took a sip and refocused her attention on Ethan. He was tuning his guitar, his hair falling in his eyes, and she smiled inwardly at the thought of running her fingers through it. She must have gotten a little lost in that particular fantasy, because upon coming back to reality, he was done tuning and was staring at her, grinning.

"Whatcha thinkin' about there? Anything I might find of interest?" he teased, running his thumb along his bottom lip, almost making her lose all sense of propriety again.

She willed her face not to blush. "Well, that depends on what you find interesting, I suppose. Maybe I was thinking about the Quadratic Equation, you don't know," she responded evenly. "So, let's hear these rock star skills everyone keeps talking about. Did you consider my myriad of requests?"

"You could say that." He started strumming a few chords, and before long, she recognized one of her all time favorite songs by Third Eye Blind, "How's It Going to Be."

She had never heard it played live before and didn't know if she could ever listen to it the same way again. Ethan didn't just play it; he owned it. His voice had exactly the right amount of roughness in it to draw her in. Every so often, he would look up and give her that smirk he had going for him, and Courtney fully understood why some women became groupies. Having him sing something specifically for her was intoxicating. She vaguely noticed other girls staring at him with the same sort of intensity, and immediately felt possessive. She tried not to falter in her newly discovered confidence, and decided to ignore the lustful glances directed towards him. He finished her song and took a few more requests while everyone ate s'mores and enjoyed the cooler temperature now that the sun had been down for a while.

What Comes of Eating Doughnuts With a Boy Who Plays Guitar

Courtney had missed this. This town, this life. The lively crackle of the bonfire mirrored the electricity running through her. The atmosphere here was completely different from that of the Scottsdale parties she had let her friends drag her to. No one seemed to be trying to one-up anyone else here. Most of these people had known each other their whole lives, and those bonds were as clear as the laughter in the air. She inhaled deeply the smell of the smoke and let it out as she looked toward the sky. Sitting on a soft blanket, listening to Ethan play, and having Vanessa there to keep her grounded was exactly what she needed. She silently vowed to not only make the most of the summer, but to somehow find her way back to this place someday.

Ethan had just finished another song, one Courtney didn't recognize but liked anyway, when she thought she should show him that he wasn't even close to having her figured out yet, despite what his smirk suggested.

"I really liked that song, what was it?" She was feeling a pretty good buzz, enhanced by her own emotions.

"That one was my own. It's not perfect yet, but this is a pretty forgiving crowd, so I thought I'd try it out. You liked it?" He looked pleased. It was a good look for him.

"You wrote that? That's awesome. I would love to hear more of your stuff if you ever want to test it out on anyone. I used to write a lot of song lyrics, but most of them were just angsty teenage drivel. Lots of over-used metaphors, you know the type. But I do appreciate someone who can put the lyrics with the right sound. I've always struggled with that," she admitted. "Can I see your guitar?" She held out her hands. He looked warily at her.

"Sure. Do you want me to teach you some chords or something?"

"Nah, I got it." She sat back down with the guitar in her lap, and began to play "Everything to Everyone," by Everclear. She had a momentary worry that she wouldn't remember the whole song, but once she got going, that faded away. Several people sang along with the chorus, and she felt the high of performing. She didn't sing often because it was never perfect, never exactly how she wanted to sound, but that night she found she wasn't afraid at all. Was it because of Ethan, or because of her?

She finished and took a bow as she handed Ethan back his instrument. In finally looking at him, she saw that his knowing smirk had been replaced by one of shock and awe. Maybe even a little admiration. "So... um, you can sing- and play guitar, then?" he questioned, laughing slightly. "That was amazing. Great choice." He kept looking at her and shaking his head slightly. She felt validated in accomplishing the goal of showing him that there was more to Courtney Ross than simply being a neurotic cheerleader.

"Well, in the interest of full disclosure, I only know about five songs. I took guitar lessons for, like, six months last year and learned how to play some of my favorites, but I wasn't particularly good. So I quit. I know that sounds bad, but I just really dislike being average at things. So, I'm not like an actual musician or anything."

"Well, also in the interest of full-disclosure, I'm kind of glad. I had a worry that you might be a better musician than me, and I didn't know if my manhood could handle that after you called me a 'boy' earlier and everything," he joked. He set his guitar behind him and pulled her onto his lap. She tried to act like this was completely normal and she sat on cute musicians' laps all the time. In actuality, though, it was difficult to know whether or not her butt cheeks should rest to one side or the other or how to maintain any sense of posture. *Normal girls don't have this problem. I am certain they don't.* She found herself a bit dizzy, though unsure if that was from her buzz or his closeness.

She decided to lean against him for balance, and he noticed her goose bumps. He started rubbing her arms to try to warm her up, but that only made the situation worse. His large hands came to rest on her thighs, making Courtney's heart jump.

"Do you want to go inside? It is a little chilly out here, especially if you normally live in the desert, I would guess." He helped her up and interlaced their fingers before heading back into the basement. Courtney let him lead her, taking in the night sky and his hand in hers and the smell of the damp grass. *This is sort of beautiful.* She was brought out of her trance when she noticed Ethan looking at her. "Did you just tell me I was beautiful? Because if you're going to start using lines from *Twilight* to hit on me, I think it's time for you to go to sleep, bear claw."

"Oh my god, did I say that out loud?" she muttered. "Well, I said, *'this is beautiful,'* Mr. Conceited, but now that you mention it, you're not hideous," she recovered.

"Oh, wow, you are well versed in the art of flattery," he teased. "It is getting late, though. C'mon, walk me upstairs before I head home?" Courtney knew she looked disappointed. She wasn't ready for him to leave and the night to end but reluctantly took him up on the offer.

They made their way to the front of the house. She turned around to face Ethan, almost wanting to brace herself for the words she was about to let out. "Are you sure you can't stay for a bit?" In her mind this was the most brazen of acts, and waiting for him to answer was enough time for her to convince herself she'd misread every signal the entire night, and he was trying to figure out how to let her down easy. *Why did I ask that? That probably sounded... oh god, why did I ask him that?!*

Ethan ran one hand through his hair and breathed out through a clenched jaw. He shook his head at her and said, "Well, I can, yeah. I just... Well, I don't want to be *that* guy."

"What guy is that?" *Please don't say the guy who hooks up with the anxiety-ridden slut girl. Just say something else.*

"The guy you'll hate in the morning because we just met and, uh, you're a little drunk." He hesitated for a long moment. "I think you're sort of... cool? So I would rather I didn't mess things up this early in the game." He finished plainly, looking surprised at his own admission.

Her head was spinning a bit, overcome with relief that he hadn't just bolted from the room. In actually hearing his words though, she realized perhaps she had been too bold. She blurted out, "I'm not inviting you to sleep with me, just to clarify. I mean, I know my invitation probably sounded kind of, well, suggestive, I just, ummm, well? Now I've created an awkward atmosphere, I guess. It's sort of my specialty."

He chuckled, appearing slightly amused. "All right, well, Vanessa wasn't kidding about your SAT vocabulary. Even when you're drunk and sort of rejecting me," he joked. "I'm good with honesty, though, no matter the form. I think I like you Courtney Ross; you surprise me."

"I do?" she asked, not sure if this was a good thing or a bad thing.

"You do. I think I should probably head home to avoid the wrath of my mom, and maybe to heal my wounded pride, but can you do me a favor and check your phone when you get up in the morning?"

"Um, sure? Why?"

"You'll see. I will talk to you soon, okay?" He stepped forward and leaned in close enough that she could see he needed to shave. He kissed her on the cheek before walking out the front door. Blankly, she turned to head upstairs, not really caring about anyone left at the party.

Courtney found herself in Vanessa's room and sank into the bed, not bothering with pajamas, enjoying the tingling spot where his lips had touched her. *Please don't let this be a dream tomorrow.*

♪ *"Sweetness"* – *Jimmy Eat World*
"Ho Hey" – *The Lumineers*

Four

Courtney woke up feeling dehydrated and slightly hung-over, but as she took in her surroundings, images from the night before started to fill her mind. She quickly remembered her promise to check her phone and frantically searched for it. In grabbing it, she groaned as she saw seven text messages from her mom. She had forgotten to call after her arrival the previous day. They read:

> M: Hey, did you land ok? Hope you're having fun!
> M: You know you're supposed to text me to let me know you're ok.
> M: Courtney Michelle Ross, I am very annoyed with you. You better hope I let you go back there next summer!
> M: Ok, I am trying to be one of those "cool moms" I read about on my blogs. I know you're 17, but you still better text me the second you wake up.
> M: I want you to know I am failing miserably at being a cool mom.
> M: CALL ME! Or text me.
> M: Please.

Courtney knew she had to face the music and decided to get it over with. She pressed *call* and waited for her mom to pick up.

"Oh my God, I am so irritated with you! Are you trying to give me grey hair?!" her mother yelled.

"I am so sorry! I got caught up reminiscing with Vanessa, and she threw a casual little gathering for me, and I'm sorry, sorry, sorry. I promise I will be on good-daughter duty the rest of my trip," Courtney swore, trying to sound as innocent as possible.

"A 'casual little gathering,'" her mom repeated. "It must have been quite the shindig for you to downplay it that much. I love Vanessa, but I know what a 'little gathering' is to her, so you just be careful, got it?"

"Yes Mother. And don't use the word shindig."

"Whatever, I'm middle-aged, I say what I want. Did you get to see any of your old friends? I know you miss living there."

"I did. It was nice to catch up, but really just…easy, to be around Vanessa again. I feel freer here than I do around my friends there," Courtney explained. "I may have met a boy, though." The words were spoken against her better judgment. She knew her mom was going to ask her a million questions, but she was just too excited not to tell someone.

"A boy, huh? Tell me more." Courtney could hear the restraint in her mother's voice and smiled.

"He has a motorcycle and owns a tattoo shop. You'd really like him, I think," Courtney said as seriously as possible.

"Ugh. My daughter the comedian. Stop trying to give me a heart attack and just tell me."

"Okay, okay. No, he's tall and dark and handsome and all of those other Disney movie adjectives. His name is Ethan and he plays guitar and sings, and I just like him, I think. Knowing me, it'll probably all go up in flames before it even starts, but I just feel excited about him."

"A musician? Well, he sounds very nice. Sneak a picture of him and send it to me the next time you meet up. I wanna see this tall and dark and handsome boy."

"I will attempt to do so," Courtney replied.

What Comes of Eating Doughnuts With a Boy Who Plays Guitar

"Now listen to me, just be *safe*, whatever you do. Do you understand? Like, you do know what I mean by *safe*, right? I don't want to embarrass you more than I have to, but I'm trying to be a realist."

"Oh my god, Mom, yes I know what you mean, and that's not a conversation we need to have right now! I am going to go. You've made me sufficiently uncomfortable for one morning."

"Okay! I'm your mother. It's my job. Have a good day, and you better text me back next time," she reminded before Courtney hit the red button. She was so emotionally scarred from that conversation that she had nearly forgotten about Ethan's request.

She snatched her phone back up and didn't quite know what she was looking for until she saw the little alarm bell on her calendar app. She opened it and checked her schedule for that day. It said she had an upcoming event in fifteen minutes. When she opened the event, she laughed. It read: "Bear claw breakfast with sexy MAN from last night." She was so caught up in wondering when he had gotten the time to put the alert in her phone that the *15 minute* warning escaped her. As it resonated that it meant fifteen minutes from right then, she flew off the bed to look at her appearance. "Oh my god," she said to her reflection. *How the hell am I going to fix this in 15 minutes?! Okay, okay, okay,* she breathed. *One thing at a time.* She searched her suitcase for the magical hair spray that would make her look less like an asylum escapee. She decided a messy side ponytail would at least seem like she had intended for it to look unkempt. She quickly took off her leftover makeup and reached for her glitter eye shadow. She would appear bright eyed and bushy tailed if it took all the glitter in the world. Finally, she furiously brushed her teeth and put on a drop of perfume before glancing at her phone. Three minutes to get dressed and calm herself down. Wardrobe options were limited, because almost everything she owned was wrinkled in a suitcase. She decided on a pair of fitted jeans before raiding Vanessa's closet for an acceptable shirt. She'd chosen a white strapless top with hot pink flowers when she realized she had no idea where Vanessa was.

Re-checking her appearance and feeling satisfied that she would not send Ethan away in horror, she went to find her friend. "V! Where are you?" she called as she bounded down the stairs.

"In the kitchen, girl!" Vanessa yelled back. Courtney walked into the kitchen and found Vanessa and Luke making breakfast. The bacon and eggs smelled so good to her post-party stomach, she almost forgot to be surprised that Luke was there.

"Annnnnd good morning to you two." Courtney looked from one to the other.

"Hey, there, any requests for your eggs? I am quite the master chef," Luke declared. To demonstrate, he flipped a fried egg in the air and caught it perfectly back on the pan.

"Impressive, Bobby Flay. I would love a fried egg. And bacon. And maybe toast too."

"It amazes me how much you eat," Vanessa interjected.

"Well, I am rather amazing. Respect," Courtney shot back, her face completely serious. Vanessa rolled her eyes playfully, and they heard the doorbell ring.

"Hmmmm, whoever could that be? I think at least *somebody* finds you amazing, anyway." Vanessa smiled as she gestured towards the door. Courtney's heart raced as she went to answer it. *What if everything I felt last night was a fluke and he realizes I'm just... me?* Courtney had a mental argument with herself and forced her brain to remember that he did show up this morning after all. She started to remember their last encounter in the kitchen and felt her chest tighten. She put on her best self-assured look as she opened the door to Ethan, who was looking incredible in a soft black fitted t-shirt and dark khakis. If possible, he was even more beautiful than she remembered. "Hello there, I believe your name was 'sexy mysterious man,' right?" she teased him, forcing her voice to sound light and relaxed. *Just don't say anything embarrassing.* There wasn't the excuse of Jell-O shots in the light of day.

"Ah, you did remember to look at your phone. So, I bought you a doughnut. I'm pretty sure you said your favorite was a bear claw, but I brought a few to be sure," he said, winking at her.

"Well, as it happens, I prefer them with sprinkles, but I will admit that I've never met a doughnut I didn't like, so hand 'em over." She grabbed the bag swiftly out of his hands and started to lead the way into the kitchen. Abruptly, she felt Ethan grab her hand and pull her back. "Yes?" she asked, confused.

"I know last night I was all about being the bigger man and respecting your virtue, but I really need to do something. Like, right now." His dark eyes were much more intense, or maybe she was just clear-headed enough to appreciate them. He stepped forward into her space, and she found herself pressed between Ethan and the wall. She dropped the bag of doughnuts on the entryway floor and wrapped her arms around his neck, pulling him closer. It all happened so quickly she forgot to be nervous, and then his lips were on hers. He tasted faintly of coffee and toothpaste, and this was now her new favorite flavor. He kissed like he had all the time in the world. His hands slipped into her back pockets and pulled her even further into the moment, and heat rose quickly to her cheeks. She had been kissed before, but this was a whole different experience. She could feel the energy radiating between their bodies as he gently kissed her lips again and pulled away slightly. She rested against the wall and found herself having to remember to inhale. She looked up at him again, and he was grinning, his eyes sparkling. "I thought about doing that all night." He kissed her once more, quickly, picked up the doughnuts, and led her into the kitchen. "Now we can have breakfast."

Courtney's brain couldn't even process what had just happened. She tried to regain her focus and act like a normal human being, but her mind was back in the entryway, reliving that moment, every time he looked at her. Vanessa raised an eyebrow at her as if to ask if everything was okay. Courtney just smiled and waved her off. She knew they could obsess about it later.

"Well, despite the fact that I really wanted you to have a bear claw as a symbol of my new nickname for you, I had a feeling you might be a sprinkles kind of girl, so there are both," Ethan explained as he put the doughnuts on the counter.

"I call the bear claw!" Luke yelled as he stuffed his face with doughnut.

"Okay then, I guess that one's Luke's," Ethan responded dryly.

"So Fisher, what prompted your little visit so early in the morning? Usually when Luke and I invite you to a post-party breakfast, you claim you have to work. What seems to have changed your mind this time?" Vanessa's voice feigned innocence.

"I have no idea what you're talking about. You must be thinking of someone else," Ethan responded. "And for your information, I do have to work in about twenty minutes, so how about them apples?"

"Nice use of an idiom there," Courtney complimented, half-joking. "I do enjoy a *man* who can turn a phrase."

"If I didn't know better, I would think you were making fun of me. But that couldn't possibly be the case, coming from a vocabulary snob such as yourself," Ethan challenged, calling her out on her big-word obsession. He slid his arms around her from behind and stole a piece of her doughnut. "That's my price for getting over your hurtful comments about my awesome idiom usage."

"My sincerest apologies." Courtney sighed to herself as he let go of her to sit on the counter.

"So, I wasn't kidding about work, and I do have to go in a minute. How else will the children learn to play guitar and grow up to be as rad as I am? But I wanted to see if anyone was up for a movie or something tonight?"

"Dude! Movies are boring- don't be lame. Let's go night canoeing," Luke said, excited as always.

"Ohhhh, yes! We haven't been in forever, and Courtney will hate it, but in this case it'll be good for her. Let's do it," Vanessa chimed in.

"Um, I'm sorry, night canoeing? As in being on the river in a very small boat, but at night when you can't see the bugs and river-creatures trying to eat you?" Courtney questioned. She was not particularly fond of nature.

Ethan chuckled quietly. "Nah, night canoeing is actually pretty awesome. I'm in. I'll protect you from all things bug-like, but you're on your own if you see any type of river-creatures. You make that sound terrifying." He gave an exaggerated shudder. "Luke, you still have the keys to the canoe storage?"

"You bet your ass. Never giving those things up." Luke took to jingling some keys in his pocket.

"Yay!" Vanessa sang as she danced around Luke in the kitchen.

"Hold up, are you telling me that in addition to bugs and river-creatures, we will also be *breaking in and stealing* these canoes? As in no one will come looking for us if we all drown in the river?"

"Come on, Bear Claw, you know you want to go on an adventure," Ethan coaxed, putting his hands on her hips, moving them back and forth slowly. She didn't want him to step away.

Courtney sighed. She didn't know that she could say no to him even if she wanted to, not when he was that close. "Fine, I'll go. But when we get picked up by the cops, I am going to throw you all under the bus, just so you're aware. And you have to agree to stop calling me 'bear claw.' Think of something that makes me sound cute," she finished.

"All right, deal." He laughed. "I will think of something else if you insist. And by the way, 'nice use of an idiom there,'" he retorted, referring to her bus comment. "Luke, I will text you later and figure out where we're meeting up. Vanessa, a pleasure as always. And girl formerly known as bear claw, I will see you tonight." He kissed her quickly on the lips, letting her know their greeting from that morning was one hundred percent real. She stared after him for a moment as he walked towards the door, and then directed her attention back to Vanessa and Luke.

"Ummmmm, what the hell was that? Since when are the two of you on casual kissing terms? I thought nothing happened last night?" Vanessa demanded.

"Yeah, I'm not really into, like, girl-talk, so I'm gonna jump in the shower before I head home. I'll leave you to it." Luke dismissed them, walking towards the basement. Apparently pumping him for information about Ethan was out. Courtney waited until he was out of earshot and told Vanessa everything. The awkward encounter from the night before, the event on her phone, the significance of the name "bear claw," and finally, the kiss in the entryway. She felt relieved after getting it all out, having been so worked up she thought she might explode.

"Shut UP! I cannot believe you two were making out at my front door and I didn't even notice! What a smoothie though. He's got some serious moves," Vanessa mused.

"So- what do you *think*? You always have an opinion, and this time I'm actually asking for it. What do I *dooooo*?" Courtney pleaded.

"Girl, you already know what I would do. The question is, what are you looking for this summer?. I can tell he's into you because he's actually trying. He doesn't just act like that around girls here, and believe me, it's not because he's lacking opportunity. You know Kim? She's been trying to land him since he got here, but he's never even looked twice. I think… I think you should have fun and let yourself be who you want to be. I can vouch for him that he's a decent guy, so, ya know, if you feel like ditching your v-card, I give you my full support, but you gotta know what you want." It was clear from the suppressed grin on Vanessa's face that she was doing her best to get Courtney riled up, but that didn't make it any less effective.

"You know how I feel about that term!" Courtney replied with a grimace. "But fine… perspective. I think I will just, I don't know, be happy for the moment. It's a new concept, but whatever. Just happy. I can do that, right?" But she was doubtful. She tried to picture Kim in her mind and felt possessive. She was cute; short dark hair, big brown eyes with girl-next-door freckles across her nose. *Well, that just won't do, will it?*

"I guess we'll find out. I know you like him because you didn't even put up a fight about night canoeing. I can't wait to see how this one plays out. Remember the camping trip when we were Girl Scouts in the second grade?" Vanessa asked, unable to control her laughter. "I thought you were going to pee your pants when you found that bug in your sleeping bag. Your face was priceless."

"Well, who's to say I didn't pee my pants just a little bit? It was terrifying; no one could have blamed me. I swear to god that bug had a mission. I made Ms. Hoffman give me a new sleeping bag and sprayed the tent with a can of Raid. Which I packed in my own bag. As an eight year old," Courtney finished, now able to laugh at how ridiculous it sounded. "Not sure whose brilliant idea it was to sign me up for Girl Scouts to begin with." Canoeing would certainly test the boundaries of her comfort zone.

"Meh, I probably insisted you come with me and annoyed you so much you agreed to ask your mom. That's sort of how our friendship works." Vanessa was now grinning openly. "So, girl, after Luke leaves, we are shopping. You, without question, need hotter clothes- no arguments!" Courtney didn't even try. She followed Vanessa upstairs to get ready, looking dreamily at the wall in the entryway as they walked by.

* * *

Vanessa exhausted her with a marathon day of consumerism. Where this girl got her determination, Courtney didn't know. She had successfully talked her into three new outfits and a bikini, which she insisted were completely *Ethan appropriate*. Courtney was learning that Vanessa was a master of manipulation.

"You know I have bathing suits, right? Like, I have a pool at my house. I do swim," she complained, looking at her purchases.

"Yeah, okay. You have 'swimming at home' suits. Not 'I want Ethan's jaw to hit the ground' suits. There's a difference, and you know it. We will be at the pool at least a couple days a week this summer, so it's sort of an important wardrobe staple." Courtney examined the very small scraps of bright yellow fabric that she had paid for, and had to at least partly agree with Vanessa. This was a far cry from the tankini sitting in her suitcase.

Courtney sat down on a bench and sighed. "Don't we need to, like, go back to your house and clean up before your parents come home?"

"Nope! One, Luke already cleaned everything. It looks better than it did before even, seriously. I've never met anyone with more energy." Vanessa paused and wiggled her eyebrows suggestively. "And two, my mom called this morning and they are staying one more night to go to some book signing thing? I don't know. They'll be home by tomorrow, no worries. That just means we don't have to sneak out."

♪ *"Leave the Night On" – Sam Hunt*
"Drunk on You" – Luke Bryan
"Free Fallin'" –Tom Petty
Performed By John Mayer

Five

When Ethan arrived that night, Courtney was actually feeling pretty confident. Okay, that was a lie. She was doing a good job of pretending, though. Vanessa had done her hair in a loose French braid, despite Courtney's initial objections to being made over. She was dressed in dark skinny jeans and brown leather sandals, topped off with a very snug fitting flannel shirt that, according to her friend, gave her "cleavage to die for." Upon hearing the doorbell, she resisted the urge to run down the steps.

"Court, you ready to go?" Vanessa called. She made her way downstairs, trying to look calm and not at all afraid of giant river bugs. Or being alone with a boy she was certain had infinitely more experience than she did.

"Oh, as ready as I'm gonna be, I suppose." She looked up to find Ethan staring at her. *So maybe the shirt was a decent purchase.* He looked seriously hot, wearing a black zip-up jacket and a silver necklace. She bit her lip as she took in the sight of him.

"Jesus, could there be more tension in this room? We are here to CANOE, people. AT NIGHT. IN THE DARK. So get it together, will you?" Luke scolded. Courtney felt the urge to punch him, but imagined that he wouldn't even notice if she did.

"We're coming, we're coming. Take a breath or something," Ethan replied, and they all piled into Luke's truck to drive to the river.

"All right, kids, are you ready?" Luke asked everyone as they pulled up next to the locked storage area for the local canoe company. Apparently he had worked there for several summers and had the forethought to copy their keys.

"Let's do it," Ethan responded, going to help Luke drag out the canoes.

"Do you need, like, water wings or something, Courtney? I don't want to be responsible for your death on the river," Luke prodded.

"Oh, shut up, I can swim just fine. It's the creatures sharing the water that bother me. But can we please try to avoid the whole falling out of the canoe situation in the first place?"

"No way, I'm flipping you guys over every chance I get. Just wait for it." Courtney couldn't tell if he was joking or not, but she was relying on Vanessa to control her man-child. "Okay, listen up, campers. Ethan and I went down to the clearing earlier today where we will end our ride and put out some giant orange flags. We also tied orange markers to some tree limbs that you will see before you come up on the stopping point. I may or may not have left a cooler with some refreshments and stuff to make a fire. I know, I'm your hero, blah, blah, blah, I won't let it go to my head. Ethan's car is parked down there so we can drive back and pick up my truck. Now let's get these things out on the water!"

Courtney was actually pretty impressed with Luke's planning skills. Even in all of her worry, she hadn't thought about what they would do when they got to the end. She started to relax a little, and just focused on not falling out of the boat. *If you can even call it a boat. More like a water hazard disguised as a means of transportation.* She helped Ethan push the canoe down to the bank and hopped in, letting him guide them into the chilly water. They sat facing each other, oars in hand, and awkwardly tried to find their rowing rhythm. Of course

Luke and Vanessa were old pros and quickly pulled ahead. *Well, at least from there Luke can't tip us over,* Courtney thought gratefully. Finding their pace, they started down the river. Courtney took a deep breath-partially because she was convinced bugs were going to attack her at any given moment, and partially because the air smelled almost sweet. There were so many things in bloom that time of year; she forgot how nice summer could feel when it wasn't 115 degrees. She was fighting off a moderate concern about being able to hold a conversation with Ethan for the entire ride without letting something completely inarticulate slip out. *Inner monologue, inner monologue, inner monologue,* she repeated.

"See? It's nice out here. It makes you feel like Tom Sawyer, right?" Ethan almost looked unsure in the last sunrays of the day. *Literature? Okay. He speaks more than one language, then. Hot guy with guitar and book nerd.*

"You know what? It kind of does. All we need now is to get lost in a cave." She smiled. "However, I'd prefer not to be chased by a homicidal maniac named Joe. Tom Sawyer was kind of a badass when you think about it."

"You're kind of an odd girl, you know that?" Ethan asked. She wasn't sure if she should be offended yet, so she went along with it.

"Well, yes, in several ways, I'm sure. But how do you mean?"

"You just, I don't know. You're crazy hot, don't get me wrong, but so are a lot of girls. You're funny. Like right now, I threw out a Twain reference, definitely trying to sound smart, and you just went with it. And you kind of knew a lot about hobbits last night, in addition to literally talking about music for a half hour. These are not typical conversations I have with females, or anyone. Do you get that?"

"I guess I do, yeah. There are very few people I can be real with. I have even, on occasion, had to pretend I care what is going on with the Kardashians in order to participate at cheer practice. But I much prefer this. I feel like I can be myself here. You are easy to talk to. And not so hard to look at either," she finished hesitantly, hoping this was how people were supposed to flirt. *I'm crazy hot? Is he for real right now?*

"Fair enough," he agreed with a laugh. "I'm glad this is the real you."

"So, what else do you like read?"

"Um, well. That's sort of classified information."

"Because...?" she continued, confused.

"Because it makes me look uncool, soooo I don't want to tell you."

"Oh come on! I'm a total book nerd; I promise I won't make fun of you. Unless it's about sparkling vampires. Then I will, without apology," she said seriously. "I also have a hard time believing there is anything that would make you look uncool. You're sort of *that* guy, you know?"

"I could say that I didn't know, but I'd sort of be lying. I'm kind of awesome. So fine. You're very persuasive for such a small girl," he commented. "My little sister is in middle school, and she's kind of, well, she doesn't have a lot of friends, but she loves to read. My mom works all the time, so since she's been little I have been the one to read with her. It's just kind of a thing. So besides books for school, I'm usually reading stuff like *Percy Jackson* or *Harry Potter* so we can talk about them," he finished reluctantly.

"Seriously? That's what you were worried about telling me? That's freaking adorable. And *Harry Potter*? If you think I have strong feelings about music, don't even get me *started* on wizards. I have a wand at home... or three," she confessed. *Too much? With the wands? Please don't let that be what freaks him out. I could have owned up to my literary candle collection too.*

"I love that you think it's 'adorable,' but if we could sort of keep that information between us, that would be awesome. And by that I mean that I will call you a liar in public if you tell people I want to be a boy wizard," he threatened playfully.

"Does it make you feel better if I tell you it's kind of really sexy that you like *Harry Potter* and are an awesome brother?" *This is definitely what flirting is supposed to feel like.* Her heart was thrumming in her chest, and she became very glad this little river adventure was at night, because her cheeks were on fire.

What Comes of Eating Doughnuts With a Boy Who Plays Guitar

"Yes." He grinned at her, amused. "Still a secret, though." He put his finger to his lips in a hushed motion. "But speaking of wizardry, put your oar down and come here for a minute." Wondering if he could see the look of *are you insane* on her face in the light of their lantern, she carefully did as he asked, willing the universe to keep her on the boat. He motioned for her to sit down in front of him. Although she was feeling her stomach contract from being that close to him, she was also curious as to where this was headed. "Let me see your hand," he commanded as he readjusted their light so he could see her better. She held up her palm and he put it in his hands. "I'm going to read your palm," he stated matter-of-factly.

"Really? You know how to do that?"

"I do. My aunt is into all kinds of mystical things- palm reading, crystals, whatever. I had her teach me how to do this so I could impress girls. You let me know if it works." He laughed. She liked hearing it. He had an easy manner about him, and it made her feel relaxed- like, actually relaxed, not the kind she had to convince herself of after frantically meditating. The oxymoron of frantically meditating was also not lost on her.

"Okay, then, let's hear it." Courtney didn't even care if he knew how to read palms or not, the sensation of his fingertips running over her hand was enough to send a shiver down her spine.

"Okay, this line here? This is your heart line, and it curves up, which means you share your emotions and thoughts freely with those you trust. And this line here," he traced the line with his thumb, "means you are full of life and energy. And this part? Means you are very interested in guys who play guitar and sing 90s songs to you at bonfires." She could practically hear the smile coming through his voice, and he picked up her hand and kissed her wrist softly. She held her breath, still having a difficult time coming to terms that this was happening.

He planted several more small kisses up the length of her forearm until she couldn't take the anticipation anymore. She came up on her knees, forgetting to be careful, and tipped the boat dangerously low, the cool water threatening to impose on their moment. It hardly registered as his lips met hers. They were actually closer to the same height with him sitting and her kneeling, and she liked the feeling of his chest pressed against hers. Ethan ran his hands lightly up the back of her shirt as she played with his hair. The kiss went even deeper, and she felt her herself melt into him. He broke their connection and his lips traveled down her neck, making her dizzy- this time without the influence of anything but his presence. Her breath hitched in her throat. He returned to kiss her several times with his perfectly curved lips and then leaned back for a moment.

She was having a hard time thinking of what to say after she finally understood why Shakespearean sonnets were written about the art of kissing. "I can categorically say that yes, palm reading impresses me," she finally got out, laughing slightly.

"I will read your palm any time you like," Ethan agreed, smoothing his hair. "Unfortunately, we should probably row to the end of our journey before Luke starts feeling bad that he didn't make you wear floaties." Courtney sighed, but she was almost thankful they had to stop. Though unsure of where she wanted this to go, she accepted that she hadn't felt a spark like that with any other guy. Ever. They managed to hold a coherent conversation as they rowed and soon began to see the orange ties in the trees. Pulling closer to the shore, they saw that Luke and Vanessa already had an actual fire going.

"Geeeez, I almost called the coast guard!" Luke shouted when he saw them.

"Oh, stop it, let them be," Vanessa reprimanded. She smiled at Courtney with a look that let her know she'd want details later. "Come and have some food." They all roasted hot dogs and s'mores while the smoke rose into the summer night air.

"Hey, run up to my car with me, I wanna grab another blanket," Ethan relayed to Courtney. He grabbed her hand and pulled her off the folding chair where she was sitting. They took a brief walk out to the dirt road that followed the path of the river, and she was intrigued when she saw his car. It was a royal blue sporty-looking thing, and she could tell it was vintage and had been re-built.

What Comes of Eating Doughnuts With a Boy Who Plays Guitar

"What kind of car is this?" she asked admiringly.

"Ahhh, this has been my obsession for the last three years. It's a 1980 Nissan Z. My grandpa helped me buy it when I was fifteen, and then we fixed it up together. You have no idea how many guitar lessons I had to teach to get it like this." He laughed, grabbing the blanket out of the trunk. "I'll take you for a drive on some back roads soon and show you what she can do."

"Sounds good to me; I happen to rather like zippy cars."

"Do you *rather* like them? You're so funny with your descriptive words. I think it's cute," he added, gauging her uncertain expression, "just amusing." He pulled her closer and kissed her before shutting the trunk, and they headed back down towards the river. *I could absolutely get used to the kissing.* As they walked up on the bank, they heard Vanessa and Luke, seemingly in a heated conversation.

"You are one-hundred percent not driving me home. I'll drive your truck, you've had like four beers," Vanessa said, her voice raised.

"Two. And I told you one hundred times, I'm FINE. Would you just chill?" Luke snapped back.

"No, actually I won't just 'chill,' I actually care if everyone gets home safely. I'll have Ethan drive us," she challenged.

"Oh my god, are you kidding me?" By this time, Ethan and Courtney had walked up closer to them, and an awkward silence followed.

"Hey, Luke, help me drag the canoes up to the road," Ethan said, diffusing the tension.

"Whatever, man." He stormed up the bank to grab a canoe. Ethan handed the blanket to Courtney and went to catch up to Luke.

"Everything okay?" Courtney asked Vanessa, concern in her voice.

"Whatever. I'm just sick of his bullshit! I don't even want to talk about it right now. I just know that he's not driving us home." She sounded almost tearful. Courtney went and put her arm around her friend. It was so rare to see Vanessa genuinely upset. It was usually all snark and wit. The boys came back a few minutes later, and Luke seemed to have calmed down.

"V, I'm sorry, please come talk to me," he pleaded. Vanessa sighed, crossed her arms, and started to walk towards the edge of the bank without waiting to see if he was following. He looked like a sad puppy trudging after her. Ethan came up behind Courtney, wrapped his arms around her, and kissed her neck briefly.

"They'll be okay. Luke always caves to Vanessa in the end," he said in her ear.

"I hope so. I like him for her; he makes her happy."

"No worries, sweet cakes."

"Sweet cakes? Still no good. Try again," Courtney chided him.

"No? I thought you'd go for that. I'll keep thinking. Here," he said, turning her around, "dance with me."

"Dance with you? Well, aren't you pulling out all the stops tonight?" She put her arms around his neck, but had to stand on her tiptoes to reach him.

"Well, that, and I really wanted an excuse to grab your ass," Ethan confessed, laughing and pulling her closer. He started to sing a piece of a Wallflowers song for her while they danced, the stars spinning overhead and her heart racing in her chest. In a moment she understood what people meant by *falling* in love. She didn't know that she *loved* Ethan, she had only known him two days, but the feeling was exactly the same. Terrifying, uncontrollable, and freeing. She didn't think about what it meant when the fall ended. Instead, she just listened to his voice and held on to him tighter.

"Ah-hem." Courtney jumped slightly as she heard Vanessa clear her throat behind them. She turned around to see her and Luke tentatively holding hands, and they both seemed less tense.

"Everything cool?" Ethan asked.

"Like a cucumber," Luke answered. Courtney did notice that Vanessa rolled her eyes at that comment. "I think we should pack up, though. It'll take a bit for me to get my truck back and lock up the boats." They agreed and started breaking down the makeshift party site. Ethan drove them back to Luke's truck, and Vanessa said she would be helping him load the canoes and driving him back to her house for the night. That left Ethan to chauffeur Courtney. She focused on her breathing. She didn't know that she was ready to be alone with him. In his car. With those stupidly soft lips and that smirk.

Think. When you get back to the house, maybe nothing will even happen. He might just go home. Do you really want him to go home? She knew that she didn't. Ethan rested his hand on her knee, drumming the beat to an unspoken song, and seemed to be free from worries. *Just freaking relax,* she told herself. *You like him, he likes you. You can always say no to anything you don't want to do. You are capable of uttering a one-syllable word.* She took another deep breath. Ethan had been nothing but respectful of her, and she repeated this in her mind until her heart rate slowed.

"What's going on in that pretty head of yours?" he questioned.

"Nothing. Well, always something. But nothing important right now," she lied. Ethan abruptly pulled the car over to the side of the road.

"Okay I have to like, apologize, or explain, or something. I can tell something is bothering you because you literally have not stopped talking since I met you until now, so hopefully I can clear up whatever is on your mind."

"Okay… you're making me a little nervous, but go ahead." She envisioned her whole summer romance dead in the water before it really even got started. *Why do you have to blow everything out of proportion?*

"No, don't be nervous, I just… this is hard to get out, but I feel this compulsion to be honest with you. First, I'm sorry for the whole 'this is a good excuse to grab your ass' comment from earlier. That was a dickish thing to say, and I feel like I gave the wrong impression. I've been kicking myself since I said it, and if I could take it back, I would." Courtney started to interrupt him to assuage his guilt, but he stopped her. "To be frank with you, I am very good at flirting with girls. I always have been. What I said to you… that's something I would typically say to a girl I was trying to hook up with. And it would work." Courtney raised an eyebrow at him. "I know I'm coming across as horribly conceited right now, I just don't know how else to explain this next part. It's like…I feel like I've known you forever. When I think that last week we weren't even on each other's radar, I wonder how that is possible. You're all I can think about. So, I don't want to 'hook up' with you. I mean I do," he corrected when he saw Courtney make a face. "God, this is all coming out wrong. I think you're, like, beautiful? I know I sound completely ridiculous right now. And of course I want to… Okay. What I'm trying to say is that I think I like you. I know that seems simple, but for me it isn't. So, if tonight, or any night I get to be with you, you just want to sit around and talk, or play guitar, or hell, play checkers, I don't care. I don't, like, expect, well, yeah. So. I think that's it. Sorry, I'm not good at words when you're looking at me like that," he finished nervously.

Courtney leaned across to the driver's seat and kissed him softly on the lips in a rare act of boldness. "I think you are picking up my talent for creating an awkward atmosphere," she teased him gently. "On the contrary, I think you're very good *words*. I was in my own head there for a minute, you weren't wrong. But I'm fine, okay? You'll know if I'm not. As you said before, I'm kind of chatty." She smiled as she kissed him again, really just relishing the fact that she could.

"So, are we good then? Like we can keep hanging out and see where this goes and whatever?" Ethan questioned.

"I think that's exactly what we do," Courtney replied. "But I hate checkers. So that's out. I would love to go back to Vanessa's and hear some of the songs you're working on, though. Can we do that? And can there possibly be cookies involved?"

"Okay," he breathed lightly. "You make me a little nervous," he revealed, kissing her one last time. "I kind of like it." He pulled back onto the road, and they drove the rest of the way to Vanessa's house at varying rates of speed so he could show off his car's abilities. She didn't know that she had ever felt more alive than racing along those back roads with all the windows down and the music up.

♪ *"All The Small Things"* – Blink 182
"Fly" – Sugar Ray
"Sugar We're Goin' Down" – Fall Out Boy

Six

Over the next two weeks, the four were inseparable. They had undertaken almost every possible dating opportunity available in the small town: the movies, mini-golf, and every restaurant in a five-mile radius. They had ordered in pizza, Chinese, and Mexican food. Ethan, true to his word, had happily chatted away during each outing, stealing some serious kisses whenever he could, but not pushing her any further. While Courtney was grateful he was giving her the time she needed to grow more comfortable, she missed some of the heat from those first few days together.

They all ventured to the city pool late one morning. The boys were playing basketball, and Courtney took the opportunity to seek out her friend's counsel while lounging by the pool. "V? I need your advice."

"I am at your service." Vanessa pushed her sunglasses on top of her head and leaned in like they were in a secret meeting.

"I feel dumb even asking this. I don't know, you are so, like, in control when it comes to how you act with Luke, and I feel like I need to be more… I don't know, confident?" She didn't know why she felt nervous talking to her best friend about it… just the whole development with Ethan was outside her normal comfort zone. *Deliciously outside your comfort zone,* she correct internally. "I know I'm good at saying 'no,' but I've never tried to say 'yes' to anything before, because, well, it hasn't really come up. Not like this, anyway."

"You don't need my advice," Vanessa replied swiftly. "You just need to make up your mind. Is he going too fast or too slow? He's been with you every night for almost two weeks, and he does exactly what you want him to do, so you're already in control. You just need to own it. If you want to move forward, you're going to have to do it yourself. He's totally afraid of doing something you don't want him to, which is sort of weird. For him, anyway. Just accept that his feelings for you are real, and then do what feels right for you." Her sunglasses went back down, signifying the end of the advice-giving.

"You're such a wise old owl. What would I do without you?" Courtney asked, lightening the mood. "But you're right. I do need to take control of what I want." She looked towards the court and appreciated the drop in her stomach when she saw him. "Speaking of which, right now I want that red-headed lifeguard to stop undressing Ethan with her eyes."

"Ah, welcome to the world of having a ridiculously hot boyfriend," Vanessa commiserated. "I want to put a sign on Luke sometimes that says he is taken. Like 'beware of dog,' but 'beware of crazy blond chick who will beat your ass if you touch her man.' I'm still working on the specifics." Courtney giggled, imagining Luke wearing such a statement.

"Well, even if he's not my boyfriend, I think I have to do something about this situation." There was something about being around Vanessa that pulled out a brave-girl-warrior side Courtney didn't know she possessed. She took to glaring at the lifeguard through the comfort of her sunglasses and chewing her bottom lip.

"Do it up, girl." Courtney slipped on her flip-flops, adjusted her skimpy yellow bikini for emphasis in the right places, and sauntered over to the basketball court.

"Hey, sexy," Ethan called, admiring her. She remembered feeling envious of other girls when their boyfriends would look at them that way. Like no one else existed. She almost had to convince herself not

What Comes of Eating Doughnuts With a Boy Who Plays Guitar

to be jealous when she glanced up at him-because everything in that stare was for her.

"Come here," she told him from the sideline. He jogged over.

"What's up? Everything okay?"

"Well, it will be in a minute." She was unconcerned with the fact that there were several people waiting for him to return to the game. Her heart was pounding for more than one reason; she just hoped what she was about to say made things clear for him. For where she wanted things to go. "See, there's this lifeguard over there, and I sort of don't like that she's drooling over you. I think she's hoping you drown in the pool so she can perform CPR." Being this directly flirtatious with any guy was unfamiliar, but it was giving her a sense of power all the same.

Ethan looked up, apparently not surprised. "And you want me to go tell her I'm taken?" he asked, confused. Courtney was slightly taken aback that he'd been okay with referring to himself as 'taken,' but she pressed on.

"Nope. I want you to show her." Courtney grinned, taking his hands and placing them very low on her back. His smile widened and he kissed her playfully. He picked her up and threw her over his shoulder, bolting back for the pool. Courtney squealed in protest, but she was secretly overjoyed. *This should make things clear,* she thought smugly. Ethan tossed her into the pool when he reached the edge and jumped in after her. When the sun hit him, light bouncing off of the water droplets clinging to his skin, she thought she might lose her mind. He swam over to her. "Well, now that I've fulfilled your request, you have to do something for me."

"What'd you have in mind?" Her thoughts were wandering as she got used to the water.

"Well, I like to think I'm pretty secure in my manhood, but since you brought it up first, do you see that group of guys over your left shoulder?" She looked and nodded. "That's half the JV football team. And while you've been prancing around in this ridiculously tempting bathing suit all morning, they've been eyeing you like they've got a shot. So just to be certain that everyone's aware you're here with

52

me..." He reached down and grabbed her thighs, wrapping her legs around his waist under the water. She laughed and indulged his wish, holding on tightly and letting him kiss her very publicly, never wanting that kiss to end. After he was satisfied, they challenged each other to various tricks off the diving board until Vanessa and Luke reappeared. They all agreed to get cleaned up, and that the girls would plan something for that night.

* * *

"So, I think I have an awesome idea," Courtney relayed excitedly to Vanessa on the way home.

"Do tell."

"I think we should have a 'Throwback Thursday' night tonight. We should make our favorite foods from when we were kids- I'm talking mac and cheese, PB&J, Kool-Aid, Ho-Hos, and Sour Patch Kids. Then we can play games from our old middle school parties. Spin the Bottle might not be so appropriate, but we could play Truth or Dare, Twenty Questions... watch Empire Records. What do you think?"

"Well, I think you are a freaking genius. That sounds even better than night canoeing. Get on your phone and text Ethan and I'll get ahold of Luke. Let's not tell them the theme though; it can be a surprise." Vanessa looked positively giddy. This was exactly what they needed. They used to plan stuff like this all the time, and it made Courtney feel like they were back in their old rhythm.

"Done and done," she said, after texting with Ethan. "This is going to be so much fun. Let's make ourselves pretty. Let me re-phrase. Let's have you make us both pretty." She smiled and batted her eyelashes at her friend for effect.

"Yes!" Vanessa agreed. The girls washed the chlorine from their hair and got ready to tackle the greatest throwback evening ever. They ran through the store, collecting anything that reminded them of the past. There was an exorbitant amount of candy, but that was to be expected, of course.

What Comes of Eating Doughnuts With a Boy Who Plays Guitar

In the last aisle, Courtney noticed Vanessa grabbing an unusual amount of toilet paper. "Um, are you planning to pee a lot in the next several hours?" she questioned.

"Nope," Vanessa replied. "Why don't you think about it for a minute and get back to me."

"OHMYGOD we're going TPing! Yes, yes, yes, yes, yes. I haven't been since we were like thirteen and your mom took us when I was here visiting. That is perfect! Have I told you lately how much I've missed you?" she questioned, and gave Vanessa a giant hug in the middle of the grocery store.

"Aw, girl, I've missed you too. And us. Tonight is going to be perfect." They paid for their nostalgia-inducing food and headed back to the house. Vanessa loaded up her iPod with songs from their past- namely Justin Bieber, Britney Spears, and a small selection of 90s pop-punk at Courtney's request. "Oh, Ethan is going to HATE this music selection," Vanessa laughed. "Wanna make a wager on how long it takes him to come over here and unplug my iPod?"

"I'm gonna go with the length of "Baby," Courtney countered.

Vanessa's mom had suggested they pull some old clothes out of the attic and dress the part, but they had decided against it. Neither of them was fond of their wardrobe choices from back in the day. "There's no reason we have to look like fashion victims. The ambience will be enough," Courtney justified as she took her new red sundress out of the closet. It wasn't her usual casual garb, but she needed a boost that night. Vanessa swore it was perfect as she picked out her own skimpy blue halter dress. V's mom was almost as excited about the party theme as they were, and had agreed to make all of the food while they got ready.

"She just likes to live vicariously through me," Vanessa complained. "Shoot me if I ever stop living my own life, will you?"

"Oh, stop, she's just being nice." Mrs. Roberts had always been good to her. She got the impression she hoped Courtney's school habits would rub off on her daughter.

"I guess," Vanessa sighed. "I do think she's coming to terms with the fact that this is who I am, though. She seems to be letting me make my own decisions more. I mean, we will be getting ready for college this time next year. How insane is that? I remember us freaking out about going to sixth grade and having lockers."

"Oh, yes. I was convinced that I would forget my combination and be humiliated in having to get the custodian to come and cut the lock off," Courtney recalled.

"You always did worry about weird stuff, friend. I was worried my braces would get stuck if I kissed a boy who also had braces." Vanessa laughed. "You have to have priorities, right?"

"Obviously," Courtney replied, wishing she had been able to go to middle school with Vanessa instead of moving. Checking her phone before leaving the room, she laughed at the text from her mom. She had delivered on the promise to send a picture of Ethan, and apparently, her mom approved.

> M: Holy crap Courtney. He looks like one of those Holli-town models. Wherever it is that you shop. Make sure he is nice to you. Or I will come there and find him. Love you <3.

"I'll have to be sure to let Ethan know that my mom thinks he looks like a 'Holli-town' model."

" 'Holli-town'? Like Hollister? That's a new one. Your mom does like to make up words. I remember us spending forever trying to get her to say 'bagels' instead of 'bay-goes'."

"I do remember that. She totally still says 'bay-goes' though. I'll have to tell her it makes her sound old, that'll make her quit." Courtney grinned. She missed her mom, despite the incredible summer she was having. "Hey, do you think I am too sparkly? I used that new glitter puff thing from the mall. I want to look like a fairy, but not a disco ball."

"Too sparkly? Is there such a thing for you?" Vanessa teased. "You look lovely, don't stress." It took Courtney a moment to realize what

What Comes of Eating Doughnuts With a Boy Who Plays Guitar

it was, but she felt something was amiss. Vanessa had told her not to stress, and she hadn't. She hadn't had a mental argument, or had to deep breathe, or felt that knot in her stomach for several days. She couldn't remember a time she had felt so... normal. The doorbell rang, interrupting her self-reflection, and the girls bounded down the stairs, excited to show the boys the night they had planned. Courtney felt so elated at her lack-of-worry that she practically knocked Ethan over when she saw him, throwing her arms around his neck and giggling.

"Okay then," Ethan smiled, stepping back to look at her. "Well don't you look pretty, sprinkles?" Ethan said, trying out yet another nickname as she twirled her dress for him.

"Yes! Oh my gosh, yes, you can call me that!" She knew it was immature, but sprinkles were just as much fun as glitter, except they went on cake. She really liked cake. "However, does this mean you no longer think I could take you in a fight? Because I'm pretty sure I could."

"Not at all," he assured her. "I've just decided you can be kick-ass and sparkly at the same time. I still have no desire to piss you off enough for you to beat me up," Ethan replied, grinning. Luke arrived shortly thereafter, and the girls made them guess the theme of the evening.

"Ummmm, crappy food and music?" Luke asked.

"I heard that, Lucas Miller!" Vanessa's mom yelled from the kitchen. "You better not be insulting my cooking."

"I would *never*, Mrs. Roberts, I didn't realize you had prepared this feast. It will obviously be delicious then," Luke said, sucking up.

"Yeah, yeah, don't overdo it," Vanessa's mom chided him. "You kids have fun tonight, but I swear to god if you get arrested going TPing I am not picking you up, got it? You'll have to sweet-talk the sheriff by yourselves," she warned.

"Got it," they said together as she left the room.

"Ok now, take a real guess," Vanessa scolded.

"Is that Kool-Aid? Like Purple-saurus? I loved that when I was a kid," Ethan shared, pointing to a pitcher on the table. After he said that, the girls could see them looking around and coming to the same conclusion. "Is the theme, like, things we loved as kids?"

"Yes!" The girls yelled in unison. "Just wait until we get to the games and activities portion later." Vanessa winked.

"All right, so it's kind of cool," Luke admitted with a half-smile. "You guys did good." They sat down to enjoy their dinner, and swapped stories about their younger years. Courtney didn't have a problem picturing Luke in his youth- he still acted like a child frequently, but Ethan? It was hard to picture him being an awkward tween, ever. Vanessa had to share the bug story from their camping trip with the boys, and everyone got a good laugh at Courtney's expense. In mock retaliation, Courtney dug up a story of her own.

"Well, Miss Vanessa here wanted to prove she was more flexible than me when we were in the seventh grade-"

"Hell yeah," Luke interrupted, grinning. Vanessa immediately punched him in the arm.

"Inappropriate!" Courtney declared. "Moving on. So yes, she tried to tell me that she could fit herself into her pillowcase. I, of course, being the responsible one, tried to talk her out of it, but she was set on accomplishing the task." Vanessa was trying to look mad at the story being told, but Courtney could tell she was about to lose it remembering that day. "She got her head, arms, and legs all stuffed into the pillowcase, and her butt was sticking out of the end when she started having a panic attack because she couldn't get out." Courtney started cracking up. "She was rocking back and forth like a turtle on its shell, trying to get out of that stupid pillowcase, and I couldn't even help her because I was laughing so hard I was crying."

"It was terrifying! How dare you all get enjoyment out of my near-death experience?!" Vanessa yelled dramatically before breaking out into a smile.

"You know, if I'm not mistaken, I have a picture of this event that I may or may not have loaded onto my phone before flying out here," Courtney said, grinning from ear to ear.

"Shut up, I will KILL you," Vanessa threatened. Courtney had stopped being scared of Vanessa's idle threats years before, so she pulled up the photo while Luke held Vanessa back. Luke and Ethan burst out laughing when they were finally able to visualize the ordeal.

"I like this chick," Luke said to his girlfriend as she scowled. It took a few minutes, but she got over it and admitted it was one of the more stupid things she had done in her youth. They all calmed down a bit and mused about becoming seniors and where they wanted to be after high school. Courtney had early acceptance from several universities, but was struggling with the actual decision part, as usual. That summer was making her even more unsure. She was a different person here. She could have the chance to go to school with Vanessa, be back in Ohio, and get out of the desert. But that would mean leaving her mom and dad and her few close friends from Scottsdale too. The thought of not seeing her mom for months at a time was enough to send her into a tailspin.

"Well, maybe I'll come out to U of A, girl, I sent my application in a few weeks ago," Vanessa admitted.

"Seriously?! Why didn't you tell me that?" Courtney asked, shocked. She had never thought Vanessa would consider leaving Ohio.

"Eh, you know how my grades are, what are the chances I'll even get in? It would be an adventure, though. I made Luke apply too, you know, just in case I need a boy toy while I'm there," she said, nudging him.

"What the hell, guys? Are you just going to leave me here?" Ethan asked, half-serious.

"Oh stop, you big baby. Apply if you want. We can take the Gem City cohort to AZ," Luke chided. Ethan looked contemplative.

"You all know I applied here too, right? Though I do love the idea of you guys coming to my world down there. It would be surreal. I got into UD, Ohio State, and BG."

"Well la-ti-da, Miss Smarty Pants," Luke joked. "So, it's all fine and well to talk about this, but what I really wanna know is what are you two lovebirds planning on doing at the end of this month? Like, you do know you're going home, right? Alllll the way across the-" Luke stopped when Vanessa elbowed him in the stomach.

"Keep your mouth shut, can't you see they are in blissful denial? Leave them alone. Don't even worry about it, you guys," Vanessa said, trying to smooth over Luke's very realistic question. An awkward silence hung in the air, and Courtney and Ethan looked anywhere but at each other. They tried to recapture the energy from earlier, but it could not be forced. "Okay, friends, I'm making an executive decision. This night was supposed to be all about reminiscing, and fun, and being young and maybe a little stupid, so I am going to give the two of you twenty minutes to deal with the elephant in the room, and then we are playing some juvenile party games and going TPing dressed as warriors of the night- do you understand?" Vanessa commanded sternly. "Luke? You and I can exchange words in the basement." She glared at him.

Shit, shit, shit, Courtney thought as they left the room. She was not ready to have this conversation; she had only known him for two weeks. There were still over two weeks left of vacation; she didn't want to imagine what it would feel like to leave him. "So, um, hi!" She was failing to sound cheerful.

"Hi, sprinkles." Ethan smiled. "Can we go sit on the couch or something? These chairs are not nearly close enough." They sank in to the over-sized sofa and he held her hands. Courtney leaned in to kiss him, thinking perhaps they could skip the "elephant in the room" conversation, but he pulled back. "I wanna know what you're thinking. I had hoped we could push this off for a while, but as usual, Luke had to force the issue."

Courtney sighed. "The only honest thing I can say is that I'm happier than I've been in... well, forever maybe. Can we just do what you said, put a pin in this until later? I know that sounds like I'm avoiding it, but, I don't know."

"Are you sure? I don't want this to be something that's hanging over our heads for the next couple weeks, I mean, I know that we are both aware that you'll have to go home, I just don't know what that means right now. I think you're incredible. I don't want you to go. That's about all my brain can process at once."

What Comes of Eating Doughnuts With a Boy Who Plays Guitar

"Is it lame if I just say 'ditto'?" Courtney laughed slightly. "I don't want to force this into something it's not, which is completely against my nature because I love labeling things- I literally asked for a label maker for my fourteenth birthday. But with you, and this, can we just be happy right now and deal with reality later?" Courtney asked, her eyes pleading.

"Well, we're still teenagers, right? This is what we do- live in a fantasy world without consequences. Or so I hear from my mom," Ethan replied with a smirk. "So, we'll just agree that this is a conversation to be had later?"

Courtney nodded, her mind already feeling relieved. "So, are you going to let me distract you now?" she asked playfully, wanting the power back she'd felt at the pool.

"God, yes. Your legs in that dress are driving me crazy," he flirted.

"Are you saying you want me out of this dress, sir? That does not seem very gentlemanly of you," she scolded jokingly. She could tell he wasn't sure if she was kidding or not, so she made him very aware of her intentions by climbing onto his lap so they were face to face. "Is this better?" she asked quietly, pushing down the wave of *what did you just do* that threatened to creep up.

"So much better," he murmured before brushing her lips with his and drawing her in. She became aware of the fact that the dress in question was very short as he ran his fingertips and down her thighs, making her whole body tingle. His hands slowly traveled places they hadn't before, and her blood forgot how to circulate oxygen properly. He moved his attention from her lips to her neck. Since their encounter in the water that morning, she hadn't been able to think about much else other than being with him. His free hand tangled in her hair and she felt her breath escape her.

"I'm just going to walk up these stairs VERY SLOWLY, in order to avoid the curse of my bad timing striking again," they heard Luke yell from the basement.

"Oh my GOD," Ethan groaned, letting his head fall back against the couch. Courtney slowed her breath and moved to stand up. Ethan pulled her back to sitting on his lap and said slowly, "I sort of need you to sit here for a few minutes if that's cool."

She almost snorted in a very unladylike manner at the implication. "You got it." She was intoxicated by the fact that he wanted her too. They both concentrated on making sure they looked presentable by the time Luke made it to the top of the stairs. Any lasting worry about her upcoming departure was pushed down deep, and she was determined not to let the future ruin her present.

♪ *"American Idiot" - Greenday*
"Here's To Never Growing Up" – Avril Lavigne

Seven

"OKAY! I AM ARRIVING AT THE TOP OF THE STAIRS MOMENTARILY," Luke announced, obnoxiously loud. "Oh, hey, guys," he said casually when he saw them. "Vanessa insists we continue on with 'Throwback Thursday' and you come and play Truth or Dare. So chop-chop- her words, not mine. I don't say lame things like 'chop-chop'."

"Yeah, dude, we'll be right there. Just give us a sec," Ethan replied with a pained expression.

Luke's face went from confused to understanding quite quickly, and then he broke into laughter. "Yeah, okay, man, see you in a minute." He continued laughing all the way down the stairs. Ethan requested that Courtney talk to him about something else, so she gave him the rundown of her hatred of fruit. He looked at her quizzically, but she was used to it.

"People are prejudiced against non-fruit eaters," she complained. "You have no idea. Soccer games as a kid? No snack for Courtney because she doesn't eat oranges. Birthday parties when weirdos put strawberry filling in the cake? Courtney gets no cake." She wasn't quite sure why she was referring to herself in the third person, but it seemed to fit her mood. She was positively buzzing after their interaction. This apparently did the trick because Ethan picked her up and claimed he was going to carry her downstairs that way.

"You are a strange girl, sprinkles, but I'm starting to think you're kind of perfect for me." His tone was serious as he put her down. Courtney blushed and squeezed his hand as they entered the basement. Vanessa was waiting for them, her arms crossed and foot tapping impatiently.

"Could you be slower? I wanna play Truth or Dare! Come, come, sit," she demanded. "Okay, here are the rules-"

"There are no rules for Truth or Dare, babe, let's just play."

"No, my party, my game. As I was saying, everyone gets one veto, you can use it on a Truth or a Dare, but otherwise you gotta play along. No one has to do anything illegal. Well, unless they really want to, I guess. And everything stays in this room. You got it?" They all nodded. Vanessa was a little scary when she was on a mission. Luke was the loudest- always, so he got to go first.

"Courtney, Truth or Dare?" he smiled excitedly.

"Seriously? Picking on the out-of-towner huh? Fine. Dare," she answered bravely, thinking it might be safer than having to answer any personal questions.

"Yes! Now it's a party. I dare you to do a body shot off of… Vanessa," he beamed.

"Oh, Jesus, veto," Courtney replied, laughing.

"What?! Veto on the first one? You're in for a long night, girly, that's not even close to my best dare," Luke warned.

"Okay, so I'm not just saying this because I desperately want to see you lick Vanessa's neck, but he's not lying. His mind is a twisted, twisted place," Ethan agreed. She knew Luke was getting a kick out of it because he thought he could embarrass her. She decided to prove him wrong.

"Lie down, V. Luke, I assume you have the appropriate set-up for this operation?" Courtney questioned, challenging him.

"There ya go. Of course I do. There are perks to having an absentee parent." He went over to his bag and pulled out shot glasses and a bottle of vodka. He sprinkled sugar on Vanessa's neck despite her squirming and put the lemon in her mouth. He held out the shot glass for Courtney, along with one for himself, and said, "Cheers," with a tone that suggested he didn't quite believe she'd do it.

"Cheers," she said back in an even tone. She licked the sugar off of Vanessa's neck, downed the shot, and picked up the lemon with her mouth. She shuddered when the alcohol hit the back of her throat. There was a reason she didn't drink vodka, but Vanessa couldn't stop giggling the entire time, which eased any leftover anxiety. "Happy?" she raised an eyebrow at Luke.

"Oh, you have no idea," he replied. "Your turn."

"Truth or Dare," she said as she turned and looked at Ethan.

"Ahhh, shit," he laughed. "Truth." Courtney was glad. She had been thinking up some questions to ask him, and the body-shot challenge was making her feel a little braver than she should.

"How many girls have you been with?" she asked, staring straight at him, her lungs refusing to take in an appropriate amount of air.

"No, no, no, no, no. Veto. Hell no," he said, refusing to meet her gaze. "We are not traveling down that road today. Next question."

"Well, now you're making me think you're a man-whore. You're better off just answering and easing my mind, don't you think?" Courtney said sweetly, determined to get an answer before she could totally commit to what she thought she wanted with him.

"She's good," Luke interjected.

"Oh my god. Whatever. You asked for this. I want immunity from any backlash that is to come, got it?" he stated very plainly to Courtney. She held up her fingers in a Scout's honor position.

"Two girls."

"Liar," Luke said under a very obvious fake cough.

"No lying allowed!" Vanessa protested.

"Damn it, Luke! Fine, four. That's the real number. You just wait, man, you are going to find your tires slashed one day in the parking lot next year, and you will remember this moment," he threatened. Courtney couldn't tell quite how serious he was in his anger. She tried not to think about the four other girls. *At least it's not fourteen,* she told herself. He was impossibly beautiful, and he had been honest about how he usually... behaved. *Is it really that bad?* Her heart calmed slightly just with the fact that she didn't have to wonder about it anymore. She tried not to let her own number of zero make her feel self-conscious. *Better zero than any number of regrets.*

"Just for the record, and to hopefully win back this girl's affection," gesturing to Courtney, "there hasn't been anyone in a while, okay? Are we good?" he asked specifically to her, toying nervously with the ring on his middle finger.

"We're good," she replied, thinking she meant it. She shook off any leftover concern and refocused on her good mood from earlier. Purposefully, she got up and went to sit on his lap to erase any doubt he had about her answer. His lips found her shoulder, making her shiver.

"Vanessa, Truth or Dare?" Ethan asked.

"I would love to stay and play, y'all, but I think it is time to go TPing! Gosh darn the luck! If only you two hadn't been upstairs for eleven hours!" Vanessa exclaimed innocently. The other three erupted in protest, but she did not waver. She sent Luke upstairs to load up his truck with their supplies while they changed into more stealthy outfits.

"Unbelievable!" Ethan said under his breath, but loud enough for her to hear him.

"Oh, Ethan, don't get so bent out of shape. I didn't like the direction the questions were headed in. My significant other may not be as understanding as the girl you have there," she informed him. "Better that we avoid it altogether."

"Well, when you put it that way, maybe you're right," Ethan conceded. "All right, let's get up there and commit a misdemeanor, shall we?" He grabbed Courtney's hand, pulled her off the couch, and the three headed upstairs to change and meet Luke outside. "So, whose house are we hitting tonight?" he asked.

"I vote for Zack Roads' place!" Luke said emphatically. Zack was Vanessa's ex-boyfriend, so the selection made sense.

What Comes of Eating Doughnuts With a Boy Who Plays Guitar

"Eh, why not? He has it coming, dirt bag," Vanessa agreed, a shadow crossing her face. "It will help Luke get through some of his anger issues too." They piled into the truck for their criminal act.

Luke pulled down the block from Zack's sizable lot with the headlights off.

"Okay, fellow ninjas, here is the game plan. TP the crap out of this yard and don't get caught. Those are the basics. If anyone comes out, we scatter and meet back at the truck when it's safe. Got it?" Luke coached.

"Yes, ninja master. Thank you for teaching us your ways," Courtney joked. Luke flipped her off and got out of the truck. The four sneaked onto the property, and soon there was a silent fireworks show of toilet paper in all directions. They were hushed and stealthy, covering the yard in under seven minutes. They saw a faint light flip on through one of the upstairs windows.

"Crap, crap, crap! Run!!!!" Luke whispered as loud as he could, and they took off running for their lives. The sound of their feet on the pavement seemed to match that of Courtney's heartbeat in her ears. They made it around the corner before anyone came out of the house, and they didn't look back as they bolted for the vehicle. Luke backed it down the street without his lights, and no one breathed until they made it out of the neighborhood and onto one of the back roads to Vanessa's house.

"Oh my GOD, that was awesome. Seriously just as fun as when we were kids," Courtney said breathlessly to Vanessa.

"Right??? This was the best idea ever," she related. Vanessa leaned across the truck and planted a kiss on Luke's mouth. "That's for being a badass," she said as he smiled. The four were abuzz with the high of almost getting caught as they drove back to the house. Courtney couldn't believe how ridiculous they all looked in black with bandanas on their heads like a motorcycle gang, but she still thought Ethan looked delicious. His lean muscles showed through his thin t-shirt and she reached over to grab his hand. He lifted hers to his lips and kissed the back of it sweetly. *How have I lived my whole teenage life without him?*

♪ *"19 You + Me" – Dan + Shay*
"Gravity" – John Mayer

Eight

They arrived back at the house, and Vanessa went to tell her mom that they had returned without being arrested. They still had an hour or so until Ethan's curfew and decided to celebrate the victory in the basement.

"So, I sort of have a surprise for you," Ethan announced.

"Oh, do you now?"

"You all just get comfy, I gotta grab my guitar." They chatted about their general awesomeness and marveled at their TPing skills until he returned. As he sat down on the ottoman in front of her, he looked a bit apprehensive.

"Ok, so I've been working on something for you. I just learned it, so bear with me, but I've been thinking about doing this since the night we met. I kind of made it my own because, well, I can't really rock a southern accent, but here you go." He breathed and started to play the opening chords of one of Courtney's favorite country songs, "19 You + Me," by Dan and Shay. The way Ethan played it made it sound more rock than country, but her heart felt like it might burst; she was so enamored with the boy sitting in front of her. As he sang about back road adventures and first loves and first kisses, she forgot there was anyone else in the room. Anyone else in the universe. It probably wasn't healthy for one's adrenaline to rise and fall this much within one night, but her heart pounded and she blinked far more than necessary as she considered the fact that he had not only listened to, but learned and perfected, this song for her.

When he finished, he looked up at her, his nerves still showing. "That's about as country as I can get."

Courtney stood up and threw her arms around him. "You are wonderful," she whispered in his ear.

He pulled her in for a quick kiss. "Anything for you."

"Why don't you ever play songs for me?" Vanessa questioned Luke.

"Well, V, I don't play guitar. But I am happy to sing for you." He burst into some god-awful version of "I Will Always Love You."

"Ahhhh! Okay, stop, I get it!" Vanessa begged, giggling as Luke tickled her on the couch. Courtney redirected her focus to Ethan and left them to their own thing.

"Hey, I know you have to leave in a bit, but do you wanna ...?" she asked seriously, tilting her head towards the hallway.

"Um, yes." As they approached one of the downstairs bedrooms, Ethan shot her an uncomfortable look. "So, I guess I should tell you that I don't really have a curfew tonight. I mean, I do normally, but I was planning on sleeping at Luke's anyway, and his mom clearly does not enforce one for him, so... yeah. I just wanted to throw that out there. Not that we need to, like, spend the night together or do anything. Am I sounding like that's what I expect by telling you this? I wasn't going to say anything. I'm going to stop talking now." She enjoyed watching him struggle far more than she should have. *At least it's not just me, then.*

Courtney did not respond to his explanation, but instead jumped on the bed and sat crisscross while she motioned for him to do the same. "Come here," she commanded with a confidence she didn't know she possessed. She tried to keep her palms from sweating, knowing what was about to come out of her mouth. *Filter. Have a filter.*

"Okay," he said, sitting down, awkwardly folding his long legs in front of him.

"I think it is sweet and wonderful that you are working so hard to make sure I'm...comfortable? I am certain that you have inferred by this time that I am not super experienced in this, ah, area." She resisted the urge to want to cover her face or sink through a hole in the floor at the intense awkwardness she was experiencing at this type of honesty. "I have never met someone where it was even a decision I needed to think about, because I've never had a real... connection with anyone. I know that sounds trite and juvenile, but I don't know what other word to use." Ethan started to say something, and she put one finger up to his lips. "Please let me get this out. I didn't say anything last time, so I feel like I have to set the record straight. So shhh," she added as playfully as she could. He looked surprised but complied. "As I was saying, I get that you don't want to pressure me or offend me and you want to be like a knight with a shining guitar or whatever. What I need for you to know is that I'm not a delicate flower or something. I know I like glitter and when you call me sprinkles, but I'm also capable of knowing what I want. I can promise you that you will not 'talk me into' doing anything I don't want to do, no matter how smooth you are." That last bit was accompanied by a tentative smile.

"I do have some pretty good lines," he bragged.

"Yeah, yeah. The other night when you had your big apology about grabbing my butt?" *Am I really talking about this right now? Is this completely necessary?* She was too far into it to turn back, so she pressed onward. "If I weren't okay with it, I would have stopped you. I kind of like that you like my ass," she told him, lightening the mood and trying to hide the blush spreading rapidly across her face. "You just seemed so set on asking for forgiveness that I let you go on about it. I just need you not to be afraid of, I don't know, tricking me into something. I'm a big girl, and I'm not so easily led astray. If you want... *more*, with us, with this, then push for it. If I'm not okay, I'll push back. Bear claw, remember?" she finally concluded, holding up her hand in a claw-like position. Ethan looked like he was processing for an extended moment. "I talk a lot. I know," she admitted, waiting for him to catch up. *So much for developing that filter,* she thought.

"You might be the most incredible girl I've ever met, Courtney Ross." He sat and looked thoughtful for a moment. "I know you can take care of yourself, I just- I don't want to screw this up."

"I will be the first to tell you if you are screwing this up. And you're not."

"Okay. I will remind myself that you are not a delicate flower," he promised. "But while we're in deep-discussion mode, do we need to talk about Truth or Dare? I don't want to lie to you, so if you need to ask me anything else, I'll tell you."

"I'm okay with your number, if that's what you're asking. So, I guess, just…did you love any of them? All of them?" The question in and of itself was enough to make her want to vomit. She didn't know what the better answer was. The thought of him being in love… being with other girls, it evoked a depth of jealousy she hadn't ever experienced.

He let out a long sigh. "I don't know. I mean, I've thrown the word out there before, before I even knew what it meant, because I thought that's what people did in relationships. But no, I don't think I ever actually did. I wasn't lying earlier when I said there hadn't been anyone in a while. I realized after I moved here that just hooking up with whomever I felt like wasn't going to fly in a town this small, and I actually started to get to know people. And I liked them. So I don't want to be that guy who messes with girls' heads." He pressed his lips together like he might actually be trying to stop the next words from escaping. In the end, he failed. "But I can tell you I have never felt for anyone what I feel for you."

"Ditto," she replied, smiling. There was a lot of smiling. She didn't know if she'd ever stop smiling. Forming more words than that proved impossible after he'd made her heart skip. "Can we snuggle now?" she asked, making him laugh.

"Whatever you wanna do, babe." She let him pull her close and intertwined her legs with his. She threaded her thumbs through his belt loops and ran her fingers lightly against his hips. He brushed a few curls out of her face and ran his thumb along her cheekbone, tangling his fingers through her hair and meeting her lips with his. She could tell the energy had shifted. Their encounters always had something electric behind them, but this was deeper. He had a new intensity as he pressed her body closer into his and peeled off her black t-shirt. The overwhelming sense of must-have-him-now overshadowed the realization that no one had ever *undressed* her before. His eyes held her gaze briefly, and his expression was one she didn't recognize, but it was *hungry*, and it sent heat through her veins.

He moved his mouth down to her collarbone, planting small kisses along the way. She let him go further than before, and was surprised at how comfortable she was with him. She released her worry about her limited experience, and found that she liked how she could affect him with her fingertips and her lips, feeling his muscles contract beneath them. His kisses were more intense, and she realized he had been holding back before. He gripped her hips with certainty instead of hesitation, and her breath got caught somewhere between her heart and her lips when he traced winding circles up her thighs. They spent the next hour testing their new limits. When she knew he was satisfied with where she was willing to go, and where she needed to stop, her worry faded into nothing but wanting and excitement.

They lay together, temperatures returning to normal, heart rates slowing, and he looked into her eyes. "There is something I want to say to you, but I don't know about my timing," he said plainly.

"Okay?" Courtney came out of the comfortable space she was occupying next to him. She attempted to smooth her hair and right her shirt. Her skin still felt hot in the places his lips had been.

"I guess you and I tend to say things when we feel them, I just…" She waited patiently for him to find his words, feeling like he didn't need her to respond. He took a deep breath. "I think I may be falling for you. Like nothing I've… well, it's new. You don't have to say it back, or even respond… I just needed to tell you that." He avoided meeting her eyes for the time being. Courtney's chest tightened. She knew this was a *moment* for them. It did not escape her that he hadn't used the word 'love,' but in knowing him, she knew that what he did say was enough.

"I love you too," she offered quietly. He let out a sigh like he had been holding his breath.

"Wow, okay, I'm glad you saw through my lie before; I totally needed you to say it back." He laughed, sliding his hand back around her waist.

"Was there really any doubt?' she asked.

"Well, one doesn't like to assume, right?" He pulled her back into his space and kissed her again. And again. And again. Lying there, they both came down from the high of being together, and fatigue set in. "All right, sprinkles, I should probably go find Luke and get us to his house before the sun comes up and V's mom wonders what the hell is going on," he admitted reluctantly. They went and found Luke and Vanessa asleep on the couch, and they got them both coherent enough to get up and go.

"I'll call you tomorrow? Or today, rather," she promised, looking at the clock.

"Absolutely." He kissed her once more before walking out to Luke's truck.

"Okay, I am not really awake right now, but I have a gut feeling I'm going to want to hear about something tomorrow. For now, make sure I don't fall down the steps," Vanessa told her, dragging her feet.

"I will," Courtney promised, and she practically floated up the stairs to bed.

♪ *"Anthem" –Good Charlotte*
"One Step at a Time" – Jordin Sparks

Nine

Courtney awoke to the sun hitting her face rather violently. "Mehhhhh, why so bright?" she asked before fully opening her eyes.

"Ladies, time to get up," Vanessa's mother answered.

"Mom, have you gone insane? It's gotta be like seven a.m. right now." Vanessa yawned dramatically.

"It's almost one in the afternoon." The girls sat up with a jolt.

"Really?" Courtney asked.

"Really. Which makes me feel like you two need a plan. No more sleeping 'till noon and staying up until god knows when with your boyfriends, so up! Get showered and I'll find you something to eat. We are making plans today."

"Ughhhhhh, 'making plans' is never a good thing when it comes to my mother." Vanessa groaned. "We might as well get ready or she'll be back in five minutes." The girls slowly woke up and made themselves presentable. Courtney hadn't realized how hungry she was until she saw the spread Mrs. Roberts had set out. Sandwiches, soup, and salad all looked delicious to her.

"Alright, girls, I spoke to Courtney's mom this morning when she called to check in-"

"She did?" Courtney interrupted.

"She did, and rightly so. She's just being your mom, wanting to know what I thought of Ethan. Don't worry, I like him just fine," she continued when she saw worry cross Courtney's face. "But we got to talking about how old you both are now and how this is one of the last breaks you have before you go out on your own. I know that sounds sappy, but we are mothers, so don't roll your eyes, Vanessa," she scolded. "I know you will both legally be adults by the end of the summer, and I have given you your space during this visit, but I'd like to propose a little road trip for tomorrow." The girls exchanged glances and waited for her to explain. "Well, I thought maybe we could pick a few colleges and go tour them before you guys have to make your final decisions about school next year. We could just make a day of it, see some local schools, and stay in a hotel overnight, maybe with a spa? We can get breakfast and come home the next morning." Vanessa looked surprised. She caught Courtney's eye and shrugged her shoulders. They shared their mutual unspoken feelings. "That actually sounds pretty cool, Mom," Vanessa replied slowly. "We're in. Right, Court?"

"Definitely, that sounds perfect. I've been stressing over college; it would be really helpful to see the campuses in person and not on a virtual tour."

"Excellent, it's settled then. We will leave tomorrow morning bright and early, so you tell your men you need to be asleep at a decent hour tonight, got it? I'm not dragging your butts out of bed again. And maybe eat a vegetable now and then, huh? You need nutrition and exercise- Vanessa, why am I paying for a gym membership if you're not going to go? Take your friends, and lift a weight or something," she chastised, leaving the kitchen. Vanessa stuck her tongue out at her and filled her plate back up with food.

"Well, she's not wrong. We have been lazy. I wouldn't mind getting a workout in, if you wanna go," Courtney admitted after chuckling at V's stubbornness.

"Fine, fine. And I know you wanna take Ethan with, so just text him already. You can look longingly at each other while you work up a

What Comes of Eating Doughnuts With a Boy Who Plays Guitar

sweat; I'm sure it will all be very 'National Geographic.' It's a good thing I think the two of you are cute together, or you might make me want to throw up."

"Have I told you today what a kind, generous, and supportive friend you are, and how much I love you?" Courtney sweet-talked. She simultaneously pulled out her phone to text Ethan as Vanessa had said. She had never claimed she didn't want him to go. Especially if she was going on a road trip the following day.

> E: Sure, I'll go. Will you let me try to bench-press you? :)
> C: Will it hurt your manly pride if I say no because I don't want to be dropped on my head? Lol.
> E: Yes.
> E: I'm just messing around with you. Maybe I can do more of that later? :) I can't stop thinking about last night.
> C: Me either. And yes to the previous question. <3 you.
> E: I love you too. I like writing that. See you soon.

Courtney almost dropped her phone when she turned her head and saw Vanessa standing right behind her.

"SHUT THE FRONT DOOR, COURTNEY ROSS!" Vanessa yelled. "He *LOVES* you??! What the hell went on last night when Luke and I fell asleep? You didn't..."

"No, no, we didn't. I mean. There were things. Good things. Fun things." Courtney blushed.

"Did you say it first or did he? I have to hear this story," Vanessa gushed. "How did you not lead with this as soon as we got up?!"

"He said it first. I couldn't believe it. I mean, do you think it's too much, too fast... does it sound ridiculous to say that I'm in love with him?" Courtney questioned earnestly. She didn't want to be that girl who just spouted off feelings before even knowing she had them. This just felt... surreal. Like he *got* her. No one had ever made her *less* nervous before. People in general just... well, she didn't like them looking at her unless she was cheering. But she really liked it when he looked at her.

"Is it shocking? Yes. But that is because I know both of you. I can't believe he told you he loves you. That is like a HUGE deal. Holy crap. I mean, I knew you guys would hit it off, I just didn't imagine… And to answer your question, yes, it's fast. But who's to say what's too fast? Don't let anyone make it seem like you're not allowed to feel what you feel." Courtney breathed a sigh of relief. She just needed to hear someone else say that it was ok. "But Court, I gotta ask. Have you guys *really* talked about what happens next week when you leave? I mean, high school and long distance, is that even something you want? I don't want to be a buzz kill, I'm just worried that there's a crash and burn in the future, and I don't want to see it happen, not to either of you."

"I know. I know the conversation is coming and I just don't want to deal with it. I'm avoiding it." Tears started to well up in her eyes. "Like, how can I just walk away? This doesn't feel like a summer fling, but maybe it is, what do I know?" *Do. Not. Cry.*

"Well, maybe you just avoid it until you can't, and ride the wave until it's done. I mean, you've already been accepted to college here, maybe you guys can just make it work until then? Like, you could fly out for prom or something! That would be so fun, and we could go together!" As usual, Vanessa was getting ahead of herself. "I guess you won't know for sure until the two of you decide to get real with each other about it."

Courtney got herself together, but knew Vanessa was speaking the truth. She didn't have much longer to delay. Her friend had opened a tiny window of hope in reminding her that college was only a year away, but her gut warned her she might be in for an epic heartbreak.

"All right, well, buck up, little pup, it was your idea to go and sweat our butts off at the gym, so get ready."

"I did think that was a good idea, didn't I? Ah well, it can't hurt. It just means we get to eat pizza and cake tonight, right?"

"Duh. But speaking of cake, do you wanna do something like a party for your birthday while you're here? It wouldn't be as crazy as the last because my parents are back, but I can put something together if you like."

"Huh, I hadn't really thought about it. I'm allowed to vote at the end of next week. Is there anything else exciting that comes along with eighteen?"

"Ummmm, you can legally sign contracts and, like, own stuff, I think."

"Well, that doesn't sound all that enticing, but let me think about it. I do want to celebrate, but I'm not feeling like a big party if that's cool."

"No prob, Bob. You just let me know." They got ready quickly and headed to the gym.

* * *

"Hey, beautiful," Ethan called as he walked up, kissing the top of her head. She thought it would be odd seeing him in gym clothes when he normally had a whole rocker-vibe going on, but it gave her a whole new appreciation for his tall, lean frame.

"How does a boy who plays guitar get a body like yours?" she asked him playfully.

"Okay, well, the two of you are obnoxiously adorable right now, so I'm going to go hop on the treadmill while you fawn over each other's perfection, 'k?" Vanessa smiled snarkily.

"I'll catch up with you in a second, V," Courtney promised as she walked away.

"Well, to answer your question, I used to be a swimmer before I moved here. I didn't want to join a new team and be the low man on the totem pole as a junior, so I just focused on finding a band."

"A swimmer, huh? Like in a speedo?" She imagined and grinned.

"Yes, in a speedo. You can just save that mental picture for later."

"Speaking of your band, don't you need to… practice? Or play somewhere. Do you call it a 'gig,' or is that, like, not a term people use anymore?"

He grinned at the question. "Yeah, you can call it a gig. One of my band mates has been out of town for a couple of weeks on vacation, so it hasn't been much of an issue, but they have been getting on my case to practice the past couple of days. No worries, though, you take priority," he assured her.

"Well you may be able to satisfy them," she explained, starting to stretch. "V and I are going on a quick college tour road trip with her mom tomorrow, and we'll be back the next morning."

"Really? That's cool. Do you, um, do you really think you'll come out here for school?" His interest was transparent, but it gave her a chill all over again.

"I don't know. It's one of those things that sounds great, and in my head I just want to do it and send in my paperwork, and then I have a stroke and flip out about the implications of leaving home and being on my own. I'm hoping actually being on campus will help me decide."

"I get that. Well, for what it's worth, I hope you like them."

"Well, it's worth a lot." She smiled. "Now come work out with me." She grabbed his hands and went to find Vanessa. Courtney put in her ear buds and started to run. It had been a while since she'd been able to tune out everything else and just sweat. Ethan, senior year, college, leaving to go back home, she let it all fade away as she got going. Breathing in and out, that was what she liked about being in the zone. While running wasn't her typical workout of choice, she did like that it simplified her perspective.

Out of the corner of her eye, she could see him lifting weights and unknowingly moving his head to whatever was playing in his ears. Without giving her brain the option to overanalyze, she knew in that moment that she really did love him. Whatever she chose to do next would be with that in mind, and it didn't matter if it was silly or rushed or unbelievable to anyone else, because she knew that what existed there was real. Even in understanding that the likelihood of having a happily-ever-after scenario with a boy she had met at seventeen was not good, her heart didn't really care. She was going to do exactly what Vanessa had said; ride the wave as long as it lasted, even if that meant it would pull her under.

Five miles later, she went to cool down and stretch, and found Ethan and Vanessa conversing.

"So, okay, I'm sorry, but my good friend Vanessa here was just telling me that it's your birthday next week? And you were planning on telling me this…"

"Ah, yeah, well. I'm sorry, I didn't want to make a thing of it. It's just a day. You don't have to, like, buy me a present or anything, I'm not eight."

"Shut up, you love presents. Ones with sparkly wrapping paper and bows," Vanessa said, calling her out. Courtney scowled at her as menacingly as she could.

"Well, I've got an idea brewing, but it's going to be a surprise. Vanessa? Not a word," he made her promise. "However, for now, I've gotta shower and go to work. Can I stop over and see you for a minute tonight? I know you guys have to turn in early; it'll just be for a second."

"Of course, just let me know when." She kissed him longer than what may have been appropriate in a gym full of people, but he didn't seem to mind. "See you tonight."

"And thanks, V, for the heads up." He smiled as he walked away.

* * *

The girls went home and got cleaned up. They decided to continue their healthy trend for the day and made a big salad for dinner, but eventually baked a batch of brownies as well. Ethan did stop by for a moment, but it wasn't long enough.

"I don't think I have gone an entire day without seeing you since you got here. I might actually see my band tomorrow, which is great because another band dropped out of the festival this weekend, so we sort of agreed to jump in. It's been a while since we've been over our set. Hopefully we haven't forgotten how to play."

"Really? Like, I can come and see you?" she asked, dreamily envisioning him singing to her on stage. "Well yes, go and practice. I don't want them to hate me because you ditched them all month. I realize I just sort of just invited myself to the festival, but I need to meet more of your friends. Or perhaps you are so ashamed of me that you want to keep me hidden away," she teased dramatically.

"You can meet them, and of course you're coming to the festival. For the record, I want everyone to know that you're with me. So if you want me to wear a label or a sign or something that says 'I love this girl,' you just let me know. It can spice up my wardrobe."

"I'll get right to work on bedazzling something special for you."

"Bedazzling? I'll really have to up my game then." He bent down to kiss her. He seemed more serious tonight despite their banter. He held her longer than normal and didn't seem to be able to make himself leave. "If this is a taste of what saying goodbye to you feels like, I'm really not looking forward to next week…I know we agreed not to talk about it yet," he insisted, anticipating her protest, "I just need you to know that I want to work this out. Okay? Whatever that means." He kissed her once more and made her promise to call him while on her college tour.

"Of course."

"Goodnight, sprinkles." His grin made Courtney sigh as she shut the door. This boy could be the end of her.

Courtney and Vanessa tried to go to sleep at a reasonable hour. About thirty minutes after turning in, Courtney heard Vanessa whisper, "Girl, are you asleep?"

"Not even close," she admitted, turning on the light.

"Let's go for a drive."

"That sounds awesome, actually. Anywhere in particular?"

"Wherever. Back roads. I wanna drive fast. We'll just say we're going out for road trip snacks."

"In our pajamas?"

"Sure, why not?"

"Okay, then, let's do it." The girls executed the plan and hopped into Vanessa's car. She chose a playlist and plugged in her phone to the audio system. Courtney laughed when she heard the first song. Apparently they were going to rock out to some old school diva anthems. They waited until the car was off of the main road, but they belted some Celine Dion to the best of their abilities. The cool, humid night air felt cleansing as her hair whipped around her face. *God, I love this place.*

♪ *"Breakaway" – Kelly Clarkson*

Ten

"Rise and shine, girlies!" Vanessa's mom shouted cheerily.

"What ungodly hour is this, Mother?"

"Five a.m., up, up, up! Breakfast is on the table, I wanna get on the road. I went to the coffee shop and picked up those drinks you like. Now, out of bed!"

"An iced mocha with a double shot and sprinkles on top?" Vanessa confirmed.

"Yes, yes, get up!"

"Okay, okay, we're coming. If I have to get up, so do you, Ross," Vanessa demanded, following her mom downstairs. Courtney was starting to regret their late-night adventure. Her brain wanted sleep.

"I'm up…" She yawned. She pulled on a light yellow long-sleeved shirt and her comfiest jeans, as it looked overcast. In glancing out the window to survey the weather, she saw Ethan's car pull in front of the house. Her heart rate picked up. He looked like he had rolled out of bed in basketball shorts and a Gem City High School t-shirt. *Yep, still hot.* She opened the bedroom window, and was unsure if the chill she got was from the cool morning breeze or from him. "Are you going to try to convince me you're always up this early and just happened to be in the neighborhood?"

"Not likely. I didn't even know things were going on in the world at this time of day. But amazingly enough, Jim's is open, and I wanted an

What Comes of Eating Doughnuts With a Boy Who Plays Guitar

excuse to see you before you left. I come bearing sprinkle doughnuts, so get your butt down here and let me wish you a safe trip and all that." She raced down the stairs and threw open the front door, all the while Vanessa and her mother were looking at her like she was crazy.

"As promised, breakfast for you all," Ethan said, holding out the bag.

"Yay! Those smell delectable! You're so good to me." Courtney's eyes shown with the kind of adoration that only comes from unexpected baked goods with high sugar content. *He just gets me.*

"Well, I'm trying. And really, with the vocabulary this early?" He grinned. "Just don't fall in love with any college guys while you're gone, okay?" he finished lightheartedly. "I won't keep you, I know you guys gotta leave, I just wanted to see you off and make sure you had your sugar fix. I am going the hell back to bed."

She giggled in understanding at that. "All right, I don't blame you. I will see you tomorrow when we get back. Have fun at band practice." She kissed him sweetly. "Love you."

"Love you, have fun." They were starting to lose the awkwardness in their goodbyes, and it seemed like the universe was rooting for them—allowing things to fall into place. Courtney wandered dreamily back into the kitchen to share the doughnuts.

"That boy has it *bad* for you, girl. I would fall over dead from shock if Luke showed up here at five a.m., even if I were leaving for the Peace Corps." Vanessa was almost fully awake and up to speed with her sarcasm. "Now hand over the pastries."

"Oh, stop, Luke adores you. Ethan and I just have this black cloud looming in the distance of our, whatever this is." Vanessa assessed her closely, and she willed herself not to get upset.

"Don't go to the dark side! Stay here and be happy and excited and amazed that your lover just brought you doughnuts. Black clouds are for next week!" Courtney took a deep breath and let those thoughts go. Today was hopefully going to be about figuring out her future.

"All right, doughnuts and mochas it is." She smiled, picking up her drink.

"Thank you." Vanessa's tone held relief. They proceeded to stuff their faces with a massive amount of calories, using the excuse that they would be physically and mentally exerting themselves over the next day. Mrs. Roberts rallied them to get their stuff and pack it into her blue SUV.

"I've made sure to pull out all of my favorite road trip tunes," Mrs. Roberts said, holding up an ancient looking CD holder.

"Negative!" Vanessa yelled, practically ripping the CDs out of her mom's hand. "I've got six playlists ready to go, and that's just for the way there. You're outta your element here, Mom," she teased.

"Such a mean daughter! I'm sure Courtney would never speak that way to her mother." She winked at her in the rearview mirror.

"Never ever. I'm a good child." Courtney received a glare from Vanessa. They got the approved music going and danced their way out of Gem City and onto the interstate. First on their list was University of Dayton since it was the closest. It was probably also the top school on Courtney's list of those in Ohio. She became more observant the closer they got to the campus. She found herself among tree-lined streets, Victorian houses, and red brick buildings as they approached.

"This is beautiful," Mrs. Roberts commented, pulling into one of the lots. Courtney just tried to take it all in. The paths were cobblestone rather than concrete, and the doors to each building were a dark walnut stained wood.

"The online tour really didn't do it justice," Courtney admitted. She had liked this school the best, even before walking on campus, because it was small and had a great pre-law program. Now that she was there, it felt like she could see herself: living in the dorms, walking the pathways to class, being near Vanessa. Maybe she was thinking of Ethan too, though she didn't want to let him cloud her judgment.

"Courtney, make sure to take lots of pictures for your mom, I know she wishes she could be here," Vanessa's mom reminded. They explored the library, the student union, and were able to get into one of the dorm rooms since they were mostly empty for the summer.

What Comes of Eating Doughnuts With a Boy Who Plays Guitar

"I don't know if I could live in one room with another human, but these are pretty nice," Vanessa declared, looking around at the sparse living space. "I think I could spruce it up." Mrs. Roberts seemed happy that Vanessa appeared to be getting into the college spirit, so she offered to take them out instead of eating the sandwiches they had packed.

"You need to get a feel for the town, so this is the best way to do it." They enjoyed lunch at a small pizzeria. They gave it a seven out of ten, only knocking off points for the lackluster personalities of the employees. Afterwards, they piled back into the car for the drive up to Bowling Green. Courtney knew this was Vanessa's school of choice. It was quite a bit bigger than UD, and Mrs. Roberts had gone there as well. "We will spend the night up there. I found a hotel with spa services and booked us all a massage for after dinner tonight."

"Your mom kind of kicks ass, V."

"And don't you forget it." Her mom smiled.

"Well, now that's just going to go to her head, you have to be careful with compliments like that, friend," Vanessa joked. Courtney fell asleep on part of the drive up, and she was glad. She woke up feeling refreshed and hyper.

"Are we there yet?" she asked, being purposefully annoying. Vanessa's mom attempted to hit her with a college brochure.

"You bite your tongue, Miss Perky. I've been up here driving while you got your beauty rest!"

"Hehe, sorry. Just kidding."

"But yes, we are almost there, ya ding-a-ling."

Courtney enjoyed walking around the BG campus but already knew that if she chose Ohio over Arizona, she would be going to UD. It was clear that Vanessa was interested, though, which made her mom happy. They all enjoyed a late dinner near the hotel and the most amazing massages. Courtney felt relaxed sipping her cucumber and mint water with her feet in the spa.

"This water is amazing. Like, why haven't we been drinking water like this our whole lives? It's just cucumber, I can slice a cucumber. But it's like magic!"

"I was literally thinking the exact same thing," Vanessa replied. "It's like an energizing elixir of some kind. I don't get it." Vanessa's mom soon joined them and sat down.

"That was fun, wasn't it? We could probably go rent a movie in the room before we go to sleep. Do you guys still want to hit Ohio State tomorrow before going home?" The friends exchanged looks.

"I think we're actually good, Mom. I like it here, and I know Courtney fell in love at UD, so can we just have a leisurely morning before we head home?" Vanessa asked.

"I think I agree," Mrs. Roberts responded. "I had an awesome time with you girls today. I know it's selfish, Courtney, because your mom would miss you so much, but I do hope you decide to go to school out here. You could come to our house for any holidays or long weekends that you couldn't travel home. You know I love you like my own. Vanessa is so happy when you're here." Her mom teared up a bit.

"Awww! Mrs. Roberts, that's so nice! I love being here, too." Courtney also felt a bit emotional. She felt Vanessa's arm link through hers and she put her head on her friend's shoulder. There was no denying that she was not ready to go home. She felt like she already was home.

♪ *"Punk Rock Princess"* – Something Corporate
"Breathe" – Michelle Branch

Eleven

After the road trip, Courtney strengthened her resolve even more to find her way back there at some point. The scales had tipped in favor of going to college out-of-state. While it still scared her to think about really being on her own, she felt a new sense of comfort in her own head. And she wasn't the only one who had noticed.

"I think I like you being in love. You're much less stressed," Vanessa touted the next afternoon. They were getting ready to go to see Ethan's band play. Courtney was excited to meet his friends, and thankfully her nerves were kept at bay.

"Well, I'm still not sure what I should wear, but I'm kind of just feeling hyper," Courtney admitted, bouncing on her toes, "not nervous."

"You realize you are not the same girl who walked off the plane earlier this month, right? Who had to take Jell-O-shots just to go to a party? The way you are now… it suits you better." Courtney thought about it while she went through her clothes. She supposed Vanessa was right, and she hoped the feeling would last. Her wardrobe choice landed on dark jeans and a bright turquoise tank top with black lace trim. She knew Ethan liked it; he said it made her look "hot as hell," and that was a good enough reason for her.

"You ready? Luke's just going to meet us there."

"Yep!" They hopped in the Camaro and drove to the next town over for the summer Strawberry Festival. It would be pretty low key, but these were the kinds of things Courtney missed most about small town life. Any event she went to in Phoenix would be jam-packed. And hot. This was much more her pace. They arrived and trekked across the dirt lot to the town park where the stage was set up. Vanessa'd had the forethought to bring a blanket for them to sit on in the grass, so they made themselves comfy and bought frozen strawberry lemonades.

"These are freaking delicious," Courtney proclaimed. "All beverages should be served in a frozen form."

"Ah-greed, friend." Vanessa lifted up her plastic cup to toast to this momentous discovery. Luke joined them a few minutes later.

"Hey babe- is that? Did you get a frozen lemonade without me?" he asked in mock horror.

"Well, I got one for you, but if you're going to be mean, I'll just drink it too."

"Aw, you're the best girlfriend ever," he said, kissing her sloppily. Vanessa dramatically wiped her mouth.

"Your kissing skills are going downhill." He went to make a reply, but Ethan's band had started to assemble, and the sound check drowned him out. The festival emcee, who was probably the local high school's student body president, came up and introduced the band.

"So give it up for Tin Roof, you guys!" Courtney just smiled while the crowd cheered. She was looking forward to seeing Ethan on stage. He looked up and smiled at her, and she blew him a kiss.

"What have you done to Fisher? He used to be a chick magnet, and you've made him all, like, domesticated," Luke complained.

"Oh, shut it, he's happy," Vanessa told him. Courtney just ignored him, and chose to forget the "chick magnet" descriptor in addition to the way it formed a small knot in her stomach. The band was actually quite good, and Courtney sang along to most of their covers. She loved listening to him sing; it reminded her of the night they had met. She cheered the loudest after their last song, and caught Ethan's eye to

What Comes of Eating Doughnuts With a Boy Who Plays Guitar

smile at him. However, to her shock and horror, he took the mic after the applause had ended and addressed the crowd.

"Ladies and gentlemen, I know that was supposed to be our last song, but I was hoping you might indulge me and help me get my girlfriend up here to sing a little Everclear. Her name is Courtney, and I would so appreciate it if you could be as convincing as possible, because she probably wants to kill me right now." His smile was lighting up his whole face. Courtney's heart was racing. *Oh, this is going to look so lame if I refuse to go up there. Breathe, breathe, breathe. Did he just call me his girlfriend? Holy crap, okay, okay, okay. So much for that self-confidence sticking around*, she thought quickly. She felt Vanessa nudge her from behind.

"Come on, girl, go sing. I'll record it. It'll be something you can show your grandkids when you and Ethan are old and gray." She was so freaking persuasive. Courtney didn't know how, but her feet started moving her towards the stage. She attempted to look self-assured while still shooting daggers out of her eyes at Ethan for doing this. People cheered when she emerged from the crowd and hopped up next to him.

Ethan wrapped her in a huge hug, and she whispered, "You are in So. Much. Trouble," into his ear.

"I know," he answered, "but it's worth it." He adjusted the mic for her and picked up his guitar. *It's just like the bonfire. There's nothing different. Pretend there's no microphone.* He flawlessly played the song she had sung for him that first night at the party, and she managed to make it through without throwing up, her voice becoming less shaky with each verse. Her hands refused to stop, however, until she was done. Once it was over, she was somehow able to appreciate the high of performing in public. Ethan kissed her, drawing more cheers, and thanked the crowd on behalf of Tin Roof.

"That was a mean thing to do, Ethan Fisher!" she told him forcefully once they were alone. Her hands were still tingly, and she could hear her heart beating in her ears.

"Oh my god, you were amazing. Having you on stage with me was, like, such a freaking rush. Please don't stay mad. Just let me bask in your awesomeness, okay?" The look in his eyes was one of complete joy, and she was smiling before she even knew she wasn't mad anymore. "Thank you. I love you. Like, I love you," he repeated as he wrapped his arms around her.

"So, this is the girl, then, huh? Not a bad showing out there." A cute boy with dark hair from Ethan's band had walked up, his hand outstretched. Courtney immediately reached out to shake it. "I'm Tyler," he said. He was shorter than Ethan, but still tall by all accounts, and he had several eyebrow piercings, making his dark eyes look harsh.

"Nice to meet you, Tyler. You guys were great. I'm so glad I got to see you play." The rest of his band sauntered up and she got a round of introductions- Silas, Jared, and Chris. They all had a similar edge to them, although Jared seemed slightly more laid back than the others. She had a hard time reconciling the Ethan she knew with the rest of his band.

"We're gonna go puff in my van, you guys want?" Tyler asked, looking unconcerned. *Puff like the magical dragon?* she wondered briefly. She assumed he was referring to weed, but she honestly had no idea.

"Nah, man, we're good. I'm gonna head out with Courtney. Do you need help loading anything?"

"We got it," Jared replied. "See you at practice." Courtney simply could not imagine her version of Ethan hanging out with these guys. The knot in her stomach made itself known again. She let Ethan take her hand and lead her back to Luke and Vanessa.

"So... those are your friends." She tried to maintain a non-judgmental tone.

"I know. They are rough around the edges, but I swear they're good guys," he promised. She didn't know if she really believed him, but she had only met them for a moment. First impressions could be deceiving.

"Okay," she stated simply. "Um, just for the record... the whole smoking thing-"

What Comes of Eating Doughnuts With a Boy Who Plays Guitar

"You caught that, huh? Yeah, they do some self-medicating. I don't though, if that's what you're asking. I, well, I have, in the past, but as a rule I don't. I'd like to keep singing in a band, so I try not to jack up my voice. That, and I think I'm laid back enough already." He grinned, nudging her with his elbow. She breathed a sigh of relief. She didn't know if that would have been something she could have gotten past at the moment and was glad she didn't have to find out. She squeezed his hand and let go of some of her worry. They caught up with Vanessa and Luke, and after much ado about her impromptu concert, they decided to stick around for the festival fireworks. It was something of a small-town fairytale to lie under the stars, fireflies roaming the skies, and watch the colors and the crackle of the fireworks burst above their heads. She found that space where she fit under Ethan's arm and just appreciated her spot on the time-space continuum right at that very minute as she traced her fingers down his chest and across his stomach muscles.

"Are you trying to tickle me?" He sounded amused. "Because I'm not ticklish. It feels good though. You don't have to stop," he said as she went to move her hand. They lay like that for a while, and she didn't think she would ever want to leave.

"Alright, lovers, Courtney and I have to get going. Ethan, you don't need a ride, do you? Did you bring your car?" Vanessa asked him.

"Yeah, I drove. Any chance you'll let me take Courtney home?" he asked, giving Vanessa his most charming smile.

"Ugh, whatever. Only because I know you're all sad and blah because she has to leave soon. I will allow you to chauffeur her to my house," she said in a parental tone. Courtney laughed and linked her arm with Ethan's, the butterflies in her stomach fluttering, happy their night didn't have to end just yet.

♪ *"Firework" – Katy Perry*

Twelve

Vanessa was acting unusually interested in Courtney's appearance the next day. She insisted that they visit the salon and both get a blow-out.

"Come on! It'll be fun. I love your curly hair, but it's good to change it up. I don't think you've straightened it once since you've been here. Ethan will love it," she added for effect.

"I'll go, I mean, whatever, I just think you're being weird in caring about my hair." Courtney did not relay the nagging voice of self-criticism about her somewhat-frizzy hair made worse by the constant humidity.

"You'll thank me later," she said in a sing-song voice.

"Why, what's going on later?" Courtney asked. She didn't remember making any specific plans for that day.

"Nothing. Just remember to shave your legs, ok?" V advised.

"What the hell? What do you know?" she demanded.

"I know nothing." Courtney attempted to bribe, guilt, and physically force Vanessa to tell her what was up while on their way to the salon, but she began to conclude that her friend should work for the CIA.

"I can't even believe I call you my best friend!" Courtney exclaimed. "This is like torture! It's like asking me to walk around all day calmly, knowing full well something is going to jump out at me!"

"Nothing will jump out at you. Enjoy your blow-out and calm down. Be happy." That was the last Vanessa would say on the subject. It took a while for the stylist to tame her massive amount of hair, but she had to hand it to her when she was done. Her dark brown curls had been transformed- now smooth and shiny, not to mention nearly down to her waist when they were straight.

"All right. This wasn't a terrible idea," she admitted.

"You can say that again. You look freaking sexy," Vanessa practically shouted. Courtney didn't totally hate that description. They walked around some of the shops in the square for a while afterwards. Courtney kept getting caught up in her reflection; it was so strange how she looked like someone else. "Yes, Court, you're very pretty, keep up, girl," Vanessa teased her. "There's this boutique-y store I wanna go in down here." The store in reference was actually very cool- a lot of bohemian and hand-made clothing and accessories. Vanessa picked up a long flowing dress in varying shades of white and ivory and started holding it up to Courtney, excited. The top of the dress barely even looked like a triangle bikini top- not Courtney's usual go-to style, but she had to admit there was something very goddess-like about the material and silver beading. "Please buy this. Like, I mean, try it on first, but I think that you need to have this dress. Today. It'll be like your birthday present to yourself." Vanessa clapped her hands together lightly.

Courtney was getting tired of all the emphasis on *today* when her friend wouldn't tell her why, but V looked so excited that she agreed to at least try on the dress. To her surprise, it fit perfectly. She would have to wear heels. *But what's new about that?* She had to give props to Vanessa. The dress was gorgeous. As she looked in the mirror, she realized how tan she'd gotten since her arrival. The white material stood out brilliantly against her skin and dark hair. She stood staring at her reflection in the little shop for a while, not wanting to take the dress off.

"Oh my god, yes, perfect. We are taking it home," Vanessa concluded. Courtney had to concur. It wasn't even a bad price, and she had saved a fair bit of money from working all year. The sales clerk rang it up, and they finally headed back to Vanessa's house.

They elected to do girly things all afternoon, and she enjoyed being alone in Vanessa's company. She realized they hadn't had much of that since she'd been there and felt a stab of guilt.

"Hey V, you know I love you, right?" Courtney asked seriously.

"Of course, don't be silly. I love you too. I've had a blast with you here this summer. I wish you were moving back now."

"Me too," Courtney agreed quietly. They watched *Clueless* to round out their relaxing afternoon, but at about four p.m., Vanessa flipped her internal switch to "insanity mode."

"Okay, so, I thought I could play it cool until the very end, but I just can't. I'm not going to spoil anything, or Ethan may murder me, but you are going to want to get ready. Like, Cinderella going to the ball ready, except Gem City style. I already hung up your dress in the bathroom, and I have silver heels and a gray sweater you can borrow. If you want me to do your make-up, I will, or whatever. I'm just dying with anticipation for you. I'm sorry I can't tell you more," she blurted out, biting her lip.

"You know you're making me nervous!" Courtney exclaimed, feeling her palms start to sweat.

"I know, I'm sorry. Don't be nervous- be excited. Just do it while you get ready."

"Just, wait." Courtney stopped her, feeling like her stomach might make a break for it. "I get that I'm doing something with Ethan tonight. I won't try and make you tell me what, because you're, like, honoring the pirate code or whatever, but V, I'm starting to freak out."

"What? Why? Don't freak out!" Vanessa said, concerned. The look on her face let Courtney know she was feeling guilty. "I'm sorry, I didn't mean to make you have an honest-to-god panic attack. It will be a good surprise, I promise."

"No, I know, I'm excited, it's just..."

"It's just what?"

"I think tonight could be... sort of *important*?" Realization slowly crossed over Vanessa's face.

"Well... I think it could be. If you want it to be. Do you?"

What Comes of Eating Doughnuts With a Boy Who Plays Guitar

"I do. Like I really do, but that makes me want to hyperventilate." The more she allowed herself to think about the possibilities, the tighter her chest became. Courtney sat down, taking purposeful breaths.

Vanessa sat in front of her on the carpet. "Court. He loves you. He respects you. If you're nervous, just tell him. It will be okay."

Courtney willed herself to calm down, repeating those words like a mantra in her head. "Just okay, huh?" she attempted to joke, swallowing dryly.

Vanessa laughed, a look of relief in her eyes that her friend's anxiety was dissipating. "Better than okay. From what I hear he's got an impressive-"

"La la la la. Not helping!" Courtney interrupted her playfully.

Vanessa smirked. "Well, if it would be more helpful, I could go get a banana for you to visualize or something."

"Shut up!" Courtney shoved her friend, trying not to laugh, and V dissolved into giggles on the floor. Courtney's stony expression eventually cracked and she genuinely smiled, shaking her head.

Vanessa collected herself and ushered Courtney into a chair so she could do her make-up. She attempted to find her Zen place and allowed the excitement to overtake her worry.

♪ *"She Looks So Perfect"* – 5 Seconds of Summer
"First Time" – Lifehouse

Thirteen

Courtney tried not to let her mind wander too far as she got ready. Vanessa was right. She was thankful she at least knew something was going to happen, and wasn't sitting around in yoga pants and a cheer t-shirt. Once her make-up was done with an acceptable amount of sparkle, she took a look at the whole package. She hardly recognized herself. The girl in Vanessa's full-length mirror looked calm... confident even. She took a few deep breaths to help her feel like she looked. She saw Ethan's car pull up and started downstairs.

"Don't you dare come down here yet," Vanessa scolded. "He needs to wait on you to make an entrance; did you learn nothing from *Clueless*?"

"So unnecessary," Courtney complained. She didn't want to make a bigger deal out of whatever this was than it needed to be. The doorbell rang and Courtney hung back, reluctantly taking Vanessa's advice.

She heard Ethan come in "Hey, V. Did you keep my secret?"

"The parts that needed to be kept, yes. The line was a little fuzzy on others." Courtney came the rest of the way down the stairs because she felt silly standing there listening to their conversation about her. She took in the sight of Ethan at the door, holding a bouquet of pink Gerbera daisies. He was wearing a dark gray button down, open over a black t-shirt. His dark hair was perfectly messy in the way that she

What Comes of Eating Doughnuts With a Boy Who Plays Guitar

liked. The look on his face was something new, though. She took it to mean Vanessa's attempt at a makeover had worked, and she blushed.

"You like it?" she asked, doing a quick twirl in her long dress, her hair brushing the bare skin of her back.

"That would be a serious understatement," he replied, still staring at her. "V, I officially forgive you for whatever part of the secret you gave away." He patted V on the head, causing her face to turn into a glare. Bending down to kiss Courtney on the cheek, he gave her the daisies. "I know nothing about flowers, but these made me think of you." *Just, seriously? Pink daises.* She melted a little bit.

"They're perfect." Vanessa took them to put in a vase in the kitchen.

"Are you ready for your pre-birthday birthday?" So that was what this had all been about. She understood the surprise element now, though her birthday was still three days away.

"In fairness to Ethan, he did want to pull this off on your actual birthday, but I told him I wasn't giving you up that night. He knows not to mess with me," Vanessa explained upon her return. She discreetly put something into Courtney's purse, but waved her off when she raised an eyebrow.

"That is a true statement," Ethan admitted. "You're a little scary when you wanna be."

"Don't you forget it," she told him protectively.

"Okay, okay. Where are we headed on this most special of occasions?"

"All part of the surprise, sprinkles, just enjoy the ride."

Courtney sighed but said goodbye to Vanessa and let Ethan open the car door for her. She turned around and kissed him in earnest before getting in. The whole thing was already something out of a storybook, and they hadn't even made it to the horse drawn carriage part yet. "What was that for?" Ethan asked, his hands still on her waist. She just shrugged her shoulders coyly. Sinking into his sporty car, she felt the energy of the evening. At that point she didn't care where they were going, as long as she got to be with him. She realized, amused, that this was technically their first date alone.

"Is this your first date protocol with all girls?" she teased.

He looked at her curiously for a moment before responding. "Nah, this is all you, baby. You make me want to make you happy." Her heart jumped as it always did when he looked at her that way. The mood shifted to something real despite the fantasy feel of its beginning. She held his hand tightly as they drove through downtown Gem. Ethan pulled his car into the drive of a small blue Victorian house, not far from where Courtney used to live.

"Is this your house? I grew up literally two streets over, on Sweetwater Drive," she marveled as she got out of the car.

"Really? I don't think I knew that. In an alternate universe, we could have been neighbors, and I would have been pulling your pigtails because I liked you in the second grade," he mused, pushing her non-pigtailed hair behind her ear. She smiled at the thought. "So, um, before we continue on this adventure, I should probably let you know that you'll be meeting my mom and sister inside." Courtney's eyes widened slightly. "Don't freak out, it's just for a minute. My mom is chaperoning Taylor's Girl Scout overnight tonight, but she insisted on meeting you first. I assume to make sure you're not a harlot trying to seduce her only son into bed." He grinned. "I asked Vanessa if I should tell you sooner, but she said you'd just stress, so here we are. Are you all right? My mom's cool, and she already likes you, I swear."

"Ummm, yeah, I'm cool." *I am so not cool. I am the opposite of cool. I am a fiery hot volcano of anxious lava.* She breathed in and out as discreetly as possible, trying to get over the initial surprise. "Parents generally like me, I just had to process what I'm walking into. It'll be fine. Let's go meet your family." This was more to convince herself than him. It dawned on her that he had just divulged that his mom would be gone for the entire night. Some of Vanessa's comments from earlier started to make more sense. He led her up the stairs with his pinky hooked in hers. They walked into the house and she was reminded of her own little Victorian around the corner. The dark stained wood floors, brightly colored rooms, and historic crown molding- this was her kind of house. It smelled of cinnamon and vanilla, making Courtney wish she had eaten more earlier.

"Ethan, is that you?" his mom called from the kitchen.

"No Mom, it's your other son bringing his girlfriend to meet you for the first time." *He used the 'g' word again,* Courtney thought. *Maybe it's just easier than saying 'girl from Phoenix I think I'm in love with,'* she told herself.

"Courtney!" His mom said knowingly as they walked through the kitchen door. "I've heard so much about you, I feel like I know you already," she relayed, shaking her hand. "You're absolutely beautiful, Ethan's description did not do you justice," she complimented.

Courtney blushed. "Thank you, Ms. Fisher," she responded.

"None of this 'Ms. Fisher' nonsense, call me Mary," she insisted. "Now, Taylor and I are heading out in a minute, so no crazy parties here, got it?" Mary gave Ethan a knowing look. "Taylor! Come and meet Courtney before we leave!" she yelled. Footsteps came rushing down the stairs.

"Courtney? Hi! I'm Taylor! Ethan says you like *Harry Potter*, is that for real?" his sister questioned precociously as soon as she entered the kitchen.

"Always," Courtney replied knowingly, a gleam in her blue eyes. Taylor's own eyes widened.

"She *is* a fan!" She giggled and helped her mom put their things in the car.

"Call if you need anything, Ethan, I'll have my cell. Try not to burn the house down. Courtney, so lovely to meet you, I hope we'll see you again." Courtney's heart sank a little when she realized she probably wouldn't get to spend much more time with his family. They backed down the driveway, leaving Courtney and Ethan alone, really alone, for the first time. They looked at each other; Ethan lifted her up onto the kitchen counter, and his lips were on hers before either of them blinked. They kissed slowly, without fear of anyone interrupting them. Heat between them built quickly, and she pushed off his button-down so she could feel his arms around her. He pulled back slightly, his arms still holding her tightly.

"So, I'm good with *this* being our whole evening, but I did actually plan a dinner and a cake and whatnot, just so you don't think I led you here under false pretenses of a birthday celebration." She wanted to ignore dinner and ask for a tour of his bedroom, but her stomach said otherwise, both from hunger and *holy crap we're alone in his house.*

"All right, what's for dinner, chef?" She played along. Ethan explained that he had observed her bizarre eating preferences, and decided upon a homemade pizza with salad, and a ginormous chocolate cake, with zero fruit, for dessert.

"Aw, you do pay attention!" she said admiringly. "I was mildly afraid you had planned for caviar and snails or something. I love me some pizza. Do you need help getting anything prepped?"

"Nope, it will be ready in ten. You can go out on the deck if you want while I finish up." She grabbed her sweater and went outside to find simple candles burning on a table set for two. Her heart melted a bit more. She enjoyed the cleansing evening air and the fact that she felt perfectly at ease there with him. Her shoulders relaxed and she let what was left of the sunset wash over her. Ethan soon emerged with pizza, salad, and cucumber water.

"You really *did* chat with Vanessa," she declared over the water. "This is amazing. I can't picture a better birthday dinner." They chatted effortlessly about his sister's reaction to her *Harry Potter* answer, his relationship with his mom, why they moved to Gem and why she had moved away. He didn't go into too much detail, but she gathered that his dad wasn't around much anymore.

Before he brought out the dessert, he offered her a disclaimer. "I realize that you're going to think I'm insane when you see the size of this cake, but you'll get why when you read what's on it." Courtney's interest was piqued, plus, well, dessert. He brought out the largest sheet cake she'd ever seen, the length of it easily spanning Ethan's shoulders, and she burst out laughing.

What Comes of Eating Doughnuts With a Boy Who Plays Guitar

"Okay, I get the warning now." He set it down carefully in front of her with a number eighteen candle burning on top. She looked down at the cake, and in pink icing it read:

Courtney Ross,
Will You Go To Homecoming With Me?

He began to explain as she read. "I know it's not until September, but I just thought if you could ask your mom-" Courtney put her finger against his lips to quiet him. She blew out her candle and said, "Yes. Whatever it takes to get there, just yes." She then left the cake and pulled him by his shirt nearer to her. Their intensity from earlier returned tenfold. She needed to be closer to him and kissed him intently, loving the way his fingertips felt on her back. When she reached for his belt buckle, though, he took a step back.

"What's wrong?" she asked, feeling confused and slightly embarrassed, hoping she hadn't misread their situation.

His words rushed out quickly. "Well, um, I had planned for a lot of things tonight, but that wasn't really one of them. I don't have any... protection? If that's even where you want this to go. I'm trying not to treat you like a delicate flower as requested, and I want you, you have no idea how badly, and I could go to the store or something, I just thought you'd want to wait until homecoming. I didn't want to, like, put pressure on tonight. I thought I could get a hotel room after the dance, or we could-"

"Right now, the dance is a beautiful hypothetical, Ethan," she interrupted. "But tonight? It's not hypothetical, and I have never been so sure of anything in my whole life as I am about you. I don't need a Cinderella homecoming night to want to be with you. I just want you." The fairy-tale reference made her think of Vanessa's metaphor from earlier, and something dawned on her. She grabbed her purse while Ethan looked on, confused, to find exactly the item they needed with a sticky note that said "Just In Case- V". She left the note on the table and pulled Ethan inside.

They continued what they had started. He seemed to treat her with a new reverence, lightly running his hands up her back. He kissed her with a gentle certainty, and slowly backed her up the stairs to his room, never letting his hands leave her skin. The space was small and simple, but it suited him. His guitars hung on the wall, a laptop sat on a small desk, and a gray graphic print covered the comforter. He guided her down on the edge his bed and kneeled in front of her, evening their height. "I love you," he said softly, kissing her neck. She pulled off his shirt and ran her hands over his chest. Letting him take the lead, he pushed down the strap of her dress with his fingertips and kissed her shoulder.

"Are you sure you wanna do this?" he asked, his eyes searching hers.

"Yes," she answered certainly, pressing into him. Neither of them looked back after that.

The event itself wasn't at all like she had expected, between health class at school and her second hand knowledge from friends and movies. There was the heat that was always between them, rising and falling, but it also felt like she now understood what people meant by making love. There were no fireworks, and the earth didn't move, but her heart did. As he held her and played with her hair afterwards, she felt like she finally knew why it had never worked out with anyone else. She was supposed to have waited for him.

"Are you okay?" he asked her, kissing her softly.

"Better than." She interlaced her fingers with his.

"Do you want anything? Water, cake?"

"Just you." He relaxed and tightened his arms around her.

♪ *"Save Tonight"* – *Eagle Eye Cherry*
"To Be With You" – *Mr. Big*

Fourteen

Ethan drove her back to Vanessa's shortly before curfew.

"So, I sort of have a present for you," he told her as they pulled up by the house.

"You really didn't have to get me a gift." The thought of him buying something for her made her feel somewhere between giddy and guilty.

"Well, if it makes you feel any better, I didn't buy it," he explained, reaching into the backseat. He pulled out two small packages wrapped in pink sparkly paper. The one on top was adorned with a big white bow. Her eyes widened at all of the glitter.

"Can I open it now?"

"Of course, hence the gift-giving."

"'Hence'? Did you download the SAT Vocabulary app I told you about?" She laughed.

"I'd rather not comment." He grinned that eyelash-fluttering grin. "Now open the present, it's killing me." Courtney unwrapped the flat package on the bottom first. It was a CD case, but when she pulled it apart, there was nothing inside. Flipping it over, the cover had her name written on it simply with black marker and a heart. She raised her eyebrows questioningly, making him laugh.

"Well, I gave the actual CD to Vanessa so she could load it onto her laptop. You should be able to transfer all of the songs easier to your phone or iPod that way. I still wanted you to open it though. I know it's very 90s of me, but I thought you might appreciate that. I also thought it was less awkward than handing you a flash drive. There are some songs I know you like, some you will but don't know it yet, and two that I wrote and recorded in the studio where I teach."

"You recorded your songs? That's awesome, Ethan. I'm so mad Vanessa knew about this before me. I wanna hear it right now."

"Well, I can arrange that," he said, plugging in his phone to the stereo system. She recognized the song she'd heard him sing at the bonfire that night.

She met his gaze. "Thank you." She listened intently.

"Do you really like it? Like it's not too cliché to basically make you a mixed tape?"

"Not in the slightest. I love it. I do wish the cover was a photo of you in your speedo though, because I'm still having a hard time picturing that one. Your mom seemed to like me; she might dig out a photo if I asked."

"Yeah, that's never gonna happen," he warned lightly, "but you can keep dreaming. You still have to open the other present, though."

"Oh! More, I forgot." She carefully opened the paper to the smaller square box. It was so light it didn't feel like anything was inside, but when she opened it, she understood. "This is the ring that you always wear," she conveyed quietly.

"Well, I was hoping that it might be the ring you always wear, for now, at least while we have to be apart. I don't know if it will even fit your thumb, but I could get you a chain or something." Courtney slid the thick silver band onto her thumb. It fit just right. She twirled it around with her finger, memorizing the black etchings on the sides.

"This is... kind of perfect."

"I wanted to buy you something sparkly, but I couldn't make up my mind, and I didn't know what was, like, 'fashionable' or whatever. Being in the jewelry section of the store made me feel incredibly out of place." Courtney smiled inwardly at the thought of Ethan perusing the jewelry counter at the mall. "I like this better anyway. I noticed this ring the first time I saw you. It's a great present." He intertwined his fingers with hers and admired the band on her finger.

"I realize you're going to be mad at me for this, but I want to tell you something. I know you've ignored the fact that I've been calling you my girlfriend, and I hope that's just in solidarity to your decision not to discuss this until the last moment. But I'm going to talk about it now."

While her initial reaction was to shy away from the topic, she kind of liked his insistence. She had felt that this was coming after the night they'd had together, so she nodded patiently and listened. There was a fire beginning in her chest, the uncertainty about what he had to say fanning the flames. "I am in love with you. Like crazy in love with you, and I don't want to be with anyone else, okay? No matter how far away you are. What's the point of having cell phones with video chat and text messaging if not to make a long distance thing work? I just can't say goodbye to you in three days and go back to how my life was before. Homecoming is like six or seven weeks away or something; we can *do* that," he stated emphatically. She kissed him hard, hoping for the bravery to say what she wanted to say, all the while worrying that he might agree with her. His plan sounded so enticing, but she knew she couldn't just jump in without covering her bases first.

She started slowly. "I want you to know that I am on board with making this work. I have never felt like this about anyone, and I don't want it to end in three days. I wasn't sure what to make of you referring to me as your girlfriend, and I didn't want to make a big thing of it if it wasn't one to you-"

"Courtney, you're so... you. You accept that I'm in love with you, but the word 'girlfriend' throws you off? I don't toss around that word casually, by the way. If I'm being honest, I've tried to avoid it like the plague for most of my life."

She laughed slightly at his admission. "I know, it just, well, it wasn't what I expected, coming here this summer. You know? And I really doubt you expected it either, let alone with someone who lives 1,802 miles away. Yes, I mapped it. So, I need us to be real for a minute. If we decide to do this, and be together and say to hell with the distance, then know that I'm all in, okay? But do you really want to *do* this? It's your senior year. You're still kind of new in town, there are probably a lot of girls you haven't met, and-"

"I don't want another girl, I want you."

"I want you too. I just don't know that you're going to want me when we can't be together, and you have girls throwing themselves at you when you play a show. Yes, I looked around at the festival, and there is no shortage of opportunity for you. I can tell you right now that's going to be difficult for me to think about, knowing I can't be here. I guess what I'm trying to say is that I'm giving you the chance to walk away with no backlash, no drama. We spend the next few days together and stay friends."

He was uncharacteristically silent for too long. "I can't be your friend, Courtney. Did you seriously just say 'let's be friends' to me? After tonight?" His eyes flashed with an emotion she couldn't quite put her finger on.

"No! Well, I mean, yes. Ugh, I'm not saying that's what I want. But would I rather have you as my friend and in my life than as my ex? Yes. If I could, I would stay here with you, Ethan, but I think it's something that you should take some time to think about. I just don't want you to resent me because you're stuck in this awkward space where you have the limits of having a girlfriend but none of the perks. Please, just think about it. I love you." *Please don't tell me I'm right. Tell me I'm wrong.* Her stomach was in her throat all at once.

"I don't need to think about it, I've been thinking about it since I kissed you in the entryway. I need you to believe me when I tell you that we can do this." His tone was insistent.

Courtney breathed slowly. She *did* want to believe him. She knew she just had to make the choice to do it, to make herself open to having her heart broken, to trust him while they were apart, and to let herself imagine a future with him. "Ok," she said simply, looking into his warm brown eyes.

"Okay, as in you will use the word 'boyfriend' and refrain from making out with any other guys?" he clarified jokingly.

What Comes of Eating Doughnuts With a Boy Who Plays Guitar

"Yes on both accounts." She smiled an actual smile. One that wasn't put on to cover up anything else. Just because she couldn't *not* smile. "Have I told you how amazing tonight was, boyfriend?" She spoke softly, pulling him towards her.

"Have I told you how ridiculously sexy you look in that dress, *girlfriend*?" he replied, kissing her. Her whole body responded to his touch, and she wanted nothing but to stay there with him, the cool breeze floating through the windows and her head abuzz with the implication of their decision.

"I really do need to go inside." Her dismay was clearly written on her face.

"I know," he answered, kissing her again. It appeared that he had no intention of ending their night just yet.

She smiled against his lips and playfully nudged him, "I knew you were going to get me in trouble the moment I saw you. Now be a gentleman and walk me to the door before Vanessa comes out here and yells at you."

"Whatever you say, sprinkles." He sighed with resignation. They walked hand in hand to the door, and Ethan continued his adoration of her until she was weak in the knees.

"You're not playing fair," she half-complained. "You know what you do to me when you kiss me like that."

"I have no idea what you're talking about. You mean like this?" and he traveled the length of her neck with his lips.

"Something like that, yeah," she replied, barely breathing. He smiled at her and kissed her quickly one last time before opening the door to the house.

"I know you don't want me to ask, but are you ok? With everything, with tonight?" He stood there, looking concerned.

"Yes. I'm wonderful. *Really*," she insisted when he still looked worried. "Call me when you wake up."

"I will. I love you." He finally turned and walked back to his car. She admired the view as he sauntered away. When she closed the door, her head was spinning. The full significance of everything that had happened that night had not resonated yet. All that was going through her mind were images of them together, and she wanted to savor every single one. Her need to talk to her friend won out, however, and she tiptoed up to Vanessa's room to see if she was still awake.

* * *

"Vanessa!" Courtney yelled in the loudest whisper possible. "Are you awake?"

"Of course I'm awake, you idiot!" Vanessa flipped on the bedside light. "I haven't been able to sleep at all. Tell me everything." Courtney tried to recall as many details of the night as possible. It was almost more for herself than for Vanessa; she didn't want to forget anything.

"Oh. My. God. That is, like, the most freaking romantic sex story anyone has ever had. And you're welcome for the last minute addition to your purse," she added. "I would give anything for my first time to have been like that."

"Why, what happened?" Courtney questioned, not liking the shadow that darkened her friend's expression. Vanessa had always been pretty tight lipped about her relationship with Zack Roads.

"Eh, nothing that needs discussing. Just saying I'm jealous." Courtney gave her a quizzical look, but Vanessa shook her off as usual. "But how are you? I mean, kind of a big night, are you feeling okay about everything?"

"I am. I'm just… contented? Blissful? *Happy*? There are a lot of synonyms. But being with Ethan felt, I don't know the word for it. Like I was finally where I was supposed to be. I do realize I sound like a really bad 80s love song, and you can feel free to stop me at any time, I am just walking on air right now."

"Not at all girl, I love it. But tell me more about 'the big talk,' what did you decide to do? It's been killing me all summer."

"I think we're going to give it a shot. He says he can do it, and if I'm planning on coming back for college… I tried to reason with him because I know this sounds insane, but he was very insistent. So I guess I'll get to ride the wave a while longer."

"What if you guys get married, and it's all because of me and my incredible match-making skills?" Vanessa asked. "Like, I want a special mention in the wedding program, maybe with a photo of me?" Her expression changed, making a model-esque face.

"Hold your horses there; I just have to make it to homecoming at this point."

"Yes! Homecoming, well, of course you'll stay here, what's the problem? It'll be so fun! We can get our hair done together, and I'll do your makeup, just like we always talked about."

"Hopefully my mom is on board with letting me come back out that soon. I will have to practice my powers of persuasion before I ask her," Courtney mused. The magnitude of how much had changed in the last eight hours began to sink in, and they both decided sleep was in order. She hoped she wouldn't wake up the next morning and find out it had all been a dream. Reliving the night in her mind, she drifted to sleep.

♪ *"Wonderful Tonight"* – Eric Clapton

Fifteen

The next two days were a blur. She had gotten a preliminary "yes" from her mom about homecoming after pulling out every persuasive strategy she could think of. There was the caveat of a "we'll discuss this more later" that came along with the "yes," but she would take it. She and Ethan spent every possible moment together. Every kiss, every inside joke, every conversation was committed to memory. She mastered the shape of his lips and the shade of brown in his eyes. Vanessa rolled her eyes a lot, and Luke came to the point of pretending to vomit, but they didn't care.

Luke's face was often arranged in mock horror or open disgust. "Seriously, Fisher, *what* has happened to you, man? You're like a bowl of whipped cream over there, I mean, it's hard for me to even watch." Secretly though, Courtney thought Luke was kind of a romantic. At least when he was looking at Vanessa and thought no one was looking at him.

"Simple solution- stop watching. It's creepy anyway," Ethan shot back, planting an overly dramatic kiss on Courtney's mouth.

"Yes, pay attention to your own relationship. Over here. With me. Looking super hot today, in case you didn't notice." Vanessa scolding him was sort of their norm. Luke agreed repentantly.

Courtney had requested a small bonfire for just the four of them for her birthday. They already had enough cake to feed an army left over

What Comes of Eating Doughnuts With a Boy Who Plays Guitar

from Ethan's house, and she just wanted to finish her summer like she started it. It was more than difficult to believe the trip was ending, but at the same time it seemed like she had known Ethan her whole life. It didn't seem possible that they had only met a month ago. She cringed inwardly when she thought about explaining that to people. They were planning on trying to sustain a relationship over the period of a year when their entire knowledge of each other spanned only four weeks. She knew she shouldn't care what anyone else thought, but imagined what she would say to a friend who told her the same tale. It wasn't exactly supportive. *This will be okay. He wants to do this with you,* she told herself as they dragged out chairs and blankets to the fire pit.

Courtney had bought a new outfit for the occasion: a short white eyelet skirt and a flowing coral tank top. She felt relaxed and like herself with Ethan's arms around her. She knew she had to kid her mind into believing this was just another night, and not the last one, or she wouldn't even make it through s'mores without breaking down.

"Do you know how incredible you look?" Ethan murmured in her ear.

"Well, now I do." She smiled, pulling his arms around her tighter.

"Is it wrong that I want to steal you away from your last night with your friend and be alone with you? Because that's all I can think about. I don't want you to go." He spoke plainly, and there was a look of refusal that was at odds the with reality in his eyes.

"Well, if it's wrong, then I'm wrong along with you, but I think Vanessa has other plans judging from the movie marathon lined up later."

Ethan sighed knowingly. "Yeah, I saw. I just wanted you to know where my head was. As long as I can be with you it'll be all right." He kissed her, and she didn't know that she could ever get over the bubbling sensation in her core during that single breath before his lips found hers.

"All right, lovers, come over here," Vanessa called. "I have some song requests for Ethan." They begrudgingly rejoined the pair, and spent some time having a rather corny campfire sing-along to anything Ethan would agree to play. Luke was the worst singer by far, but always the loudest, until Vanessa made him take turns with everyone else. As the stars came out, Ethan declared he was playing his last song for the evening, and began a version of "Wonderful Tonight," by Eric Clapton. It was one of Courtney's favorites, and by the time he made it to the first chorus, silent tears were threatening to cascade down her cheeks. She tried to smile through them, but by the end she had watery streaks lining her face. Vanessa sat next to her and rubbed her back while Ethan finished.

"Come here," he motioned to her. "I didn't mean to make you cry, I'm sorry. I knew you liked the song," he explained, gesturing for her to come and sit on his lap. Vanessa and Luke gave them some space, claiming they were going to pick a movie to get started. She buried her face into Ethan's shoulder and tried to cry as ladylike as possible. He wrapped his arms around her and pulled the blanket over them both. "It's going to be okay, baby, I swear. By this time next year you'll be living here for real, and this time and this space apart will just seem like nothing. You're the first girl I've ever met who I could see myself having a future with. Please don't cry, these are all good things." His fingertips traced the curve of her spine as he spoke.

She slowed her breath and dried her tears on the blanket. "I can't decide if your optimism is endearing or annoying." She laughed in spite of everything. "I will try to get on board with the positivity."

"Good. And obviously it's endearing, I mean, look at this face," he said, giving her a cheesy smile. Feeling lighter, she laughed softly and curled back into him. She made mental notes of how his arms felt around her, how his heartbeat sounded with her head on his shoulder, and how his scent reminded her of pine trees in late fall. An audible sigh escaped her.

"I guess we should go inside?"

"One minute, I want to give you something while we're alone," he confessed, pulling an envelope out of his pocket. "I sort of wrote you a letter. Well, it's part letter, part rambling, part song lyrics." She took

What Comes of Eating Doughnuts With a Boy Who Plays Guitar

it from him and turned it over in her hands. "Don't read it now, I just, I was afraid I wouldn't be able to get out what I needed to say tonight, and I wanted to make sure I wrote it all down." She held onto the sealed letter and wrapped her arms around his waist.

"I love everything about you." His eyes shone briefly when she made that declaration.

"Well, I don't know if that's entirely true, but you bring out a better side of me than I've shown in a long time. Maybe ever. You're very good for me." He brushed a few stray curls out of her face. She smiled as he kissed her.

"So, if this is the present portion of the evening, does that mean I can give you yours?"

"You got me a present?" Excitement lit up his face.

"I did!" She grinned. "Stay here, I'll be right back." Courtney skipped to grab the package from the basement, put the letter in her purse, and avoided Vanessa's raised eyebrow. She promised they would be in momentarily. She took in the sight of Ethan as she walked back out, stretched out, looking at the stars. She sat down beside him, and she handed over a rectangular package wrapped in craft paper. It had never occurred to her how to wrap a present in a manly way, but she figured it would work. She had written his name in sharpie on the front and decorated it until black-markered designs took up most of the space.

"This looks cool," he commented. "You want me to open it now?"

"Yes, now, 'hence the gift-giving,' " she repeated with a gleam in her eye. He laughed and opened the package, careful not to disturb the design she'd made. He took out a distressed leather-bound notebook, running his fingers over the cover. She'd had his name branded into the bottom corner. He flipped open the hand-cut pages and noticed what she had created. The first three pages were already full. She had printed several three-by-three pictures of the two of them from their adventures: night canoeing, mini-golfing, and singing together at the festival among others. She had written her memories from each event in sharpie as decorative word-frames around each photo, filling the paper.

"This is... I don't even have the words, Court, to explain what this means." He almost sounded choked up.

She reached for his hand. "Well, I've seen you scribbling lyrics on random scraps. I thought you might want to keep them in one place," she explained. "If the photo part in front is too uncool for people to see, you could always take it out and keep it somewhere else."

"Uncool? This is, like, *the* coolest thing anyone's ever done for me. If anyone thinks I'm lame for worshipping the ground that you walk on, they can screw themselves."

"The ground that I walk on, huh? I kind of enjoy that." She laughed. "I'm glad you like it. It makes me happy. However, it does not make me happy that this night is almost over, and we should probably head inside. On the plus side, though, there's cake in there. I didn't really get to eat any the other night." She struggled to keep her tone casual.

"Hey, I offered!" he protested, taking her hand and starting towards the house.

"Eh, I was preoccupied with your hot body."

Ethan struck a "serious male model" pose. "This old thing? I just had it lying around, you know." Courtney giggled and they made their way into the basement. It was sort of weird that talking about having sex wasn't at all weird. If anything, she felt like this version of their relationship had been waiting in the wings the whole time until she'd been ready. It felt...safe.

Vanessa hadn't waited for them to start the first movie, and she and Luke were partway into *The Breakfast Club* when they walked in. Her friend didn't even comment, which made Courtney think she and Luke had needed a moment too. Ethan took it upon himself to bring down massive pieces of cake for everyone, and they sang her 'happy birthday.' She didn't even know what to wish for when she blew out the candles, other than for the next year to fly by so that she could find herself there again.

♪ *"Your Body Is a Wonderland"* – *John Mayer*
"Sugar" – *Tonic*

Sixteen

At some point during the second movie, Courtney fell asleep, and she awoke to Ethan tracing the lines on her palm.

"Hey, babe. I didn't want to wake you up, but I have to head home in a bit." Her heart immediately sank. This was going to be their goodbye. This had been her last night with him, and she had missed part of it.

"I don't want to go." Tears filled her eyes, her breath coming quickly.

"I don't want you to go, either." He kissed her for a long moment. "Here, walk me to my car," he suggested, pulling her off the couch. "Vanessa, Luke, I'll catch you guys later, ok?"

"Later bro."

"See ya," Vanessa relayed sadly.

They trudged slowly up the stairs and out to his car. She tried to smooth her hair and willed herself not to cry. Ethan looked thoughtful. "I can't believe it was only a month ago that I drove over here for Vanessa's party. I didn't believe her when she said you'd be perfect for me, you know how she exaggerates. But you are. You're it for me."

Her willpower crumbled, and the tears welled up. "Homecoming's less than six weeks away at this point, Court," he said in a calming tone. "You'll be so busy with cheer and school it will fly by. We can video chat or talk or text everyday." She had completely forgotten about cheer and the beginning of her senior year. It was like her whole Scottsdale universe had ceased to exist since she met him.

"I know. I know, I just miss you already and I haven't even left yet. I want to be able to do this whenever I want." Blinking back tears, she leaned in with a look of determination. Demonstrating, she began by running her hands up his shirt and her fingertips over his hips. His breath caught as she traced her fingers lower.

"Courtney..." he groaned with no real purpose.

He kissed her hungrily. Her heart raced, and her entire body told her she needed to be with him. She couldn't leave without feeling that close again. "Ethan," she murmured, "get in the car with me."

He stopped for a moment, "Wait, really? Because you want to make out in the back seat? Or..."

"Yes, *or*. Assuming you brought-"

"I did. Not because I assumed, just, I wanted to-" She interrupted him with a kiss and opened the car door. He pulled her in, onto his lap, and closed the door behind them. "You are the most magnificent woman who has ever existed," he told her seriously in between kisses, his hands at her waist, bringing her closer. The mood was very different from their first time. With the promise of tomorrow's loss hanging over their heads, they alternated between a powerful need to show the other how they felt, and the urge to laugh through the awkwardness of their lack of experience together- heightened by the limitations imposed by his small car. In the end, however, she felt loved and content as he played with the silver ring around her thumb.

"I love you."

"I love you too."

"I know you're probably very late for your curfew. I'll get out of the car in thirty seconds, I swear," she promised as she wrapped her arms around his neck.

"Being grounded is worth this," he assured her, his breath slowing. He rubbed her back lightly. Minutes later, she tried to exit the car gracefully, fluffing her long hair and fixing the white skirt as he climbed out after her.

"I will call you when I get home tomorrow."

"Please do. You can read my letter on the plane if you want."

"I will. Just. I'll miss you. I love you. Drive home safe. I'm running out of 'last words' to say. So just, I'll see you in six weeks, I guess."

"I'll miss you, I love you, I'll drive safely, and I can't wait until homecoming. Did that cover it all?" he joked gently. He kissed her once more and got back in the car. She started slowly up the walk, back into the house, and waved at him.

She heard Vanessa and Luke talking quietly when she got back downstairs, and it looked as though Luke was getting ready to leave.

"Well, Courtney, I'm heading home, but I can say this summer has been awesome, so I, for one, will miss you." Luke's admission came in a rare moment of seriousness. He gave her a giant hug, lifting her off of the ground, reminiscent of their first meeting.

"I will miss you too, Luke. Thank you for being a good sport and sharing Vanessa with me."

"Okay, enough sappiness! I'll walk you up," Vanessa declared. Courtney started cleaning up the basement and looking for any last-minute items of hers that hadn't made their way into her suitcase earlier. She looked at her purse and saw the letter sticking out of it. There was an incredible urge to rip it open right then, but she decided perhaps it would be better to do in private in case she spontaneously burst into an ugly cry. Instead, she sat down and started going through the literal hundreds of photos she had taken the past month. She couldn't believe they had talked her into going night canoeing, and that she had survived without falling in the river. Then Vanessa came back and interrupted her walk down memory lane.

"You tired?" Vanessa asked.

"Mentally? Yes. Physically? Not really."

"Feel like sneaking out and driving around for a bit? I made the perfect playlist, and you're the only one who will appreciate it. It's going to be weird without you here tomorrow. You're like my sister, you know that?"

"You too, girl. I can't believe I'm going home." Silently, she thanked her for not pressing for an explanation about being outside with Ethan for so long. She wanted to keep that to herself for now. The girls got in the Camaro as quietly as they could and backed it out without turning on the lights.

Once they made it on the road, Vanessa flipped the lights and started her playlist with "Famous in a Small Town," by Miranda Lambert. "I think you're gonna like this mix." She and Courtney drove around under the moon for a while, listening to their own personal summer songs. By the time they coasted back into the driveway, she was exhausted. The girls took some photos to commemorate their last night together.

♪ *"If Only"* – Hanson
"Boys of Summer" – The Ataris

Seventeen

Courtney reached for her phone to shut off the alarm, wondering for a brief moment why it was going off. Her heart sank as reality snuck up on her, and she remembered she was leaving for home-if that term even applied anymore. It was early, a little after five. Vanessa was planning on taking her to the airport in just under an hour, so she knew it was time to get ready to go. She lay there for a minute, comfortable on the trundle bed she had frequented so often during sleepovers when they were kids. *Time is so weird*, she thought, reflecting on the thirteen years they had been best friends. Their last names were close in the alphabet, so on the first day of kindergarten they had been seated next to each other. Vanessa had taken out her Lisa Frank pencil box with a sparkly pony on it, and the rest was history. Courtney had always thought Vanessa was the coolest girl she'd ever met, and she'd seriously coveted that pencil box. *She's still the coolest*, Courtney reminded herself as she finally sat up.

She tried to be quiet, gathering the last of her things from around the room and making sure she had her boarding pass and ID ready to go. Checking her phone one more time to see if it was necessary to wake up Vanessa yet, she saw a text from Ethan. Excitement coursed throughout her body.

E: Hey, I know you're leaving super early this morning, and we already did our goodbyes last night, but I wanted you to have some sustenance, so go check the front door when you get up. You'll always be more of a bear claw to me, but you'll find sprinkles there too :).
C: You are amazing. <3

Courtney rushed downstairs and pulled open the front door to find a "Jim's Donuts" bag on the front mat. Taped to the back of the bag was another envelope that read, "Letter Part Two." She carefully unstuck it and took it inside to put with what was apparently "Part One." On the front of the bag there was just a heart and Ethan's name in pen, and it looked like he had written it in the car. No matter how dorky, she was saving that bag in her carry-on. She wished she had been able to see him, just for a moment, but knew maybe it was better they left last night as their goodbye. It had been perfect. She set the treats on the counter and turned around to find Vanessa sleepily clunking down the stairs.

"Flights this early should be deemed unconstitutional."

"Here, have a doughnut, it'll make you feel better about it."

"Where'd you get- ahh, I'm telling you, that boyfriend of yours is good," she said, answering her own question. "Gimme."

They ate doughnuts in near silence, knowing they had to leave momentarily. Vanessa's mom had given her a goodbye speech the afternoon before, assuring her she could stay there anytime: homecoming, college, or otherwise. She may have even shed a few tears.

This is going to be hard, Courtney thought.

"All right, friend. Let's do this," Vanessa said. They loaded up her car and headed to the airport.

Once there, Vanessa helped Courtney get her bags inside and threw her arms around her. "You know I'm not a hugger, but I am going to miss you. Text me or call me when you land, and I will keep an eye on Ethan for you. I'm not going to stalk him or anything, but you better believe he will walk the straight and narrow if I have anything to say about it."

"I'm going to miss you the most, V. I don't even know how to thank you, or your parents, for letting me come and stay with you. This has been... well, there's no word for how this summer has been. Life-altering, maybe. So thank you." Tears threatened to fall already.

"Okay, girl, you're gonna be back for homecoming, and I can't wait, so let's just focus on that, right?" Vanessa stood there wiping her eyes.

"Right. Not even six weeks. I will see you then." With that, Courtney walked away to check her bag and get to her gate. Stupidly, she put in her ear buds and started listening to the songs Ethan had recorded. She was crying before he even sang the first word. Embarrassingly, she proceeded to cry like a girl, which she was, so at least that part was acceptable, all the way through the first hour of the flight. *Freaking get it together, Courtney, nobody died, this is not the end of the world. Stop crying, stop crying, stop crying. Deep breaths.* Eventually, she was able to calm down and flip through the magazine she'd bought in the airport terminal. Feeling grateful that no one was seated next to her, she took advantage of the space and decided to sleep.

She awoke with her eyes still red from crying to the captain's voice saying they were on their final descent into Sky Harbor. Fruitlessly, she tried to make herself look presentable. Her mom was going to have a heyday pumping her for information already; she didn't need to add fuel to that fire with a cry face. *Sunglasses it is,* she thought as she concluded that the puffiness was a lost cause.

* * *

Standing curbside, Courtney was looking for her mom's red VW bug. She constantly complained that it was a teenage girl car, but the woman didn't appear to care. The 115-degree heat was invading her lungs, and she actually longed for the humidity of Ohio. The car finally pulled up, and her mom got out to look her over and give her a hug.

"You got tan!" she exclaimed. "You look *good.* Ohio agrees with you."

"Thanks?"

"Are you tired? Hungry? We could grab some food on the way home if you want," she told her, loading her bags.

"Hungry, yes. I want Mexican food. Taco Bell's about as good as it gets in Gem. I need chips with real salsa and something greasy from Ajo Al's."

"Courtney… it's nine-thirty in the morning."

"Ughhh! Stupid time change! Fine, I want French toast and eggs then. And maybe a muffin. And bacon." She grinned just thinking about it.

"Well, good to see you haven't changed too much," her mom commented as they got in the car. "So, do you want your birthday present now or later?"

"Ohhhhhh, now please!" Her mother handed over a plain white envelope. Courtney stifled a gasp as she realized she hadn't read Ethan's letter on the plane. Instinctively, she began to reach for it, but thankfully stopped. That wasn't a moment she wanted to have in front of her mom. She took the present and opened it. Inside were two printed plane tickets with a September date on them. She looked up, realizing one was for her and one for her mom.

"You're coming with me?"

"Absolutely. You didn't think I'd miss seeing you get ready for your senior homecoming, did you? I tried to get your dad to come too, but he'll be in Brazil, so it'll be a girls' weekend. I've booked us a room at a B and B on Main Street and a rental car already. I wanna meet this Ethan." Everything was stated quite matter-of-factly. Courtney's heart warmed at the idea of getting to have her senior homecoming experience complete with her mom to fuss over her hair and makeup.

"Best birthday ever, Mom." For the rest of the drive and on into breakfast, Courtney chatted on, satisfying her mom's need for information about the trip. She showed her Ethan's ring and several pictures. She was especially interested in the ones from UD.

"You're gonna go, huh?" her mom questioned, referencing her college decision.

Courtney sighed. When she was there, she'd been certain. Now that she was back in Phoenix, the line had become blurry again. "I don't know. I have some time before deposits are due. I need to sit on it for a while longer."

"Okay, just let me know so I can prepare for my empty-nest syndrome."

"That's not a real thing."

"Oh yes it is, I heard it on Dr. Oz." Courtney laughed. Part of her felt relieved to be back among familiar surroundings, as long as she ignored the other part that knew she wasn't going to see Ethan or Vanessa that night. They finished breakfast and headed home. Courtney had to admit it was nice to peruse her own closet and jump into her own bed for the first time in a month. As soon as she got comfy, she grabbed Ethan's letters out of her bag. She opened the first one carefully. He had clearly ripped the pages out of an old spiral notebook; the tears on the sides had a confetti effect. She read through it once, trying to take it all in as quickly as possible, and then more slowly, looking at all of his scribbled lyrics and doodles in the margins.

Courtney-

Well, this is the third letter I've written to you. The last two just keep coming out wrong. I can't seem to say what I need to say, so I'm just going to be blunt about this. I want you to know that I don't normally do this stuff. I don't think I've ever written a love letter in my life. I am all kinds of whipped thanks to you. First of all, I've had the best month ever since you've been here. I won't forget anything from this summer. I'm sad to see you leave, but at the same time I'm beyond happy that you came. I'd give anything to keep you here with me, but I guess I shouldn't worry too much since you'll be living back here before long :). I just have to focus on that, because I still don't know how I'm going to handle not seeing you. I can't even take being away for a day much less another year. I will have to figure it out. I can always play a little Eric Clapton or Third Eye Blind and think of you. I've been working on a song for you, by the way. I wanted to keep it a surprise, but, well, I really suck at keeping things secret. It almost killed me planning your birthday date. I hate this so much!!! I love you more than anything, and I don't want you to leave. See what you do to me?

I can't wait until homecoming. If I have anything to say about it, I will fly you out here for prom too. I will teach every single kid in Gem City how to play guitar if I have to. I have grand plans for our weekend together; I just hope everything works out how I want it. But it'll be great because I'll be with you. We can do this :). I don't let minor details slow me down, you know, like several state lines. I don't know what else to really say, so I guess I'll just wrap it up. I want you to know I love you and I'm going to miss you so much.

Love Always,

Ethan

P.S. I know this is probably incredibly sappy and reputation-crushing, but you know you like it :). If you think this is bad though, you should get inside of my head because I still can't seem to get out what I really want to say. You get the point.

That was the end of "letter one," and Courtney was having trouble forming thoughts. Having him spell out everything he was feeling on paper was wonderfully overwhelming. It was all of the things she wished she could know when she looked at him, and it was perfect. All of the doubts that were already creeping up since she'd crossed the threshold of her room were kept at bay with his words. She marveled at how in love she was with this boy. She couldn't even imagine what more he had to say, but tore open "Part Two" with much less caution than the first. She had to know what was in there.

What Comes of Eating Doughnuts With a Boy Who Plays Guitar

Well, it's Thursday night, and I just left Vanessa's about an hour ago. I tried to sleep, but it's not working. I can't stop thinking about you. Tonight was incredible. I've never done <u>that</u> in my car before, and I'm not gonna lie, it was hot. I hope that doesn't sound bad. I mean, you know how I feel about you, so I hope it's not like disrespectful or something. I just need you to know that you are the most amazing girl. I don't know how to do this long distance thing, but I am going to work it out. I love you. I'm really going to try and sleep now so I can get up and buy you doughnuts in a few hours. I miss you already.

Love You,

Ethan

Courtney didn't even know when she started crying, but her throat was tight and down the tears came. It sort of felt like they hadn't stopped since the night before. She wanted to call and hear his voice, but knew hers couldn't make it through that conversation, so she texted instead.

> C: I just read your letters. I love you so much. I don't know how I can feel like this about you and be so sad at the same time. I want to get on a plane and come back. Tell me again how it's not that long until I can kiss you.
> E: I feel the same, so at least know you're not alone in this. I keep getting the urge to jump in my car and drive to Vanessa's, and then it hits me that you're not there.
> C: Did you really mean what you said? About prom? And all of it?
> E: Every word, of course. I don't think you understand what you do to my head.
> C: Well, I think I might if it's anything like what goes on in my own.
> E: Can we video chat? I need to see you. I feel like I'm

losing my mind over here.
C: Ahhhh, can we do it later? Like when I haven't been crying? And maybe after I fix my plane hair?
E: Don't cry :(. And yes, that's fine. I wouldn't want to be scared away by your 'plane hair.' What a waste of a summer that would be ;). jk. I'll be home tonight so call me whenever, ok? I love you.
C: I love you too. Thank you again for your letter. <3

Courtney tried to calm herself by taking a shower and unpacking. It did work for a bit, and she focused on doing laundry and organizing her room. Her mom was going to think that a pod person had taken over her body while she was gone. Her freshly made bed was calling her name, and she lay down to think about Ethan and what the next year could possibly look like.

♪ *"Sugar"* – Maroon 5
"Ain't It Fun" – Paramore

Eighteen

There were four days until Courtney went back to school. She really hadn't given it a second thought while she was gone, but now the stress of getting everything together, planning for the first cheer meetings and practices of the year, and picking up her hours from Krispy Kreme was starting to get to her. She downloaded her school schedule in the middle of the chaos, and was thrilled and relieved when she remembered that she'd be out by twelve-fifteen every day. This meant she could work a few four-hour shifts after school, rather than until eleven p.m. *I might actually be able to go to sleep before one every night. And I'll have more time to talk to Ethan.*

She heard her phone vibrate and pounced on it, hoping for a message from him. Instead, it was her friend Ashley inquiring about her schedule.

> A: Hey! You're home now right? Who'd you get for English? I'm with Mr. K. Can we please do something before school starts? You're like a stranger to me, I was worried you were taken captive.
> C: Lol ya I'm home. I have Mr. K too, third period. I'm up for whatever, what did you have in mind? I missed you!
> A: Let's go to Desert Ridge and let cute guys hit on us. I'll pick you up at 6.

C: You are special. See you then. Is Molly coming too?
A: She's on her way to my house now. We'll see you later.

Courtney felt bad she hadn't really kept up with her friends while she was gone. It wasn't that she hadn't missed them. Well, it sort of was. But now that she was back she realized that her life needed Ashley's dramatic nature. She was excited to see them both. She had second thoughts about regaling them with the details of exactly what she had been up to for the past month for fear that they would think she was insane. *Well, they might already think that, having known you this long. You might as well take advantage of the opportunity to brag about Ethan.* She felt a smile cross her lips in knowing they would think he was beautiful.

She had a while to get ready, so she picked out some of her newer clothes from her trip to wear and decided to straighten her hair. Eagerly, she thought she would try to get in a video chat with Ethan before her friends arrived too. While the phone rang, she sat, trying to look cute. He picked up quickly and adjusted until she could see him clearly.

"Hey, beautiful," he said with a slight delay once they were both on screen.

"Hey yourself."

"I missed seeing your face. Technology is amazing."

"If only there were a teleportation device attached to our phones, we would be set."

"How awesome would that be? I would totally sneak out every night and teleport there to crawl in bed with you. You know, to, like, snuggle. And sleep."

"Yes, snuggling and sleeping are both options, though perhaps not the most interesting ones. Speaking of which, let me give you a tour of my room," she told him, moving her camera. Her walls were a sunny yellow, and she had a wide bench under her large, shuttered second-story window. Her room was actually clean thanks to her earlier need to be busy. The bed was covered in a white duvet with a rainbow of

What Comes of Eating Doughnuts With a Boy Who Plays Guitar

colored ribbon stripes. The walls were filled mostly in picture frames, and her dresser mirror with concert ticket stubs.

Her pom-poms were thrown carelessly on the floor, and when she scanned them, she heard Ethan say, "Hoooold up."

"What?" she asked, worried she'd left out something embarrassing.

"Are those your pom-poms? Like rah-rah whatever?"

"Um, yes. That's actually our most popular cheer. We all stand around and say 'rah-rah whatever' in a bored tone. Huge crowd pleaser."

"Does that mean you have, like, a whole cheer uniform in that closet of yours?" It dawned on her where he was going with his questioning.

"Why yes, yes it does." It sort of amazed her how easy it was to flirt with him; that even a thousand miles away, the chemistry held up. *But for how long?* She shushed the pessimist that lived in her brain and refocused.

"Do you have any reason to put on said uniform, like right now, and do a cheer?"

"I think I'd consider it if someone asked me really nicely."

"Please, please. Please put on your uniform."

"Ok. It'll have to be fast, though, because my friends are picking me up in a few minutes."

"Fast is fine, I just have to see this."

"I assume this means that during our next conversation you'll be modeling your Speedo. Just sayin'." She heard him laugh as she put down the phone. It briefly crossed her mind to be a tease by changing in front of him, but she heard the warnings of all of those Internet safety assemblies she'd had to attend ringing in her ears. She went into her closet and picked out her favorite white cheer skirt and cropped white shell. She returned and picked up her phone. "Are you ready for some serious spirit?"

"Absolutely, let's hear it," he said, rhyming purposefully and making a fist. He attempted to mimic a cheer pose. She set her phone on the dresser and, as seriously as she could, broke into a cheer. For emphasis, she threw a standing back tuck at the end. "Did you just literally do a back flip?" he asked. *Mission accomplished.*

"Oh, that? Yeah, no big deal," she lied. She had worked on landing it for three years.

"Jesus, you're like a cheerleader superhero."

She laughed in response. "Hold on, I gotta change back in case my friends get here and think I'm a head-case for wearing this around the house." When she came back, he was messing with tuning his guitar.

"So, where are you going looking all hot, and should I be jealous?" he asked.

"Just up to Desert Ridge." Seeing his confusion, she realized he wasn't from Scottsdale. "It's like an outdoor mall. It's hotter than hell outside, but for some reason they keep building things that force us to be outside. And we keep frequenting these establishments. So anyhow, that's it, with my friends Ashley and Molly. And you don't really strike me as the jealous type- you're sort of a tall, dark, and sexy rock star. Did you know?"

"I don't know if that ranks as high as cheerleader super hero, but I'll take tall, dark, and sexy," he laughed. Seeing his smile made her heart flutter. "I'll let you go, I don't want to keep you from your friends. I love you, though. I wish you were here. Or I was there. I kind of want to see this outdoor mall concept," he contemplated, raising his eyebrows.

"I love you too. Anytime you find that teleportation device, you just let me know. I'll text you later." She made the promise and blew him a kiss into the camera.

After they hung up, she tried to recapture the excitement about seeing her friends that she'd felt earlier, but it proved difficult with the pit growing in her stomach. *Five weeks, five weeks, that's it,* she repeated, rounding down the time she had to wait. She heard a car door outside and ran down the stairs.

"Friends!" Courtney shouted as she opened the door for them.

"Oh my god, you got dark!" Ashley exclaimed. Her own skin was as porcelain as ever, and her strawberry hair curled down her back. She and Molly came inside to get out of the heat.

What Comes of Eating Doughnuts With a Boy Who Plays Guitar

"So you better have some good stories about your small-town escapades," Molly insisted, her blue eyes showing interest. The girls walked through Courtney's vast entryway into the kitchen. Her house was open and airy, with vaulted ceilings and a bit of country flair in the décor. Almost the entire back of the house was glass, looking out onto her family's pool.

"I might have a few," she hinted. "You guys want water or something?"

"Yes, please! I am parched. Can this weather just be over already?" Ashley complained. Courtney got waters and chips and salsa for them to share.

"Tell. I wanna see pictures of cute boys who drive tractors or something." Molly sat flipping her white-blond hair over her shoulder.

"Well, not too many tractors in Gem City, but I've got pictures galore." She let her friends flip through her phone and answered questions when they asked.

"Um, excuse me, who are these beautiful men that look like Greek gods?" Ashley's voice was intent. Courtney looked to see, and it was a picture of Luke and Ethan that she had taken when they went mini-golfing. They were posed like catalog models trying to sell golf clubs. She laughed out loud.

"Ah, yes. That one is Luke, he's Vanessa's boyfriend, and that one is Ethan. He's, well, I guess he would call himself my boyfriend if you asked him," she admitted, knowing she sounded ridiculous.

"Your *boyfriend*?! How the hell do you not call or text with this information?" Molly's eyes went wide and then she glared at the faux pas of not sharing said news.

"He is seriously gorgeous. You're dating him? How is that working, just long distance and whatever?" Ashley asked, zooming in to inspect the photo more closely. She breathed. They were much more accepting than she had anticipated. She shared an abridged version of the story with her friends, ending with their video chat from only minutes before.

"I want to go to this town. It's like a magical place with hot boys who don't use more hair products than me. I'm so sick of guys in this city, I want a farm boy or something." Molly looked wistful, and Courtney had no doubt she was picturing something out of *The Notebook*. Courtney laughed, relaxing. They finished their food and chatted more about her trip, their school schedules, and the following week's cheer practice on the way to Desert Ridge. The sun was setting, but the dash on Ashley's Volvo still read 105 degrees. Despite this, Courtney knew they'd run into half the student body while they were there. They saw several of their squad members who were out shopping and a third of the basketball team getting dinner at Smashburger.

Ben emerged from the group and headed over to her. He looked very collegiate with his broad shoulders in a tight white polo, his auburn hair newly cut. "Hey, Ross, long time. How's your summer been?"

"Her summer was awesome, she's got a smokin' hot small-town boyfriend," Ashley answered for her before bouncing towards a nearby table. Courtney's cheeks burned. If she could have murdered her friend with her mind, there would have been quite a scene in the courtyard. Ben looked slightly confused for a moment, and Courtney decided to continue on as if Ashley hadn't spoken.

"Well, then, my summer was good. Cheer camp was exhausting, but vacation was fun. Yours?" She hoped it was dark enough that her mortification was not showing. She didn't even know why she was this embarrassed. She loved Ethan; she just hadn't planned on broadcasting her their relationship to the masses.

"Decent. Went to the lake quite a bit. My dad bought a boat and he wants to take it out all the time. I, uh. Well, I kind of missed you." He didn't seem to be anything but sincere. "I had hoped you'd be in town for your birthday, I got you a present. I mean, it's nothing too exciting, but I'll bring it next time I see you if that's cool." He shuffled his feet a bit, looking down. *Is he flirting with me?* she thought, shocked.

"Oh my gosh, you didn't have to get me anything, that's so nice."

"Well, if you don't want it, I'll just take it back I guess." His eyebrows narrowed playfully.

"No no no! I like presents!" she joked back, mock-pushing him in protest. They had known each other for years, and the only time he had given her a birthday present was at her last "invite the whole class" birthday party when she had moved there in the sixth grade. *Very interesting.*

"All right, well I'll bring it to school next week. I assume you have Mr. Kramer for English? I've got him third period."

"Same. Save me a seat if you get there before me. I don't wanna be in the front with Leah. I can't take the brown-nosing, it makes me nauseous."

"Hah, you got it. Good to see you." He looked unsure, like he didn't know whether to shake her hand or hug her or just walk away.

"You too, have a good night." In the end he strolled back to his teammates. Courtney skipped toward the fountain in the middle of the courtyard to find Ashley and Molly sipping coffee at a side table.

"Here, I got you an iced mocha," Molly said, putting the coffee in front of an empty chair.

"Ahhh, you know me well."

"What did Ben want? He's looking kind of hot lately, he got big," Ashley noted, mimicking large biceps as she spoke.

"Yeah, he kind of did," Courtney remarked. "Just catching up. He apparently has a birthday present for me."

"I think he would make a good boyfriend, he seems sweet. I don't know him well, just saying. How into Ethan are you?" Molly questioned curiously.

"Hold up, jumping the gun a little there. Ben and I have known each other forever; I'm sure it's just a friendly gift. And I am *very* into Ethan."

"All right, I'm bored here. We already know all of these people. You wanna see a movie?" Ashley suggested.

"Sure, you pick," Courtney replied. The three went and bought tickets for a token chick flick and loaded up with candy.

"It's a good thing practice starts next week. I'm going to blow up like a balloon if I don't start working out again," Molly said once they sat down.

"Amen, sister," Courtney retorted. They made comments throughout most of the movie, which irritated those around them, but this was not unusual. Courtney's jet lag was in full force, and she fell asleep soon after they dropped her off.

♪ *"A Thousand Miles"* –Vanessa Carlton
"You Get What You Give" – The New Radicals

Nineteen

Courtney tried to enjoy her last weekend of summer, but in reality she just wanted the next five weeks to Freaking. Hurry. Up. Her friends wanted her to fly Ethan out for their homecoming, which was considerably later, scheduled for the end of October. Unfortunately, it didn't seem that either of their parents were down for that trip. She just wanted to see him again. They made a point to text every chance they got, and talked or video chatted whenever they could, but it was never enough.

> E: Hey baby, whatcha doin?
> C: Well, I was working on a routine for my first cheer practice, but now I'm thinking about you.
> E: Lucky me :). I was just fine-tuning your song. I wanna have it perfected before you get here.
> C: Well, let's plan on you playing it for me when we're alone.
> E: Why? It'll be good! Do you have that little faith in me?
> C: Lol, I know it'll be good, that's what I'm saying! I'm either going to cry or going to need some VERY alone time with you afterward.
> E: Ahhh, ok, I like those reasons. You know I think about you all the time, right?

C: Well now I do <3. I think about you too. Non-stop. It's actually getting kind of ridiculous.
E: Well let's keep it that way, all right? I love you.
C: Deal. I love you too. Call me later?
E: Yeah. I have band practice, but I will when it's over. <3
C: Have fun.

Most of their conversations went on like this during the following days and weeks, though some were a bit more intimate. The thing she loved the most was listening to him sing, and she asked him to do it often. She had actually been glad when school, cheer, and work began again, because they kept her mind occupied and made the distance less difficult to manage. The first week of school brought several AP course loads to contend with, and she threw herself into creating cheer routines for the upcoming football season. Ethan took all of her spare moments, and she felt like she had found a rhythm in their unconventional courtship.

As promised, Ben had saved her a seat on the first day of school in Mr. K's class. Sitting on her desk was a small box with ribbon around it.

"So you weren't lying, you did get me something! And pretty ribbon!" she exclaimed, bouncing to her seat.

"Would I lie?" He was abnormally cheerful. He gave her a real smile as he waited for her to open it. Quickly, she unwrapped it, not wanting to last bell to ring before she saw what it was. She pried open the white cardboard box to find a pin. It was a gold megaphone with her name and graduation year on it. "I know you guys all put pins on your cheer bags or whatever, so I thought-"

"Ben, it's amazing! Seriously, thank you, I'm going to put it on my bag as soon as I get home." She leaned over and hugged him, though the desk made it awkward. He tentatively hugged her back.

"You were so nostalgic during the last study session we had before finals, so I hoped it would, I don't know, commemorate your senior year or something. So, you like it then," he confirmed. His eyes were bright and he seemed pleased with himself.

What Comes of Eating Doughnuts With a Boy Who Plays Guitar

"Love it," she reassured him as the bell rang. She faced forward to listen to Mr. Kramer go over the syllabus, and she began to wonder how she would feel if a girl gave Ethan such a thoughtful gift. *But we've been friends for so long. He won't think it's a big deal, will he? Ugh.* She knew she was committed to Ethan, so why did this feel weird? She hoped she would keep the lid on her crazy if one of his friends gave him a birthday present, even if that friend was a girl. *It's fine. Ben just remembered what I said about feeling like time was moving quickly. It's a friendly gift, no big thing.*

* * *

School picked up, and she and Ethan continued their routine. The weeks were moving slowly, but at least they were moving. The squad's first football game with her as the captain went swimmingly. People commented on the quality of the stunts and how clean everything looked. She felt relieved that at least she had that under control. Her stress started to die down. She would be missing one game to go to Ohio, but that was a sacrifice she was willing to make.

"Hey, love," Ethan greeted her during one of their Saturday-morning calls.

"Oh, I like that. It makes you sound British."

"Would you like some tea and crumpets then, love?" he responded, playing along with a horrible attempt at an English accent.

Courtney laughed. "That's truly terrible. Like you should not do that to impress girls."

"Well, that's the only British thing I could think of to say," he replied, defending his effort. He suddenly changed his tone, however, when he continued. "And, um, just to be clear, there are no other girls, okay? Like, I get that this is hard, but I just wanted you to know that, in case your comment about impressing girls was worry disguised as a joke."

She took a breath. "Maybe it was, even if I didn't mean it to be," she admitted. "And you're right. This is hard. I just need to see you, like, really see you, in person. How much longer?"

"Only six days."

"Really?!" She had a hard time believing it was that close. It had taken serious rejection of all of her compulsive tendencies not to dwell on the calendar because she knew it would drive her insane, but they had almost made it. "I get to see you in six days. Thank god." She breathed an actual breath. With oxygen and everything.

"I second that." They seemed to gather a renewed energy after this realization, and spent the next hour discussing every detail about homecoming, from where they would meet when she arrived in town to where they wanted to go for the after party. She let out a surprised laugh when he asked her what color her dress was, so that he could place an order for her corsage.

"I forgot to buy a dress! Oh my god, what self-respecting girl is this excited about homecoming and forgets to buy a dress? All I have been thinking about is seeing you; the actual dance part hasn't even registered. Holy crap, okay, so something else for the to-do list. Jesus Christ."

"Do you know that you are a special girl?" She could hear him trying not to laugh.

"Shut up, you should be flattered that all of my thoughts were on you. Now I'm going to hang up and get my mom to take me dress shopping, like immediately."

"All right. You can keep thinking about me while you try on dresses. And I mean that in the most inappropriate way possible."

Courtney thundered down the stairs to find her mom folding laundry.

"Mother, are you aware that we leave for Ohio in six days and I don't even have a dress for homecoming?!"

"Well, I was kind of wondering about that. I thought maybe you had plans to shop with your friends."

"I don't! I need you to stop doing this laundry. This is a life-threatening fashion emergency. I need your marathon shopper gameface on, Mom. Can you accept this mission?" Courtney knew she was over-selling it, but she was so excited that the event she had been waiting for was almost upon her. She was punchy.

What Comes of Eating Doughnuts With a Boy Who Plays Guitar

"What did you put in your cereal this morning?"

"Mom!"

"All right, let me grab my purse and we'll go. I accept the mission!" Courtney's smile went all the way to her eyes. They spent the next five hours in as many stores as they could manage at Fashion Square. She tried on a mountain of gowns, trying to picture herself dancing with Ethan. Her mom patiently waited for her outside each fitting room, exhibiting saint-like behavior. They ended up in a small dress shop in the corner of the mall. Courtney had never even heard of it before, but she picked up a floor length black silk gown and had a feeling she might have found the one. It was strapless and fairly plain in the front, but the back was open and had skinny horizontal rhinestone straps to hold it together. Her most favorite part was the slit up the back that had black sparkly tulle inserted under the seam. She had to get glitter in there somewhere, and it was perfect.

"This is beautiful, Court," her mom confirmed.

"Oh, I hope it fits me." Courtney literally crossed her fingers. She tried the dress on, and it fit like a fairytale. She was going to have to wear the highest heels still safe to walk in, but that was a small price to pay to look as good as she did. Her mom was even happier when they learned it was twenty percent off, making it one of the least expensive gowns she had tried on all day.

"It was meant to be. All of it. I am so excited to meet Ethan and to see you off to homecoming. It's nice to see you so… joyful, honestly. It has been a long time," her mom admitted. Courtney hugged her until she complained that she couldn't breathe.

"Sorry. I'm just so freaking excited. I can't even stand it." They paid for her dress, found the perfect heels, and went home exhausted. Courtney texted Ethan later to tell him about her purchase.

> E: Send me a pic!
> C: No way! It has to be a surprise.
> E: That's not a rule! Come on, I wanna see it.
> C: Nope. I want to see the look on your face when you

pick me up.
E: All right, all right. You win, sprinkles.
C: Hehe :). I can't believe I can finally say "I'll see you on Friday."
E: Sounds good to me. Do you still wanna do the whole football game?
C: Yes! I have to see Vanessa cheer at least for a little bit. Then I'll leave our plans up to you. Annnnnything you want :).
E: <3 You don't know what you do to me.
C: Yes I do. And I like it.
E: Cruel cruel girl. All right, I will talk to you tomorrow, okay?
C: Of course, love you.
E: Love you.

Courtney spent the next five days keeping herself as busy as possible, even picking up extra shifts to make the time go by. She had never felt so tired but so indescribably happy in her entire life.

♪ *"Ready to Go" – Panic! At the Disco*
"Till I Hear It From You" – The Gin Blossoms

Twenty

Courtney was already awake to greet her alarm. She'd hardly slept. They were leaving for the airport in a few hours, and she didn't even know what to do with the electricity bouncing around in her brain. She had talked with Vanessa late into the night before, and was excited to be able to get to do a Gem City homecoming with her oldest friend. She had learned from their conversation that Ethan was, in fact, walking the straight and narrow.

"Seriously, Court, he doesn't even so much as blink at another girl. I know that you've been witness to his skills of flirtation, but they were even more intense when he wanted them to be. Guys just started calling him 'The Fisher,' last year because he could 'reel in' anyone he wanted. I honestly didn't think he could do the whole long distance thing, but he is. He loves you," Vanessa said. Hearing that made Courtney feel… sort of guilty. After she got over the sophomoric play on his last name, she was of course glad he wasn't out hitting on every girl he came across, but his flirty nature also sort of made him who he was. She held onto the worry for a while after they'd hung up, but decided she could address it with him when they saw each other.

She ran through her checklist to make sure she'd packed everything that was needed. Her mom drove her by school so she could drop off an essay that was due. She ran into Ben in the office on her way out.

"Hey there, are you not at school today?" he inquired.

"No, I'm actually on my way to the airport, I just had to turn in the paper for history before I left," she explained.

"Are you going to Ohio?" he asked knowingly.

"I am. I'm doing homecoming there this weekend." She didn't know why she was so reluctant to talk about Ethan to Ben, but it felt all kinds of awkward.

"Well, I hope you have fun. Have a safe flight," he relayed, a disappointed look playing out across his usually cheerful face.

"Will do. I'll see you on Monday, have a good weekend!" she replied, leaving the building. "Let's hit the road," she told her mom, putting on her sunglasses. They had an uneventful flight, and her mom slept most of the way. Courtney tried to work on homework, but her mind couldn't focus long without thinking about Ethan kissing her. She eventually gave up and gave in to her daydreams.

She pushed her mother along once they landed, wanting to get to the B and B as soon as possible to get ready before Ethan picked her up. It seemed like everything was moving in slow motion: getting their bags, picking up the rental car, and driving out of the airport. *We are literally never going to get there.*

"Courtney. You are going to have to calm down or you'll have a heart attack. We will get there, I promise." Courtney glared at her mother in case she had become a mind reader.

"I know, I just. I don't know. I want it to be perfect."

"Well, it won't be. Nothing ever is. Just let it be what it is and have fun, okay? You'll regret it if you spend the whole weekend worried about perfection when you should have been enjoying being with Ethan and your friends."

Courtney took a few deep breaths. "When did you get to be so wise?"

"I know, right? I have to stop saying things like that or people will start to guess my age." Courtney laughed and resolved to be calmer. She didn't want her overactive mind to ruin homecoming. They finally arrived, and she was able to do her makeup and get dressed. The

What Comes of Eating Doughnuts With a Boy Who Plays Guitar

weather there felt much better than Phoenix when she'd left. It was in between summer and fall, a slight breeze winding through the trees. It made her hope there would be a bonfire after the game that night. She texted Ethan when they arrived at their room and told him to give her a half hour. He disagreed, and insisted on coming right away until she threatened to make him sit outside until she was presentable.

She had decided to be festive and dress in red and black for the football game to support Gem City High. From her suitcase, she took out a new long-sleeved black shirt that hugged her just right, and slipped into her favorite jeans with a sparkly belt. She had even brought earrings with red flowers to complete her ensemble. Being able to grab a hoodie for after sun went down made her so glad she wasn't in Phoenix.

"Okay, Mom, *seriously* don't embarrass me in front of Ethan please. Just please. Be cool, and don't, like, ask him what his intentions are, or something from a bad Lifetime movie. He'll be here in a minute." Courtney's heart was pounding and she began to fidget. While it felt like only yesterday she had been with him, it also seemed like they'd been apart a long time. *What if it's not the same? What if he sees me and realizes all of this long distance crap isn't worth it, and there is just awkwardness and we don't know how to hold hands anymore, or the kissing is different?*

"I'm not going to embarrass you. However, I did fly you across the country to go to a dance with this boy, so I think that if I *did*, it would be well within my rights."

"Just promise!"

"I promise," she said, sighing. As if planned, there was a knock on their hotel room door. Courtney sucked in her breath. She opened it to find Ethan looking just as delicious as she remembered. He was in faded jeans, a tight black shirt, and a very sexy black leather jacket open over it. He looked like Soda Pop from *The Outsiders*, and in seeing him, all of her worries faded. She threw her arms around his neck and he picked her up and twirled her around, allowing her nerves to escape in the form of giggles.

"Oh my god, I missed you so much." It amazed her that he looked even better than in her memory. Definitely better than on screen.

"I think I can relate," he replied, not letting go of her hands. He looked at her intently, and then his eyes traveled to the open door of her hotel room.

"If you're wondering if you can kiss me, you can." She grinned in knowing that her mom would give them a moment.

"Oh, thank god." He responded by bending down and placing her arms around his neck. He pulled her in close, and it felt like they hadn't been apart at all. Everything was right with the world. The way his thumb brushed her jaw, his fingertips causing a fizzy sort of shiver up her spine, it was all just… right. It was the right place at the right time with the right person, and she fell in love all over again. The leather jacket didn't hurt either. They reluctantly broke the kiss before things got too intense. "So, do I get to meet your mom, or are you ashamed of me?" he teased, somehow not out of breath.

"If you think you can handle it." She grabbed his hand and pulled him inside. "Mom, this is Ethan Fisher, Ethan, this is my mom, Julie Ross."

"So nice to finally meet you, Ethan. I've heard a lot about you." There wasn't one embarrassing word that left her mother's mouth. She silently thanked the universe.

"Nice to meet you, too. I can't thank you enough for letting Courtney come back out here for homecoming. You've saved me from going stag and dancing with my English teacher or something."

"Well, I couldn't allow that to happen, could I? Plus, if you know Courtney, then you know that she's rather persuasive. I'm not sure I had a choice."

"Um, yeah, I'm still in the room. Just so you're aware!" Courtney interjected. "Can we go now? I want the whole small-town homecoming weekend experience. We can't miss kickoff." The worries that had piled up on her shoulders were dissipating quickly, and she just wanted to *be* there already.

What Comes of Eating Doughnuts With a Boy Who Plays Guitar

"Yeah, actually, we should go. I sort of made reservations for dinner before the game, if that's cool," Ethan admitted.

"Oh, this one's a keeper." Courtney's mom sounded more than impressed.

"I know." An is-this-real smile spread across her cheeks. "Reservations, huh? Do I need to dress more fancy?"

"Not at all, you look perfect. Again, nice to meet you, Mrs. Ross," he said sincerely.

"You guys have fun. Courtney, call me if you are going to be later than curfew, ok? I'll be out catching up with some friends." They made their way slowly out to his car, fingers interlaced. There was the smell of fall in the air. She knew her mom had been impressed with Ethan, but that was confirmed when she read the text that came in several minutes later. An amused sound escaped her.

"What's funny?" Ethan asked.

"My mom thinks you look like a movie star, that's all."

"Well, I guess that's better than thinking I look like a hoodlum trying to take advantage of her daughter. Which I totally want to do by the way," he joked, squeezing her hand. Courtney blushed slightly as her chest tightened. She couldn't believe she'd been away for over a month. Every part about being with him felt like home.

"So, do we really have reservations somewhere? Or were you just trying to get me alone for a large block of time?" The flirting came back just as easily as she slid into the car. "I'm good with either, just to be clear."

She'd achieved the ultimate goal of getting his lips to form the self-satisfied smirk that made her crazy. "The reservations really do exist, but I like the way your mind works. I'll cancel them if you'd like," he assured her. "It's nowhere fancy, just this café. They have great food and it gets really packed whenever there's a game, so I saved us a table."

"Well, I can't miss that. You know how I feel about food."

"That I do." He started the car and rested his hand on her knee as they drove. Not much was said on the way, but it was an easy quiet. They found themselves singing along to the song on the radio, and

Ethan instantly rolled down the windows and turned it up louder so they could fully appreciate it. That earned them some stares from the other drivers, but it didn't even register for them to care. She was almost sad when they reached the parking lot. The breeze had felt rejuvenating after being in the scorching heat of the desert, and she finally felt like she could breathe again.

♪ *"Come To Me" – The Goo Goo Dolls*
"Heaven" - Bryan Adams
Performed by: Boyce Avenue feat. Megan Nicole
"Kiss Me" – Ed Sheeran

Twenty-One

"I can't believe how much I missed you." He stated this like a confession, turning off the car. "Can I just, like...can I touch you?" He laughed. "I realize how that sounds, I just, ugh. We've been apart for so long and I don't want to, like, accost you in the restaurant, but I need to really know that you're here. I'm tired of video chatting and texting, and I'm sorry if-"

"Yes," she interrupted, "you don't have to explain." She watched his entire demeanor change. He became much more serious, placing his forehead on hers and cupping her face with his hands. She kissed him softly several times, pushed off his jacket, and let her fingertips travel the length of his arms.

"I love you. God, I love you so much." He kissed her again, and she matched his intensity. She let him show her what he needed, which was clearly just for them to be close. Purposefully, she soaked in every moment of him stroking her back, playing with her hair, and kissing her neck. She reciprocated, needing him just as much. "Thank you," he said quietly after pressing his lips against hers again, his seriousness dissipating some.

"For?"

"I just needed that." A small smile returned to his face. "But we can eat now. I don't want the bear claw to come out," he teased her. "We're not even late for our reservation."

"It was worth it, even if we were." She hoped everything was okay, and that it was just him missing her that had prompted the shift in his mood. *Just enjoy it, stop overanalyzing.* He came around to her side of the car and opened the door.

"Right this way," Ethan said formally. She giggled and hopped out, grabbing his hand. The café was adorable, everything she had expected from downtown Gem City. It had a collection of reclaimed wood signs, mismatched tables and chairs, and fresh flowers in tall steel vases. They found their table and sat. Courtney was ravenous. She rubbed Ethan's leg with her bare foot, having slipped off her adorable but less-than-comfortable shoes, while she perused the menu. As was her custom, she ordered a ridiculous amount of food, including cake, macaroni, and fried chicken. Ethan just shook his head and smiled. He played with her fingers across the table.

"You're still wearing my ring."

"Of course, I wear it all the time."

"Good. That makes me feel better."

"Better? Were you feeling not-so-good?" Concern traveled into the question without permission, but things were going too well for her comfort, really. They couldn't possibly stay this way. *Shut up.* It was time for her to get bossy with that pessimist in her head.

"No, no, nothing in particular, just hard being away from you and imagining you having to beat guys off with a stick. It makes me crazy."

"Well, I find your craziness endearing, but the worry is unfounded, I promise. I'm yours," she said. Concern started to form a knot in her stomach, but she ignored it and focused on Ethan. "But if we wanna be in deep-discussion mode right now, can I ask you something?"

"Anything."

"This is going to sound insane, but, well, our situation is different. So… So. Well. This is just more than awkward to say, so I'm going to just blurt it out. Are you ready?"

What Comes of Eating Doughnuts With a Boy Who Plays Guitar

"I was. Now I'm less than sure. But lay it on me." His eyes were not convinced.

"Do you feel like you can't flirt with other girls? Or, like, I don't know if 'flirt' is the right word." His face fell as soon as the words were out, and she wished she could take them back.

"I haven't flirted with anyone, so if Vanessa said-" he started in, sounding upset.

"No, no, no, I'm not explaining this right. V said you hadn't so much as looked at another girl, so please don't be mad at her, that's not where I'm going with this. I just want you to be able to be yourself, like, I don't want you to feel like you can't go out and have fun because of us. I mean, if you want us to be together, then obviously I don't want you to go crazy, but if you would normally joke around with your friends who are girls, then you don't have to stop because you feel guilty. I think that's what I'm trying to say," she finished nervously.

"Really?" She couldn't read his expression. "I mean, I don't want to hit on anyone or anything, but I have been feeling like I don't know how to act at parties or around other girls. I just don't want to screw things up. And Vanessa scares me a little." This made Courtney laugh.

"Well, take comfort in knowing that you're not the only one who's scared of her. I think we're just going to have to find a way to be, well… ourselves. I love you. I don't want to be with anyone else, but we also have to be able to have a senior year and not walk around on eggshells all of the time. Like, can we just be honest about that?"

"Fair enough. Can I selfishly say I don't want you to flirt with other guys? I know you're being so open-minded right now, but it makes me, like, insane to think of you smiling at another guy the way you smile at me." This came out with him looking slightly embarrassed.

"If that's how you feel, then I will refrain from smiling at anyone. Frowns only from here on out," she joked, trying to pull him out of his mood. He did give her the grin that she loved and admitted it might be possible for him just not to think about it. "No more of this talk, though. This is our homecoming weekend, boyfriend, can we just be in love and ignore that I'll have to leave again?"

"I am one hundred percent good with that plan." He kissed her hand sweetly, and their food arrived. He hadn't lied, it was amazing, and they enjoyed each other's banter for the rest of the meal. Maybe they just enjoyed looking at each other in person and making everyone around them uncomfortable. Either was plausible. "Are you ready to watch some football then?"

"For a bit. Then I might be ready to make out under the bleachers, or something equally as cliché, if that's okay with you." She put on her best innocent expression, raising her eyebrows at him.

"Best. Girlfriend. Ever." She let him take her hand, and they walked back to his car. Feeling full and happy, she hoped that their conversation would alleviate the worry that had been weighing on her.

"Thank you for dinner."

"Well, you did fly 1,800 miles to see me, so it was sort of the least I could do."

"When you put it that way, where are my diamonds?" she teased.

"Patience, grasshopper," he said, winking at her. That was not the response she'd expected, and it made her heart beat out of time. They had to park down the street from the football field because the game was so packed already. *These people love their football.* She enjoyed the sea of red and black on the bleachers and the energy of the crowd as they walked up. It made her feel like she was part of something. She saw Vanessa stretching on the sidelines, and ran up to the fence.

"V!" she shouted. Vanessa looked up and ran over to them.

"I can't believe you're actually here! Are you going to watch the game?"

"For a bit. I wanna see you cheer. Otherwise, call me after and maybe we can all meet up?"

"Sounds good, girl, I'm so excited you're really here. Nice to see you too, Ethan," she added as an afterthought, running back to her team. They found a spot in the jam-packed stands. It was a new experience for Courtney to be a spectator at a game. She had a great time watching the routines, smelling the freshly cut grass, and breathing in the cool air. All of this coupled with Ethan's arm over her shoulder made her feel like she was in one of her daydreams.

After the first half, however, she was done with the crowd.

"Hey, let's get out of here," she whispered in his ear. He was up and down the stairs of the bleachers almost before she finished the sentence. They sauntered over to the town park adjacent to the football field. There were a few other people milling around, but for the most part they were alone.

"You wanna push me on the swings?" she asked him playfully.

"Hah, sure, why not?" Courtney had loved the swings at that park since she was a kid. She and Vanessa used to climb as high as they could into the air, always a competition, and then hang their heads backwards. It had been like flying, the ground rushing up. It was amazing neither of them ever broke their necks. Having Ethan push her was like flying in a whole other sense. He attempted to kiss or tickle her every time she swung towards him, making blood race through her veins. He eventually stopped and wrapped his long arms around her waist. "Come with me."

"If I want to live?" she finished, unable to resist. He just shook his head, apparently used to her nerd-dom.

She followed him towards a jungle gym-looking apparatus, and put on her hoodie, as the air had turned chilly. He climbed up to the top and held out his hand to pull her up. "It's quiet up here," he explained, and he sat against the entrance to one of the tunnels. Courtney sat on his lap, immediately finding his lips with hers. His warm hands felt good on her skin under the sweater. She was vaguely aware that they were in a semi-public place; she just didn't care. Her hands slid up under his shirt, and she marveled at the fact that he was hers. She pressed her weight against him, pushing him into the tunnel. If he was surprised, he didn't show it. He pulled her in on top of him and sat up on his elbows. She drank him in, seeming to get lost in a world all their own for a while. Her brain was at war with her hormones in deciding whether or not to push it any further when she heard voices below the jungle gym.

"Oh, I will KILL him!" Ethan exclaimed.
"Who?"
"Who do you think?"
"You're joking," she said, disentangling herself from their moment. But he wasn't. She looked down and saw Luke with another guy who looked vaguely familiar.

"Hey there, Miss Courtney Ross!" Luke shouted up. "Fancy meeting you guys here, whatcha up to?"

"Dude, I know you're bigger than me, but I swear to god I will beat you with pure rage if you do not stop messing up my life," Ethan lashed out, sounding genuinely pissed after following her out of the tunnel. Luke seemed a little unsure of how to react to this version of Ethan, and Courtney wasn't certain either. She turned around and put her arms around him before they climbed down.

"Hey, I know, okay? I know," she said softly, her fingers in the hair at the back of his neck. "This wasn't a great place to be alone anyhow. We can go somewhere else if you want. It's fine. Let's go for a drive or something before we meet up with anyone." She felt some of the stress leave his body.

"Yeah, you're right. I'm sorry, I just…"

"Me too. But it'll be fine." They started down the jungle gym to meet Luke.

"Hey, I'm sorry man, I didn't mean to piss you off. Vanessa asked me to come find you guys and see if you wanted to hit up a party at the river in a bit. The game'll be over soon." Luke's tone was apologetic.

"It's fine. Sorry I lost it." *So this is how boys argue. So much easier than the way girls do it.*

"Hey, Courtney, this is Jeff, Jeff, Courtney."

"Yeah, I remember you," Jeff said, sounding bored.

"You too," she automated. "I think we may head out for a drive, but we could meet up at the party later."

"Sounds good, I'll tell V. Good to see you, I know she's excited for you guys to do… whatever it is girls do to get ready for dances tomorrow. It's cool you could come."

"Me too." Courtney laughed at his description. "We'll see you guys later." She grabbed Ethan's hand and held it tightly, sensing he was not entirely over his anger from before. They made it to his car and were alone again.

"I'm sorry. I'm a little worked up right now."

"So I noticed. Talk to me."

"This is one of two nights that we get together, and I just, ugh, I don't know. I'm sorry."

"Ethan, I'm here with you. And as far as being worked up…let's take care of that." She flirted shamelessly, sort of reveling in the power that she had to change his mood. She was going to snap him out of his funk if she had to use every one of her girl powers. Satisfactorily, his attention shifted back to her.

"Oh, yeah?" he asked, sounding like himself again.

"Mhm."

"You are good for me. Do you know that?" he asked, holding her close. "Let's go for that drive." She agreed and kissed him intently before getting into the car. They drove out to the edge of town to an area she was certain had a ridiculously stereotypical name like "Lookout Pointe," or something like that. Her mind flashed back to the last scene that played out in the back of his car, and she intended to recreate that mood. She had fun teasing him, liking that she could make him react in the way that she wanted. It was less funny, but just as enjoyable, when he did the same to her. She felt alive again, having almost forgotten what it was for her insides to turn to glitter. Everything tingled when he put his hands on her, his lips on her skin. By the time they came up for air, she felt his energy the way it had been before. He seemed lighter, more trusting in their relationship, and she was glad.

"You are…a goddess."

"You are… a cornball."

"Yes, that's probably true," he admitted, kissing her head. "But I wasn't this way until I met you. I was a badass."

"Well, I still think you're pretty badass. Especially wearing that leather jacket. Did I mention that it was driving me crazy all night?"

"You liked that, huh? It made me think of *The Outsiders*."

"Shut up! That's exactly what went through my head when I opened the door and saw you tonight. You look like Rob Lowe when he was Soda Pop in the movie."

"Really? Well, shit, I'm going to wear it every day, then." He grinned easily at her, and she smacked him playfully. "So sprinkles, do you wanna go to that party?"

"Not particularly, but I should probably go say hi to Vanessa for a minute if that's okay."

"Sure thing." Courtney made herself look presentable as he drove. They made an appearance at the party, but neither was in the mood to mingle or talk about the game they didn't watch. She complimented her friend and chatted for a while, making plans for the following day to meet at her house for primping and taking pre-dance pictures. She saw Ethan with his guitar out of the corner of her eye, and her stomach flip-flopped at the sight. *Jesus, I love him,* She bounced over to sit down in front of him, asking what he was going to play.

"Well, I thought I might play the song I've been working on," he divulged, winking at her. *The song he wrote for me.*

"Do you think that's safe in front of all these people? Who knows what I'm liable to do?"

"I will take full responsibility for your actions," he promised, kissing her quickly. She sat back, excited, and mildly terrified that she would cry in front of a large group of mostly strangers. *They don't matter, just focus on Ethan,* she told herself. Carefully, she listened to him start to pluck out a slow but happy melody, and liked it right from the beginning. She tried to memorize the lyrics as he went, but knew she'd have to ask for a recording of it later.

> "*When she smiles at me,*
> *I can see who I'm supposed to be,*
> *Here or there, however hard it is*
> *I can see what she can't see...*"

He continued singing, and she was enchanted with the idea that the entire song was written for her. She kept it together, save for a few tears at the end, but she was too impressed to cry for long. She fell into his lap when he was done, kissing him in front of everyone. He dipped her back dramatically. Several party-goers whistled at their display, making her cheeks redden. Ethan laughed and sat her back up.

"Well, girly, I should probably get you back to your hotel before your mom decides not to like me anymore."

Courtney sighed slowly. "Fine, but know that I'm only agreeing this easily because I am so tired I might fall asleep standing up at some point." The previous sleepless night was catching up to her. He promptly threw her over his shoulder, grabbed his guitar, and carried her laughing back to his car.

"There, now you're awake."

"Touché," she said, out of breath. "Your song was... well, I don't have a word for what it was, which is rare, because you know how I feel about vocabulary. It was magical. I need a copy of it to make my friends at home super jealous."

"I can arrange that," he promised, pleased with her reaction. "But for now, let's get you back. I don't want to waste a missed curfew on tonight when it would be so much more fun tomorrow." The hardcore flirting made the butterflies in her stomach react when she thought about the following night.

"Why can I not get enough of you?" she questioned, more to the universe than to him directly. They had been saying goodnight for more than ten minutes in front of the B and B.

"Because you're insatiable. I like this about you... don't change it," he told her between kisses.

"Okay, okay, I really have to go in or I actually will be late." Ethan walked her up to her room and pecked her cheek.

"I will see you tomorrow," he said meaningfully, for they both knew it would be the last time those words could be spoken truthfully for a while. She woke her mom up to let her know she was back and got ready for bed. Her dreams were filled with blurry love songs and images of Ethan in his leather jacket.

♪ *"All For You"* – Sister Hazel
"Home" – Phillip Phillips

Twenty-Two

Courtney cursed the jet-lag gods when she awoke later than planned the following morning. The breakfast service at their hotel had already ended. She threw her hair in some sort of braided experiment and attempted some basic make-up- the good stuff would have to be saved for later.

"Do you want to go to brunch? You can invite Vanessa, or Ethan, or whoever," said her mom.

"Whomever."

"Daughters who correct their mothers' grammar tend not to get free breakfast," her mom warned.

"Sorry, habit. Vanessa is on the decorating committee or something for homecoming, so she's spending the morning at school, but can I ask Ethan if he wants to meet us?"

"Of course. Should we invite his mom too? Or is that uncool?" her mom said uncool-ly.

"Ummm, no, I think that might be nice. Let me ask him." Courtney stepped outside to make the call.

"Wow, okay. So you wanna do the whole family thing?"

"Why, is that lame?"

"No, not at all, I'm down. It just seems, like, *for real*, you know? But in a good way. Let me ask my mom." In the end, they all agreed to meet a half hour later at the restaurant next to the B and B. Courtney was kind of excited to see Ethan's sister again, but as it turned out she had spent the night at a friend's. Ms. Fisher seemed very excited that Taylor had a friend, and Courtney agreed. She seemed like a cool kid. Their moms immediately hit it off, as it appeared Mary was a member of several town committees that Courtney's mom had served on when they lived there.

"So Courtney, where are you thinking of going to school?" Ethan's mom asked her.

"Well, I've been accepted to a few places both here and in Arizona, but the actual process of deciding has been difficult. I really, really like UD. I went and visited the campus over the summer."

"I think she'll end up there, even though she keeps giving me hope she'll stay nearby and go to U of A," her mom added. "I think we should drive by UD again tomorrow so I can see it too." This suggestion surprised Courtney, but it was a great idea. She wanted to share that with her mom.

"I actually went there," Ms. Fisher said. "Great school, great atmosphere. I think you'd love it. Of course, staying near your mom is important too; I just wanted to throw it out there. Maybe you'll entice Ethan to go," she said, elbowing her son lightly, "his new SAT scores were certainly good enough to get in."

"New?" Courtney shot back, looking at Ethan.

"Ahhhhh. Thanks Mom," Ethan said, trying to sound annoyed. "Yes, I re-took them. The SAT app you made me download was kind of addicting, so whatever, I did better on the verbal. My math was always good, so, well, yeah." He stopped, looking uncomfortable.

"That's awesome. I told you that app was amazing." Courtney was trying not to embarrass him further, but she felt so proud of him.

"So, new subject, really, anything else," he pleaded.

"All right, all right. Courtney, tell me about your dress," his mom inquired.

"Cover your ears," she directed towards Ethan. He smiled and put in his ear buds as she described her dress for his mom. "But you'll be there tonight, right? Before we leave? You'll get to see it."

"Am I invited?" she asked, looking pointedly at her son.

"Of course!" Courtney's mom assured her. "Meet us for pictures over at the Roberts', and knowing them, there will be margaritas. I promise you won't be disappointed."

"Well, you sold it." Ms. Fisher laughed, pulling Ethan's ear buds out of his ears. "You almost made me miss margaritas, kid." They spent the rest of brunch talking easily, and Ethan found Courtney's hand under the table. *How much easier would life be if we had just never moved?* She could envision her whole world there, cheering with V, being with Ethan, and getting ready to go to UD.

Courtney convinced all of them that Ethan should drive her to Vanessa's to get ready. She ran back up to the room and grabbed her dress and bag, and Ethan was waiting for her when she came back down.

"Our mothers have decided to order another round of mimosas," he told her.

"They're BFFs!"

"That's horrifying," he joked. "So, do you need to go straight over there, or can you drive with me for a few minutes?"

"I can spare some time, I think." It always seemed to come as a surprise that he was as desperate for time together as she was. A nervous drop of thought rippled throughout her happiness that wondered when he'd stop. *Seriously. Quit it.*

"Oh, you think so?" He raised an eyebrow at her.

"Well, you're gonna have to work for it." He smiled and leaned in, making her shift her weight to rest against the car.

"Like this?" he said in her ear, putting one hand in her back pocket and the other on the car, blocking her in. He traced her jawline with his lips and finally found hers. He had won her little game because she was completely at his mercy. Her arms were covered in goose bumps and she was having a problem breathing properly.

"Mhm," was all she managed to get out, kissing him back.

He laughed, breaking the spell. "Nice to know I can still have that effect on you. You were getting a little cocky there for a minute, sprinkles." He gave her the smirk that drove her crazy, and she admitted defeat. She could not out-flirt Ethan Fisher. As she settled into the car, her heart was still pounding. "You pick the music, I just wanna drive around for a bit before all of the craziness begins."

"I'm sorry, who are you? You're going to let me pick the music?"

"Come on, I let you pick sometimes."

"Never, not one time, ever." She brushed off his argument and looked for the song "Home," on her phone, feeling it was appropriate. She plugged it in, knowing he would sing along. He drummed his fingers on her leg as they drove, and she tried to soak in every feeling: his hand on her thigh, the grassy scent of the air, and both of them singing more to each other than to themselves. They drove up and down the back roads to Vanessa's several times before he actually dropped her off.

"I'll see you in a few hours, okay?" She agreed, kissed his cheek, and started up the walk. He grabbed her hand, gently spinning her back around. "Hey," he said plainly.

"Hey," she responded, confused.

"I'm really happy you're here. Like, you actually made this happen, and we are going to homecoming together tonight. You sort of rock." He finished by pressing his lips to her palm.

"I sort of do, huh?" She grinned. "I love you."

"I love you. See you in a bit." He kissed her again and was gone.

♪ *"Underneath It All"* –No Doubt Ft. Lady Saw
"Here's To The Night" –Eve 6

Twenty-Three

Courtney and Vanessa spent more time talking about getting ready than actually doing it, but they had fun in the process. Vanessa had her blond hair up in a beautiful arrangement, complete with flowers to match her slinky purple dress. Courtney took a different approach and worked her long dark curls into a short side braid, the ends flowing down her shoulder. She chose to accessorize with a tiny rhinestone headband to match the back of her gown. Vanessa did her makeup darker than normal, and she hoped it wasn't too crazy. When she finally slipped into her dress and looked in the mirror, it felt like she was looking at a completely different person. Gone was the scared girl with the knee-length jean skirt from earlier that year, and in her place stood a beautiful, confident young adult. She twirled in a circle, almost falling over, shattering the 'adult' portion of the image, but she was still amazed at the transformation. She was just going to have to tell Ethan that he wasn't allowed to let her fall. *Ironic*, she thought, considering how hard she'd already fallen because of him.

Courtney's mom had arrived a bit earlier, taking pictures of the girls mid-makeup and hair. Since then she had been happily catching up with Mrs. Roberts in the kitchen. Courtney came downstairs to find Vanessa already there, looking for her lip-gloss.

She heard a gasp from her mother. "Oh my god. It's perfect! I mean, I knew in the store it was a beautiful dress, but all of it together is incredible, Court." She then proceeded to take seven million photos of the girls until they complained enough to make her stop. The boys were due to arrive any minute to take them to dinner. For once in her life, Courtney wasn't starving. Knowing she was going to spend the night dancing with the first boy, or man, as Ethan would insist, she had ever loved, meant there was nothing left for her to think about. She breathed.

Vanessa's mom let them in when they arrived, and seeing Ethan's face when he took in the sight of her was priceless. She smiled and did a slow spin, showing off the skin-baring design of the back. "You look. You look… phenomenal." His eyes were unmoving from hers. He moved closer and bent down to kiss her briefly. He looked delicious in a black suit and a skinny tie. His hair was messed to perfection, reminding her of the night she had met him.

"Thank you," she said, smiling. "You clean up pretty nice yourself." His mom arrived a few minutes later, and she too marveled at Courtney's dress. They all posed for pictures for their parents, the ideas getting sillier by the minute. Their moms finally allowed them to leave when she and Vanessa suggested they build a human pyramid in the living room.

"Be *safe*," her mother reminded her quietly before she left. "And you can stay out until two, but don't push it."

"Yes, Mom. And thank you so much. For everything," she said, hugging her. Her mom teared up a bit, and Courtney knew she had to leave before she cried and ruined her makeup. She turned and crossed her fingers with Ethan's, attempting to walk carefully with him out to his car. "So, um, you're sort of in charge of me not toppling over tonight. I just needed to make you aware. These shoes are very high, making the ground a lot further away than I'm used to."

"I can absolutely assure you that with you looking like that? I will not be leaving your side at all tonight." He tipped her chin up, bringing his lips to hers. They drove separately from Luke and Vanessa in case they wanted to leave the dance early, but they were all meeting at Olive Garden because, well, pickings were slim in the realm of dining options. Courtney looked down and admired her corsage. The flower was hot pink, but with all black and rhinestone embellishments. She let out a satisfied sigh, and Ethan reached for her hand.

"What was that for?"

"Just happy."

"Happy is good." He traced circles on her palm as he drove. "I do want to warn you, while we're alone, that my dance skills are pretty off-the-chain. I mean, I don't want you to be intimidated or anything, but I'm sort of a big deal out on the floor." He looked so mischievous she couldn't tell if he was being sarcastic or completely honest.

"Oh really? I had you pegged as sticking with the typical white-guy-head-bob. I'm excited to see these skills in action."

"Hah, well, maybe you're right. I guess time will tell." He grinned. "But in all seriousness, I did want to tell you that, um... I went ahead and got a hotel room. I mean, I hope we're past the point of me offending you, I just thought, if we wanted to be alone, it would be less stressful if we had-"

"Well, look at you. Vanessa always does say you're smooth, and this time I'll have to agree. It's perfect." She smiled with butterflies in her stomach, resisting the urge to pinch herself that this was actually happening. *Me with the hot date in the fast car and a hotel room after the dance. This is a strange new world.* "Everything. You, tonight, just everything is perfect." She fluffed her hair. Thoughts of being alone with Ethan solidified her lack of appetite as they pulled into the restaurant parking lot.

He looked relieved to have shared the secret. "Well, hold onto that feeling of perfection, because I'm not sure if Vanessa told you that we're also meeting Tyler and Kim for dinner. But, well, we are."

"Kim, as in your biggest fan, the girl who has been trying to lure you into bed for a year?"

"Nah, V exaggerates. Kim is cool; it'll be fine. Don't worry, okay?"

"Okay..." Courtney said, not quite meaning it.

"Really okay?"

"No. But yes. I'm a girl, that's a logical statement."

"All right, whatever you say." He laughed, getting out of the car and opening her door. Courtney got out, having every intention of letting go her frustration about the dinner situation, but her mouth got the better of her.

"So, um, before we go in. I just need to, like. Did you ever hook up with her?" she asked timidly, not sure if she really wanted the answer. She willed herself to appear more confident than she felt and looked up at him to find his signature smirk.

"Courtney Ross, are you jealous?" He smiled. "No, I never hooked up with her. If I'm being honest? Yes, I enjoyed the attention for a while, and I perhaps encouraged it, because well, I've been known to be kind of a dick like that, but it never went past there." She finally let out the breath she'd been holding.

"Okay, then. Let's eat," she decided.

"I kind of like you jealous, it's good for my ego," he admitted, making her push him away playfully as they walked. That backfired, however, because she sort of needed him for balance, so she pulled him back moments later.

"Is it just me, or are Tyler and Kim a really odd paring anyway? How did that even happen?"

"It's not just you. It's incredibly awkward. And to answer your second question- Vanessa."

"Of course Vanessa."

With her game face on, she was determined to make it through dinner without letting Kim, or anyone for that matter, see any insecurity. She sat between Vanessa and Ethan and did the best she could to control her facial expressions.

"So, you guys are doing the whole long-distance thing? That has to be hard. It's cool you could come out for the dance, though," Kim commented. She seemed sincere, but Courtney's instinct was to distrust her, so she let Ethan field the question.

"Yeah, it sucks. Not gonna lie, but nights like this make it worth it." His face was confident and he squeezed her hand under the table. Courtney wondered how difficult it would be to eat one-handed so that she wouldn't have to let go at all.

"Yeah, so, enough about how owned Fisher is," Luke interjected, causing Ethan to throw a breadstick at his head, which he blocked rather forcefully. "Even that shot was lame. Disappointing, man."

"Luke's just projecting. He's worried somebody else will win Homecoming King tonight," Vanessa shared.

"Please, no one is beating me. Have you met me? I'm awesome," Luke stated, throwing an olive into the air and catching it in his mouth. They all laughed and chatted easily for the rest of the meal. Courtney found herself letting her guard down and actually not minding the extra company. It felt...natural. It was rare that anything felt that way for her. She was usually replaying things she'd said in her head to make sure none of it was stupid. But that night, she just fit. Again, Courtney could see flashes of her life as if she had never moved away. Moments like these might be commonplace instead of a rarity. Her energy was high when they paid the bill and left for the dance. The fact that she was leaving the next day was hardly a worry in her mind.

♪ *"Shut Up and Dance"* – Walk the Moon
"Crash Into Me" - Dave Matthews Band
"Lullaby" –Shawn Mullins

Twenty-Four

Courtney and Ethan arrived at the dance after the others because they had to finish singing the song on the stereo first. She almost laughed at how perfectly iconic the gym looked. Streamers, colored balloons, glitter, all of it right out of a teen movie. The theme was "The End of the Rainbow," which was actually pretty original, but no less cheesy than any other dance theme. They took their photo with a backdrop of rainbow colored streamers and a pot of gold, and neither of them could keep a straight face long enough to get a good shot. Ethan kept looking for a leprechaun.

"Seriously, I hated that movie as a kid, and I would not put it past Luke to plant some creepy little man back there to jump out at me." Ethan shook his head as he double-checked the props dramatically.

"You're totally destroying your street cred by being afraid of leprechauns."

"Court, I have so much street cred, I own the street bank."

"Did you literally just say that?" Her smile was going to break her face, she was sure of it.

"Yeah. Sorry. That was lame," he replied shamelessly, laughing. Being with him was so easy; she wished she even had a hope of breezing through anything the way he did. They finally got a photo in after holding up the line. She wasn't even sure she wanted to see that piece of photographic evidence.

The music was typical: contemporary, lots of mainstream hip-hop, but at least it had a good beat. Courtney stashed her too-tall shoes under a table and pulled Ethan out on the dance floor.

"So let's see those moves, then, boyfriend." It was issued as a challenge. Her mouth almost hit the floor when he busted out some pop and lock moves coupled with a bit of break dancing. He did end his little routine with the "token white-guy-head-bob" as he grinned at her. "You have been holding out on me!"

"Well, that was a bit misleading. I only have a few moves I'm really good at, but I do like to bring them out to impress the ladies. Or lady, in this case," he corrected, grabbing her hands to put them around his neck. "Have I told you that I like your ass in this dress?" he added, his hands traveling down her back, pulling her close.

"I don't believe so." She blinked, loving every second of his attention. She brought out a few of her own moves when songs came on that she particularly liked, and Ethan was a fan of anything that got her to shake, well, really any body part. After a while they went to find their "cloud." A small wall of the gym had been dedicated to paper clouds with each attendant's or couple's name on them. It was apparently a Gem City thing, as Courtney had never heard of such a tradition.

Ethan stood behind her, his arms wrapped tightly around her waist as they searched the wall. She couldn't concentrate because he kept kissing her neck and running his hands places not entirely appropriate for a school dance.

"I'm never going to find the stupid cloud if you keep doing that."

"I don't care. I can't keep my hands off of you. You seriously have no idea what you are doing to me looking like that."

"Well then, do you want to get outta here soon?" she asked, needing to be with him. "I could get out of this dress, since it is so distracting."

"I thought you would never ask. Jesus, yes, let's go," he agreed, reaching up and grabbing their cloud.

"Did you know that was there all along?!"

"You'll never know." She glared at him playfully.

"You are sneaky," she concluded. "I gotta find Vanessa and tell her we're leaving."

"Lead the way." Courtney found Vanessa and Luke easily, being that they both had crowns atop their heads.

"Excuse me, your majesties, I just wanted to let you know we were heading out. Congratulations, by the way, royalty suits you both."

"Okay girl," Vanessa said, "Are you coming to the after-party? And will I get to see you tomorrow before you leave?"

"Undecided about tonight, but I'll stop by tomorrow, no worries." As they chatted and said goodbye, Courtney saw Kim walk up to Ethan in her peripheral vision.

"Hey, if you guys are going to go, do you mind if I steal a dance?" Kim asked, more to Courtney than to Ethan. Courtney's insides contracted. If only she could have said no.

"Not at all," she replied instead. Ethan raised an eyebrow at her, but she waved him off.

"Here, why don't you dance with Luke? I have to go and have my picture taken with the crown, anyway," Vanessa offered.

"Sure, sounds good." Courtney cut in and stood on her tiptoes to put her arms on Luke's broad shoulders. A slow song had come on, and Courtney willed herself not to look at Ethan and Kim. She knew there was no way it would make her feel better.

"He's standing like a mile away from her, just so you know." Luke smirked. "It may be annoying, but he's really into you. I wouldn't worry too much about Kim."

"You're surprisingly perceptive."

"Yeah, you can save your fancy words for your Scottsdale crowd, speak like a person," he demanded, making Courtney laugh. "So after tonight, what happens?"

"Do you mean, like, will I turn into a pumpkin?"

"No, I mean, like, do you and Ethan keep going until whenever you can see each other again?" She had to hand it to him; he knew how to ask the hard questions.

"I guess that's the plan. It's not a good plan, but it is one."

"Well, even though Ethan has lost all of his cool points since he, like, fell in love with you or whatever, I like you, so I hope it all works out."

"Thanks, Luke. I think that's the nicest thing you've ever said to me."

"Don't get used to it." The song ended, and he twirled her around dramatically. She felt Ethan come up next to them.

"Thanks for keeping my girl company." Ethan turned his eyes back to Courtney, seeming to ask for forgiveness. "He didn't get handsy with you, did he? Because I'll throw down right here." He stood there, puffing his chest.

"Bro, don't joke. You're embarrassing yourself," Luke responded. Ethan let out his breath, laughing.

"Are you ready to go then?"

"Well… sort of." He looked at her quizzically. "This is going to sound stupid, but I don't want your last dance to be with someone else. So we have to stay for one more." Ethan laughed softly.

"Anything you want, baby," he assured her, pulling her close even though the music didn't call for it. She let him hold her like that until the next slow song and tried to commit every moment of it to memory. He pulled up a chair for her to stand on eventually, so she could be at his height. Taking advantage of the equality, she pressed her lips to his with as much intensity as she could, and he responded evenly. "You ready to go *now*?" She just nodded her head. They found her shoes and her bag and waltzed out of the gym.

* * *

They checked into the hotel, ignoring the judgmental glances from the night clerk, and took the elevator to the seventh floor. As soon as the doors closed, Courtney grabbed Ethan's hands and pulled him into a very serious kiss. She needed him more than air at that moment. It felt like they were free, with nowhere to be and no one to check in on them, and she didn't want to talk anymore. The elevator opened and he wordlessly led her to the room and pushed the door open. The moment they were over the threshold, Ethan had her back against the wall, his lips finding hers magnetically. She breathed him in, pushing his jacket off of his shoulders and unbuttoning his shirt. She wasn't sure how, given the amount of time it took to get dressed that evening, but Ethan had her dress off in three point seven seconds, and they didn't bother unmaking the bed. There was no giggling or awkwardness this time. The level of intensity between them never waned, and it left her exhilarated rather than fatigued when it was over. She caught her breath slowly. He traced her palm with his fingers, and let them travel up her forearm lightly.

"That tickles," she said softly. Those were the first words either of them had really spoken since they were in the lobby, and it ended their suspended moment in time.

"I'm sorry," he said, kissing her lightly. "That was…"

"It was." She smiled at him and kissed him again, longer this time. He got up to grab some bottled water, and Courtney looked around the room for the first time. It was simple but nice. Bright linens, a small desk, and turquoise curtains with an intricate yellow print. She explored the bed and wrapped the sheet around herself, feeling chilled without Ethan next to her. He dropped a kiss on her head when he came back.

"I got three texts from Vanessa, by the way; I'm guessing you probably have more. She wants us to come to the after-party at the river." His expression was unreadable.

"Vanessa is just fine without us," Courtney responded, surprising even herself with her tone. "We are not leaving this room until curfew." She watched his smile widen and knew she had said the right thing. He downed the rest of his water and tossed the bottle on the floor, burying a kiss on her neck and pulling the sheet over the both of them. She giggled as he resumed tickling her, and her hands found their favorite spot in his hair. They made love twice more that night. Once playfully, with smiles and banter, and kisses through laugher. The last with the knowledge that their Cinderella evening was about to come to an end, and they did not know when they would see each other again. There were kisses through tears, and Courtney tried to memorize the way his lips felt when they met hers, and the way her skin blazed when he touched her.

The hour became late, and she knew the spell was about to be broken. She wrapped her arms around him tightly and laid her head on his shoulder.

She awoke to her phone vibrating on the desk across the room. It took a moment to recognize where she was before alarm bells started going off in her head. She shook Ethan awake and stumbled across the room, pulling the sheet tightly around her, to see that her mom was calling. She also became aware that it was two-thirty in the morning. Her mind raced. She willed her voice to sound like she hadn't been sleeping, and thought it best to start off with an apology.

"Mom, I know it's late I'm sorry I lost track of time I'm on my way back right now please just be okay you know I never break curfew I swear I just hadn't looked at my phone and I didn't know it had gotten so late just be cool, okay?" she blurted out as quickly as possible before her mom could say a word.

She heard a sigh. "You're okay, though?" she asked. Courtney's heart slowed down, knowing she wasn't in that much trouble if there wasn't yelling happening yet.

"Yes, I'm fine, I'm great. It just didn't seem that late. I'm sorry. I'll be back ASAP, I swear."

"I really want to ground you, you know."

"*Ground* me? From what, work and school and cheer?" Courtney smiled over her pounding heart.

"Yes. You've revealed the flaw in the plan, I guess. Just get back here, all right? And don't you dare complain that you're tired tomorrow when we leave, or I will kill you."

"Not a word. I'll see you in a few." She hung up with her mom and turned around to see Ethan getting dressed. "Well, that wasn't part of the plan."

"Everything okay with your mom? I'm sorry, I should have set an alarm or something. I didn't think I'd fall asleep."

"Everything's fine. Can you stop doing that for a minute?" she asked him.

"Doing what?"

"Getting ready to leave. Can we just have one more minute before reality sets in?"

"Yes, we can have that." He sat down and pulled her onto his lap. "So, um...we can talk about this tomorrow, or today, whatever, if you want. But, like, what's next? For us, I mean."

She kissed his lips, knowing that this had been coming. "How do you feel about New Year's?"

"Well...that it's far away. But that it's better than next summer. Can you really come back?" he asked tentatively.

"I have to solidify things, I wanted to talk to you first, but I've been working an insane amount of hours, so I have the money. Vanessa's mom said I could stay with them anytime, so that's my plan. I'm sorry it's not sooner or more concrete."

"Hey, I'll take it. Don't apologize. I'll feel better dropping you off tonight, knowing that's where things are going." He kissed her again. She knew they had to leave, but she couldn't force herself to get up. "I love you," he concluded simply.

"I love you too." She gave him one last kiss before gathering her things and changing into the clothes she'd brought for the party. They hurried getting to the front desk and the car. Courtney knew leaving a hotel at almost three a.m. was not a super classy thing to do, but figured there was that old saying about desperate times and measures for a reason. She attempted to fix her hair in the car into something that looked like she'd been at the river and not a hotel. She wasn't sure if the endeavor was successful, but knew it was probably as good as it was going to get.

"Do I get to see you tomorrow before you leave? Or do I have to leave doughnuts outside of your door in a couple of hours?" he asked. She could tell he was fighting to keep things light, but the weight in his voice had changed. The thing they'd been holding onto, waiting for, was over. And now there was the unknown.

She smiled at the memory anyway. "Of course. We are heading out at about ten-thirty for UD so my mom can see the campus before heading home, but call me when you get up. I'm not leaving without seeing you, boyfriend." She placed her hand on his bicep and leaned over to kiss his cheek.

"All right, good." He managed to muster up half a smile. He pulled into her hotel parking lot, and got out to open her door. "If your mom is up, I want to apologize for having you home late," he told her nervously.

"You really don't need to, everything is fine," she assured him, but knew he probably would anyway. He grabbed her hand, his long fingers pressing into hers, and walked her to her room. She let herself in and saw that her mom was up watching TV. Well, that and glaring at her.

"You're lucky it's a lot earlier in Phoenix or I would be way more pissed," her mom spouted when she walked in.

"Hi to you too, Mom. Ethan wants to come in and apologize, if that's okay."

Her mom looked surprised, but acquiesced. Courtney grabbed Ethan from outside the door and he walked in looking more confident than she imagined he felt.

"Mrs. Ross, I'm so sorry Courtney is back after curfew. We should have checked the time. I knew it was getting late, and I was careless. So, I'm sorry."

"Thank you Ethan, I appreciate the apology. I suppose you're only young once, though. Thanks for getting her back safely, albeit an hour late. Now you'd better get home too before your mom is worried."

"Will do," he told her, reaching for the door. Courtney followed him back out to say goodnight.

"Tonight was the best homecoming I could have dreamt up. I hope you know that," she told him sincerely. She knew she would start crying if he stayed much longer, but she tried to keep it together.

"You are the best girl I could have dreamt up, and I hope you know *that*," he told her. All bets were off at that, and her smile faltered dangerously, tears filling her eyes.

"I love you, Ethan Fisher."

"I love you, Courtney Ross. I'll see you for a bit in the morning, okay? Get some sleep." He kissed her once more and walked away. Courtney trudged back into the room to get ready for bed.

"Was it everything you imagined? Did you get your perfect homecoming?" her mom asked sleepily.

"Yes and yes. Absolutely. Mom, I am in love with him… and I don't know what to do about that. Leaving here is going to kill me this time," she admitted and started crying in earnest. Her mom hugged her, knowing there wasn't much she could say. Courtney let the tears come while she took out her hair and washed off her make-up. It felt very final when she stood in front of the mirror, all evidence of the night's magic gone. She eventually calmed down enough to go to sleep, but her heart was heavy as she closed her eyes.

🎵 *"Here Without You"* – 3 Doors Down
"More Than Life" – Whitley

Twenty-Five

Courtney woke up with the pit already present in her stomach. She had become quite adept at avoiding thoughts about leaving and just kept burying them. When she had left that summer, she and Ethan had known exactly when they would see each other again, and it had been less than two months away. This time, the goodbye would be different. She started to pack up her things silently. *You have to get it together,* she resolved, looking at herself in the bathroom mirror. *This is going to be fine. You will make New Year's work, and then it's only five months to graduation. This is possible.* She took deep breaths and kept up that inner dialogue until her mom interrupted her thoughts.

"What's on the agenda this morning? Do you need to go and see Vanessa before we head out?"

"Yeah. I think Ethan may bring over some breakfast and then we can go and say bye to V."

"I know today is going to be hard. I'm sorry, and I wish I could make it easier. I'm really glad I got to meet Ethan, though. I understand why he's so important to you." Courtney did her best to turn up the corners of her mouth at the support. Her mom gave her space while she finished getting ready. Ethan had texted to say he would be by soon with doughnuts, and she mentally prepared for their last encounter. She threw on a soft gray hoodie and a pair of jeans and tried to make unruly hair go into a ponytail. A knock sounded at the door, and she steeled herself for the onslaught of upcoming emotions before opening it.

She put on a smile, taking in the sight of his tired eyes holding a bag of doughnuts.

"I think this has to count as a labor of love. My body does not want to be awake right now," he said with a weary smile. She gave him a sleepy hug, wanting to curl up next to him.

"Wanna go for a walk?" she asked him. "Or maybe just a sit, over there, in the grass?" pointing to a small area under a tree.

"I could go for a sit," he agreed, slinging his arm around her shoulder. His black jacket was warm against her skin. They took the pastries for a makeshift picnic. *Jesus, he even makes bed-head look good,* she thought appreciatively. She loved that her heart still fluttered when he looked at her. Courtney found herself staring into his dark brown eyes, wondering how they got to this point. "What's going on in there?" he asked, interrupting her thoughts.

"Just admiring the view." She gave a half-hearted attempt at flirting.

He grinned back. "It's not too bad from over here either."

"I love you. You know that, I know. I just," she breathed. "I'm not sure how to do this again. How to leave. I can't leave," she managed, tears threatening to roll down her cheeks. He grabbed her hands and pulled her close to him.

"I know the feeling," he murmured. "It'll be okay. We'll work it out. Please don't cry." Him asking her not to cry made the pain burn brighter, and she buried her face into his shoulder, trying to even out her breathing.

"It's just so unfair. I know that's like a spoiled teenager thing to say, but it's true," she choked through her tears.

"You have to stop crying, or you're going to be responsible for me losing *all* of my street cred and crying with you," he told her. He guided her chin upward to kiss him. She attempted a smile.

"Ok, I'll stop. I swear. But I thought you were the bank," she joked, wiping her eyes. "Give me a sprinkle doughnut."

"That's my girl," he grinned. They consumed a large amount of frosting and kissed, and then kissed some more, both of them knowing that was it. Ethan took a deep breath. "This is going to sound really corny, and I'll probably deny I ever said it if this gets back to Luke or my band, but last night was the best night of my life. You have changed everything for me." His voice broke. "Wow, that was harder to get out than I thought, but it's true. I find myself thinking about the future in a completely different way since I met you. You're amazing."

"That's not corny. It's exactly how I feel. I can't imagine going back to my life without you in it. This thing, it's not just infatuation, or whatever it is people would call it. My whole life is better with you. I don't even have to meditate before I leave the house anymore," she joked.

He looked at her with a confused expression. "Do I even want you to explain that?" She waved him off, laughing at her own craziness. "Well, love, you know I'd stay here all day, but you probably need to get going if you're going to beg Vanessa's forgiveness for ditching the after-party last night *and* still make it to UD before your flight."

"Uggggghhhh, I forgot she was mad." Courtney groaned. "Whatever, she'll feel so sorry for me she'll have to forgive me."

"Good luck with that. Have you actually met Vanessa?" he laughed. "Lemme walk you back." His warm hand encompassed hers until they got to the room door. "Call me when you land, ok?"

"Ok," she said, taking steady breaths. "This is killing me. I'm gonna keep it together until you get to your car, all right? But I love you," she told him, pulling him in for a kiss neither of them wanted to break. He finally stepped back.

"I love you too. I'll talk to you in a bit." He kissed her cheek, shoved his hands in his pockets, and meandered back to his car. Courtney leaned against the door to her room and slid down to the concrete, her face in her hands. The ground was chilling, even through her jeans. She wasn't sure how long she sat there crying before her mom opened the door, startling her.

"All right, Courtney. I know you're falling apart right now, but you're going to have to figure out how to put one foot in front of the other. I told Vanessa's mom we'd be there in twenty minutes so you guys could spend a bit of time together." Courtney got up reluctantly and tried to fix her face with glitter. The attempt failed miserably, but at least she was sparkly.

Vanessa was in the basement when they arrived, and Courtney trotted down the stairs, ready to beg for mercy. Vanessa pulled out her ear buds and gave her a pointed look. "You better have a story for me, best friend." Courtney relaxed, knowing she could win her over with the details from the night before.

"Jesus! He's got stamina, doesn't he?" She laughed. "I don't really blame you for skipping the party. If I didn't know when I'd see Luke again, I doubt we'd come up for air. I did miss you though."

"I'm sure your royal subjects took good care of you."

"Well, being queen is a lot of responsibility, but I'm sure I'll bear the burden gracefully." Courtney got the scoop on the after-party and eventually asked her what she thought about her New Year's idea.

"Hell yeah! That would be awesome. My mom totally wouldn't care." Courtney breathed a sigh of relief, feeling like having a concrete plan to return was within her grasp. The girls gossiped about everyone else's homecoming dresses and the drama that Courtney had missed being wrapped up with Ethan. Apparently Kim and Tyler just went as friends, but he ended up leaving with someone else, causing quite the scandal and forcing Vanessa to put a bounty on his head. Courtney sighed when she heard her mom calling. She always felt better after talking to Vanessa, but it didn't make leaving any easier. Vanessa promised to ask her mom about New Year's and made Courtney swear to call when she got home.

Courtney's mom tried to get her excited about visiting UD, and she was, but was far more preoccupied with taking in the last mental images of Gem City on their way out of town. She breathed the last of the almost-fall air and forced her mom to drive by their old house. Her heart contracted knowing Ethan's house was nearby, and she contemplated running in to see him just for a second, but unfortunately understood they had to get going eventually. She was able to get out of her own head long enough to show her mom around campus and the cute neighborhood she had liked. It was apparent that Mrs. Ross was impressed because she didn't say much when they got back in the car. Painfully, it was clear that she didn't want her to leave Arizona, but it had become undeniable that her heart belonged in Ohio. They were both in their own worlds for most of the trip home. Courtney took something to help her sleep on the plane, knowing she couldn't cry it out like she had over the summer. In touching down in Phoenix, it felt like the dry heat might suffocate her. The best parts of her remained in a small town off the Ohio interstate, and she didn't think she would be whole again until she went back.

♪ *"I and Love and You"* – The Avett Brothers
"Pompeii" – Bastille
"Don't Wait" –Dashboard Confessional

Twenty-Six

Courtney sequestered herself in her room for two hours when they arrived home, allowing all of the injustice of the situation to take over. She didn't care that she was being melodramatic. Every possible argument for her going to live with Vanessa for the rest of senior year was spinning around in her head, but she knew that "I'm in love" probably wasn't going to convince her parents to allow their only daughter to move out eight months before graduation.

She forced herself to get up, put on make-up, and do something productive: shopping. She wanted to mail Ethan a care package of sorts, full of guitar picks, red vines licorice, pictures of them from homecoming, a sappy letter, and a copy of *Tom Sawyer* to remind him of their canoe trip. It was the reason giant sunglasses were invented, she was certain of it.

Once home, she wrapped them all individually in brown craft paper and decorated them in sharpie as she had for his last gift. Her mom gave her a quizzical expression while she worked on filling the box in her kitchen, but said nothing. Courtney decided to get up early the next morning and overnight the package at FedEx. She briefly contemplated how much it would cost to overnight herself there in a box as well.

She knew she was going to have to figure out how to make it through school the next day, and went over a mental checklist to make sure all of her homework was completed, and even picked out her outfit ahead of time. The less thinking required, the better. Only small thoughts were acceptable at that moment: eat, breathe, Ethan. *How can one person miss another person this much? He can't be feeling the same way or he would be calling every five minutes.* That's exactly what she wanted to do, but she didn't think she'd be able to hold an entire conversation without sounding like a stalker. She longed for him like she was in some Jane Austen novel. Actual *longing*. It was so bad that she took to putting her phone in her mom's purse and instructing her not to allow her to have it back for two hours. At one hour she went and stole it back anyway, worried she would have missed his call. *Life and geography are completely and utterly unfair.*

Finally feeling like she could feign happiness long enough to get through a call, her finger pressed his number on her phone after dinner.

"Hey, baby," he said, answering the phone.

"Hi, there. What are you up to?" *Cheerful, positive girlfriend, that's what I am.*

"Just messin' around on my guitar, thinking about this awesome girl I know."

"Oh yeah? What about her?"

"How hot she was last night. I wish I had a time machine and we could go back and do the whole weekend over again, exactly the same."

"Me too. I'd totally get in the DeLorean for that."

"Hell yeah," he agreed. "What are you doing?"

"I just finished a present for you, actually. I'm going to overnight it tomorrow, so you'll have it shortly."

"A present huh? What is it?"

"Well, that would ruin the whole surprise, now, wouldn't it? It'll arrive soon enough." She sighed heavily, running her fingers through her hair. "I miss you. Like, this is so much worse than last time. I'm sorry to be a downer, but I can just only be upbeat for so long."

"I miss you too, Court. All the time." *Cue the sigh of relief.* Maybe they were on the same page.

"I will sit down with my mom about New Year's tonight and get an answer. Then at least we'll have something to look forward to."

"That will help. Not knowing when I can touch you again is painful." She silently wiped a tear that threatened to drop and asked him to sing a song. He started to play "I and Love and You" by The Avett Brothers, and she just listened, trying to imagine she was in his room having an ordinary afternoon.

* * *

Courtney returned to school and went through her days mechanically. She studied for tests, went to work, and prepped for football games. She smiled and socialized with her friends when her mom told her she needed to get out of the house. She even had fun sometimes. Ashley and Molly kept her entertained, Ben kept her on track at school, and she worked her ass off as cheer captain. But part of her knew what she was missing. If Ethan were in Phoenix, or she were in Gem, her entire life would have more color. Her mom had agreed to New Year's if Courtney paid for the ticket herself, so she was waiting until prices came down to purchase one. At least it gave her and Ethan a bright spot to focus on when they spoke, but the days between them just seemed overwhelming. Every time he sighed on the phone or didn't pick up when she called, her mind raced with how to prepare for whatever he was going to confess. The constant rollercoaster of anxiety and relief was completely exhausting.

Regardless, they settled back into their routine- texting, talking, and video chatting whenever they could, but life got in the way sometimes, as life does. She'd get out of practice to see a missed call, or would catch him in the middle of rehearsal. It wasn't perfect, but things seemed to be working. At least, she hoped they were working. There was a growing part of her brain that was waiting for the other shoe to drop. It seemed like too much to ask of the universe, to allow her this insane amount of happiness that was just beyond her reach. *Do people really*

What Comes of Eating Doughnuts With a Boy Who Plays Guitar

get that? Do things end up in a happily ever after... with the musician with the fast car? In a novel, sure, she'd assume it would work out after the trials and tribulations, but this was real life, and no one had ever held the power to hurt her like this. She thought about Ethan more than school, cheer, and college combined. More than chocolate and sprinkles. *Just breathe and focus on what's good.* There was so much good. Just the sound of his voice on her phone had a ripple effect on her entire day. She just had to count down the days until winter break. Seventy-two to go. *Seventy freaking two.*

> E: Hey sprinkles, just wanted to let you know I was going to hang out with Jared and the guys tonight, so I won't be around. Can I catch you tomorrow morning?
> C: No problem. Anything fun?
> E: Just a party. They complain I never go out anymore.
> C: Well you should. Have fun with your friends. I wish I could be there.
> E: Me too :(. I'll call you tomorrow.
> C: Love you.

She was determined not to let her head get the best of her. *He can go to a party. What do you want him to do, sit at home every night? You've been out with your friends plenty of times, and he's never complained once, so quit it,* she argued with her heart. Her mind flashed back to the conversation they'd had homecoming weekend when she'd basically told him it was okay to flirt with other girls, and she felt nauseous. *Don't think about it. You either trust him or you don't.* She knew he wouldn't hurt her. *You need a distraction.*

> C: Ash, what are you up to tonight?
> A: I don't know, there's supposed to be a thing at somebody's house. I can get details if you wanna go. Not usually your scene though.
> C: I gotta get out of here. Lemme know where and when

and I'll come along.
A: Sounds good. I'll come by around 7.

Courtney had no real desire to go to a party, but knew she'd go insane staying home on a Saturday night worrying about what Ethan was doing. Even at seven p.m. in October, the weather was stifling, so she picked out the red sundress she'd worn that summer. She couldn't decide whether it was heartwarming or depressing that literally everything she owned reminded her of him. A sigh escaped as she finished getting ready and went downstairs to wait for Ashley.

"Are you going out?" her mom asked when she saw her.

"Yeah, Ashley's picking me up. I'll be home before curfew, don't worry."

"Well, I'm glad. It's not doing you any good sitting around every weekend."

"Yes Mom, so you've said. And said again."

"Doesn't make it any less true," her mom retorted.

Ashley came over, but let Courtney play the designated driver. She'd procured the address of a house near school belonging to a basketball player named Tim. "So, Ben will be there, you know," Ashley informed her.

"Oookay, and?"

"Whatever, you know he's into you, right? Like, you'd have to be blind not to see it."

"He is not, we're just friends."

"Sure, whatever you say." Ashley smiled tentatively. "I know you're in love with this Ethan person, I'm just saying that you have options here too. It's your senior year, and I thought you should know there was a possibility." Courtney knew her friend's admission was coming from a place of concern, but she wished she hadn't brought it up. The longer she was away from Ethan, the harder it was to hold onto the electricity between them. She didn't want to entertain the idea that he would certainly have other "possibilities" as well. She loved him more than ever; she just needed to physically see him.

"Well, thank you for the information. I just can't imagine being with anyone else. I know it seems insane."

"Not insane. Just want to make sure you're happy." Something in Ashley's tone let Courtney know she wasn't quite done. "So, are you? Like you're happy?"

Courtney sighed. She hadn't anticipated the car ride to turn into this heavy a conversation. "I think I'm as happy as I can be given the circumstances, yeah." But the question weighed on her.

"Okay, well good. Let's go to a party, then." Ashley turned up the music, attempting to lighten the mood.

"You got it," Courtney responded, parking the car. They pranced into a large Spanish-style house filled with music and guys playing video games. Out back it appeared that people were swimming or in the hot tub, and others were playing corn hole. *So, like every other party in the history of the world.* She turned down a Jell-O shot, making her think of Luke, and followed her friend out back. She saw Ben sitting with a group over at a large patio table and tried to decide if she should say hi or avoid him and any awkwardness that might abound. In the middle of her indecision, he caught her eye and waved her over. *Well, there goes that.* She walked over to the group without quite caring if everyone there liked her or what they thought of her dress. Missing Ethan took up too much of her brain space to care what other people were thinking. "Hey," she greeted lightly, looking for a chair.

"Here," Ben said, offering his.

"Oh no, you're fine, I can stand or scrounge up a chair, no worries." He insisted, however, so she took his seat and he pulled up an ottoman to sit beside her. He offered her a beer and she declined, so he brought water instead. She tuned in to the conversation going on around her, and found them to be talking about the varsity football record so far that year. Their team was good. Actually, they were really good; she liked cheering the games, because, well, it was always more fun when her team won. She brought up a particularly impressive play that resulted in the defeat of one of their rivals from the past week.

"Yes! That's the shit I'm talking about," Tim agreed wholeheartedly.

"You pay attention to the games?" Ben asked, amused.

"And what else would I be thinking about down there on the sidelines?"

"I don't know." He smiled. "I guess I never really thought about it. Maybe unicorns and pillow fights?"

"You're such a boy." She rolled her eyes.

Surprisingly, she found herself actually enjoying the gathering as she mingled a bit more and left her anxious persona behind. She went to grab another bottle of water and Ben walked up behind her.

"You seem to be having a good time. I don't usually see you out much."

"Yeah, it's not typically my thing, but I am having a decent time tonight."

"Oh, yeah? What is your thing?" The question was sincere.

"Um, well, I don't know, I guess. I'm more of a small group person than a party girl, I think."

"I hear you. Sometimes this is all a bit much," he agreed, nodding towards a particularly rowdy game of beer pong. "Speaking of small groups," he started, "there are a few of us going to homecoming, just as friends, if you want to come. It should be a good time." Courtney searched her brain for a way to respond, noticing his emphasis on the word '"friends".

"That does sound fun. I just have, well, like, a-"

"You have a boyfriend, I know," he said, surprising her. "If you don't wanna come, it's okay, I just thought you shouldn't miss out on your homecoming here, you know? If you want to think about it, that's cool too, it's not a big deal."

"I will think about it. Thanks for asking." She found herself meaning it. She hadn't thought about what it would be like to cheer the homecoming game and not be going to the dance. It wasn't really in her character to go alone, but a group might be tolerable, even enjoyable. She resolved to talk to Ethan about it.

"Anytime," he told her before strolling away.

What Comes of Eating Doughnuts With a Boy Who Plays Guitar

She needed to find Ashley and get some advice. Well, what she really needed was to talk to Vanessa. She texted her to call in the morning when she got up. Courtney found Ashley flirting with Tim's older brother who was home from ASU. She caught her eye and pointed to a pretend watch on her wrist. Ashley nodded, so she made another lap around while she waited for her friend. Spying a guitar leaning against the wall outside, she asked its owner if she could play it. Courtney knew him casually from school, and he looked at her somewhat confused. Unfazed, she ignored his expression and picked it up anyway. She hadn't played since that bonfire with Ethan, and she hadn't sung in public since her unplanned concert at the Strawberry Festival, but the sight of the guitar brought about such a feeling of longing that she couldn't *not* play it.

Casually, she sat down on a chair by the pool and strummed the beginning chords to "Wonderwall," by Oasis. It was one of the five songs she knew. She sang along quietly at first, but by the end, the words were at least audible to those who made a point to listen. Some light applause from around the pool sounded as she finished, so she stood up and curtseyed, not even really feeling embarrassed. The "not caring" side effect of her missing Ethan was a benefit, and she briefly considered that her life in Scottsdale might have been very different if she could have found this version of herself sooner. She returned the guitar to its owner, his expression now admiring instead of confused, and went to drag Ashley to the car before they were late getting home. She started for the house, but found Ashley outside instead, looking at her curiously.

"Who are you and where has Courtney gone?" She crossed her lightly freckled arms. "You just gave a concert to a party full of people, when a year ago you couldn't even be convinced to come. You're blowing my mind right now." Courtney just shrugged off her comments. She waved to Ben as they left and managed to get them home on time.

* * *

Vanessa called her early the next morning.

"Hey girl, how are you?"

"Eh."

"Yeah, I kind of figured. I was going to call you today anyway. I assume you've talked to Ethan, obviously, but what is going on with him?"

"What do you mean?" Courtney asked, alarm bells sounding in her brain.

"I mean, nothing too dramatic, just he's either been walking around like a zombie, ear buds in, not speaking to anyone, or he's getting wasted with Jared at a party, or so I hear. Like, it's just not *him*. Well, not the new him, anyway."

Courtney frowned. "Well, I guess I'm probably guilty of the zombie part too, and I knew he went out with the guys last night, but I haven't really sat down and talked to him since Friday. I'll call him this morning. Thanks for the heads up, though." Her gratitude was half-hearted, as there was a wave of guilt and *I-told-you-so* cascading over her head.

"I'm sure he's just adjusting. What you guys are doing is hard. He'll perk up. You'll be back in December, that's only..."

"Seventy-one days away."

"Right, no big deal," Vanessa told her, trying to sound cheerful.

"Thanks for trying to make it sound reasonable," Courtney said.

"I'm sorry. I didn't sell it very well, did I? I'm sure everything will work out, I just want you both to be together and be happy!"

"Me too, girl. Thanks for calling, I gotta get up and get ready though, I'll text you later, okay?"

"'K. Good luck talking to Ethan," Vanessa added, hanging up. Courtney rolled back over and put a pillow over her head. She wanted to crawl in a hole. The person Vanessa described didn't sound like her boyfriend. She took a steadying breath, and braced herself for a potentially difficult conversation. She pressed Ethan's name and listened to it ring.

"Hello," he answered, having clearly been asleep.

"Hey, I'm sorry, I woke you up. Go back to bed, I'll call you later."

"No, no, it's fine, I needed to wake up anyway. What's up?" he asked her, yawning.

"Well, that's sort of what I was going to ask you. Are you okay?"

"Of course, why?"

"I don't know. I talked to Vanessa. Don't get mad at her, she's just worried about you. I don't... well, the way she described you, just, I don't want you to be unhappy. Are you... unhappy?" *Nothing like diving right into awkward and anxious.*

"Ah, Vanessa, of course. Look, I got a little drunk last night. I had a ride home, I wasn't out like being reckless or driving or anything. I just needed a break, you know? It's not the crisis situation Vanessa is making it out to be. And it's kind of hypocritical of her too, since Luke drinks like a fish every weekend." His tone held irritation. "So yes, I'm okay, I'm happy. Please don't read too much into this, okay?" he said more softly. She felt guilty for waking him up and questioning him. Maybe Vanessa was just overreacting. After all, she had gone out the night before too, and he wasn't interrogating her about it first thing in the morning.

"You're right, I'm sorry. I shouldn't let her get into my head like that. I just miss you, that's all." She hope he could hear her asking for an unspoken forgiveness.

"Don't worry about it, babe," he replied more cheerfully. "I'm actually glad you woke me up, I have to be at work in a bit. How was your night?"

"Good, actually, though I didn't expect it to be. I went to a party with my friend Ashley. I usually hate that scene, but I even played a little guitar and sang some Oasis. You would have been proud of me."

"That's awesome, I wish I could have seen it. Do I need to question you about your party behavior?" he asked, mocking her slightly.

"Shush, you know you don't." He laughed and the sound made her happy. She thought about bringing up homecoming, but felt they were a little off-balance and decided to wait. They talked quickly about their plans for the day and agreed to video chat later that night.

"Love you," he told her.

"Love you."

♪ *"Landslide"* – Fleetwood Mac
Performed by Hannah Trigwell Ft. Nick Howard
"How's It Going to Be" – Third Eye Blind

Twenty-Seven

They continued in the same pattern over the next week or so, but Courtney still had an uneasy feeling. They hadn't seen each other in more than six weeks, but the space felt much larger. *Like the Grand Canyon larger.* She knew he had been going out with Tyler more, and his band had played a couple of shows. Though he swore everything was fine, the worry remained. They had missed each other's calls two days in a row, and she was bound and determined to talk to him as soon as humanly possible. She dialed his number and got into her car after practice. Voicemail. *Dammit.* She couldn't focus on anything else until she heard his voice. Her phone buzzed.

> E: With the band, call you later?
> C: K. I miss you.
> E: You too

Ugh. She knew she would feel better after they were able to speak, but she hated waiting around. She went home and ate dinner with her parents, a rare occurrence. Still no call. Her phone was with her at all times; she even set it on the floor next to the shower so she could jump out if it rang. But it didn't. *Don't freak out, don't freak out, don't freak out. He's busy, he got held up, nothing catastrophic has happened.*

The words didn't alleviate the constant nausea she was experiencing because she couldn't imagine any scenario other than school where she wouldn't call or text him back right away. She was getting ready for bed and about to break down and call him again when the screen lit up on her comforter. She took a breath before answering.

"Hey, I was starting to think you'd been kidnapped or held hostage or something." *Light, funny, nonchalant.*

"Nah, just got held up. What's up?"

"Just getting ready for bed. It's late there," she realized.

"Yeah, I should head to bed soon too. It was a long day." Her heart sank. She had hoped to be able to talk for a while. She needed to feel close to him... not being around him was driving her crazy.

"Oh, okay, then. Well, I guess I'll try and catch you earlier tomorrow," she said softly.

"Courtney-" he stopped.

"Yeah?"

"I lied to you the other day. I've never lied to you before, and it's just, I don't know. You asked me if I was unhappy, and if everything was okay, and I told you I was fine. But I'm not. Like I'm really not fine, I'm miserable here without you." His words rushed out quickly, like a dam had finally burst.

Courtney winced at the admission, visualizing that elusive shoe hurtling towards the ground. "Okay... I don't want you to be miserable. I know this sucks, I just... I don't know what else to do. I know New Year's seems far away." Her heart started pounding and her palms were sweating. He was quiet for too long. "Are you still there?" she asked, knowing the answer.

"I just don't know that I can do this," he said slowly. "I want to *be* with you. More than anything. But I'm not *with* you. You're there and I'm here, and I thought... I don't know what I thought. I didn't imagine it being this hard because I know I can talk to you and see you on screen, but I *need* to touch you and kiss you. I'm losing my mind." He paused. When she didn't offer a response, he continued. "God, am I the only one finding this impossible? Can you honestly tell me that you're loving life right now, with the way things are?" Ethan was almost shouting, his frustration evident.

Courtney focused on taking steady breaths. *Please don't do this,* she pleaded in her head. "So, what you're saying is, is that you're done?" Courtney asked as evenly as she could. The pit in her stomach had grown exponentially, as if to gloat.

"Are you saying that's my only option? We either continue as we have been or I never get to talk to you again? How is that fair?" he responded, not bothering to keep his volume in check any longer. "I haven't done anything *wrong*. I haven't cheated on you, I haven't hurt you. I have loved you from the moment we met. Am I an asshole for wanting my senior year to consist of more than waiting for the one call we have a day and feeling guilty every time I talk to another girl because you're not *here*?" The intensity of his emotions was coming through in the shaking of his voice.

Her mind raced, processing everything he was saying. His mention of other girls was like a punch to the gut. She felt helpless. She couldn't go to him, she couldn't kiss him and assure him everything was going to be okay if he would just *wait*. She didn't want to have to convince him she was worth waiting *for*. There was a choice to be made, and she chose to protect what would be left of her heart rather than throw it at his feet. Her adrenaline kicked in, and she chose not to let him see what this was doing to her. Stubbornly, she wasn't going to beg for him to love her enough to make it until graduation. She knew she had been quiet for a long time, afraid to make a decision, afraid it would be the wrong one. She continued on.

"It doesn't make you an asshole. It just makes you single," she replied coldly, attempting to mask her panic. *Keep it together, don't cry, don't cry, don't cry.* "I don't blame you; this makes sense. In fact, I'm pretty sure it was me who gave you an out at the end of the summer to walk away and have your senior year. *You* were the one who insisted on taking it to this level. And I *believed* you. I believed we could do this for a year." She struggled to maintain her composure, all the while wondering if she should stop. If it was even possible to stop. "No, it's not sunshine and daisies over here either. I miss you *all* the time, but there's NOTHING I can do about it," she stated emphatically, almost losing the control in her speech. She begged the universe to let her get off of the phone before she couldn't hide her tears anymore. Her heart was going to burst. She briefly contemplated just driving to the airport and showing up at his house the next morning. She knew if she could just *see* him, she could make him feel better.

"I don't want to lose you forever, please don't shut me out. Please, please just listen to me! I'm trying to be honest; I never want to hurt you. You're going to be here for school. Can't we see where we are then? Maybe-"

"No." She interrupted him very clearly, snapping out of her delusional fantasy of taking a red-eye to Ohio. She *loved* him, but if he told her to "wait and see" until she got to school… she would. She would wait and hope and pray until she got there. And she'd be completely wrecked if he didn't wait for her. The idea helped her stay the course and poured on a layer of anger to everything else. "You don't get to have it both ways. You can't go whore around the rest of this year and expect me to take you back in September as if nothing happened. You don't get to keep me on your hook. It isn't fair. It's not called a 'pause,' Ethan, it's called a break-up for a reason, because we will be broken. You cannot ask me to agree to that, you have to understand where I'm coming from, right?" Reality was beginning to set in. This was it. She didn't even get to appreciate their last happy conversation because she hadn't known there'd never be another. Everything they had was about to be over, and it felt as if she were being sucked into a void. *Maybe this is the opposite of falling in love. You have to be pulled back up. Painfully, all the emotions in reverse.* She contemplated this truth as the tears rolled down her cheeks.

"Courtney, please…" He was crying now. Hearing that was almost unbearable for her- he was always the one who kept it together. "You can't tell me you're ready for this to be completely over."

"I'm not, not even close. You made this decision. I don't want to be in the business of trying to convince you to stay in love with me, I can't-"

"I *am* in love with you, this is *not* about how I feel for you. This is about distance and being realistic-" he argued.

"Ethan, intellectually, I get where you are coming from, okay? I know that this is impossibly hard. But being with you never felt 'realistic' to me, it felt like, I don't know, a fairytale. In my heart I worried that I couldn't hold onto it, and now that is coming to pass. You've made your case; it seems that we just need to stop before we start saying things we don't mean." She gulped silently.

"Just, okay, slow down. Please don't hang up. I'll do it, ok? I'll do whatever you want. I will make it through this year, just please don't make this the end. I've never… I can't imagine my future without you being a part of it. Please, can we just forget this? I'm sorry. I was just freaking out, I can do this, with you. I can."

Her entire heart wanted to believe his words, but she knew they weren't true. She envisioned having the exact same argument two months from then, or worse, finding out that he cheated on her.

"Ethan-" she stopped to hold the phone away from her mouth to catch her breath. "I love you. I have given you *everything*. I don't know, I suppose I should thank you, because the old Courtney would be ready to accept anything you offered, just so that I wouldn't… I wouldn't lose you, but you have been so good to me that I know what I'd be missing. I know how it feels for things to be so *good*. I couldn't have asked for a more perfect first… well, everything. But you know that you're lying right now. If you aren't all in, then you can't do this. Which means I can't do this. Above anything else, I want you to be happy-"

"Please stop. Stop saying that. Don't refer to us in the past tense. Just believe me, please. I would do anything for you, you know that," Ethan begged.

"I do know that. Which is why I know it's best for us to be done. I don't want you to give up anything for me. You will only be resentful later, and I don't want us to end that way." Her entire body was resisting her logic, her stomach churning. *You don't have to do this, Courtney, you can just accept that what he says is true and forget about this by tomorrow,* she told herself. It was so tempting. But there was a reason she'd had that little speech prepared for a while. In her mind, there was always a contingency plan in case that wave she'd been riding came to an end before she was ready.

"Please, just don't," Ethan whispered, starting to accept her words. "I'm not ready to get off the phone. I can't let this be it."

"You will be okay. You deserve someone you can be with, and for it to be easy. I know this isn't easy anymore. I am going to hang up in a second, okay? I just, um, I need to process," she told him, her voice breaking. "The hardest part is that you are the first person I would call to tell something like this, because I'd know you would make me feel better. I'm going to miss you more than you can imagine." Her voice betrayed her in that last sentiment, tumbling into the territory of the ugly cry.

"No, you're not, I am always here for you. You're breaking my heart, Courtney. You know you can call me, text me, anything, anytime."

She laughed softly through her tears. "You know it's not the same. I do love you, Ethan, but I need to go. Goodbye."

She could hear him say her name as she dropped the phone from her ear and ended the call. The full magnitude of the loss seemed to hit a few moments later, and she allowed the waves of heartbreak to take over. She dragged her blanket and pillow into her closet so her mom and dad wouldn't hear her. If she thought it had been difficult coming back in September, she didn't even know what word to use for this. She was shattered. This wasn't just losing him; this was losing everything she had given him. Every happy moment, every kiss, every first she had experienced with him was being taken back. She shut off her phone as she saw text messages from Ethan start to fill up her screen. She knew she couldn't be trusted to stick with her decision if she started reading them. Her gut was already questioning everything. *Should you have fought harder? Could you fly out sooner? Maybe it wouldn't hurt to text him back.* It was too much. But she also knew she couldn't stay in a long-distance relationship if he wasn't in one hundred percent. It had been impossible enough when they were both on the same page. Convincing herself of these facts proved to be a challenging endeavor as she curled up to cry into her comforter, wishing he were there to hold her. She kept it up until her throat was raw and her eyes swollen shut.

She didn't remember falling asleep, but at some point woke up disoriented. The whole sequence of events came rushing back and her stomach turned. She managed to get back in her own bed and tried to escape this new reality, but she couldn't fall back asleep. She watched the sun come up through her shuttered windows and waited for the alarm to go off. Her brain couldn't even function enough to roll over, let alone think about how she was going to make it to school that morning.

She turned her phone back on and had seven text messages from Ethan. Her head told her to delete them, but she couldn't. She had to know if he was as broken as she was.

> E: Courtney. I love you. Please let me take back what I said.
> E: I can't not be with you. Just please tell me that you're ok, or call me back.
> E: I didn't want to hurt you.
> E: Just can we talk about this some more?
> E: I know you said you needed to process. I don't know what else to say.
> E: I don't think I'll ever get over you. How can this even be happening?
> E: I'm sorry.

Her brain had been right. She should have deleted them. She knew by the "I'm sorry" at the end that he had realized it was over. He was done fighting for them to continue. She fought the urge to write him back, and deleted what he had written. She started to delete every message he'd ever sent, but her heart wouldn't let her. They were proof that what they'd had really existed. That he had loved her and she had made him happy. She sighed tearfully back into her pillow and decided to try and find sleep.

♪ *"Goodbye To You"* – Michelle Branch
"Dog Days are Over" – Florence + The Machine

Twenty-Eight

Courtney's alarm did go off a short time later; she just didn't care. She didn't need to look in the mirror to know that it wasn't feasible to leave the house. Her mind braced itself for her mom's footsteps in the hall, but they never came. She slept off and on over the next couple of hours, but there finally came a knock at her door.

"Yeah." Her mom poked her head in her room.

"I called you out of school earlier. I think you should eat," she said plainly. Courtney couldn't believe there were no questions, but was going to roll with whatever this was.

"I can't eat. I'm too nauseous," she croaked, sitting up in bed.

"Well, get dressed anyway and come downstairs. We're going to brunch. You can just have some orange juice if you don't want food."

"You're joking, right?" Her voice was scratchy from crying. "I cannot leave the house looking like this."

"Then fix yourself up. It'll make you feel better anyhow. We're leaving in a half hour," her mom finished decisively, leaving the room. Courtney lay there for a minute, wondering how much she knew. It had seemed a stealthy move, hiding in the closet the night before, but it wasn't like her parents couldn't have heard her anyway. She thought about ignoring the command to get up and get dressed, but she didn't really have it in her to argue. She threw on a gray t-shirt and jean shorts because it was still in the 90s at the end of October. Her hair found its way into a messy bun atop her head, and she pulled out the largest, darkest sunglasses she owned to cover her swollen eyes. She only bothered with lip gloss, but she did feel better after putting herself together, if only slightly. She clomped down the stairs, making her feelings known. Her mom was already waiting, purse in hand.

"Good, you look less zombie-like. Let's go." She ushered her into the car. Courtney turned up the music. Loud. She figured this would delay the need for her to answer questions. Her mom pulled into the parking lot at Butterfield's, one of Courtney's favorite breakfast spots. Her stomach growled despite her protests that she wasn't hungry. They were seated outside at Courtney's request so she could wear her sunglasses without being weird, and she decided food might be her friend after all.

"What are you gonna get?" her mom asked.

"I don't know. Sort of everything and nothing sounds good at the same time."

"Well, let's go with a little of everything, then, shall we?" Courtney gave a half-hearted laugh. She was shocked when the waiter returned. "Yeah, so we want a cinnamon roll, this pancake special thing you have going on, some chorizo and eggs- a side of sour cream with that too, please, annnnnnnd two asiago bagels." The waiter looked amused.

"You got it," he said.

"Mom, I thought you were joking. That's like enough calories for the next two weeks!"

"Who says we have to eat it all? You said you didn't know what sounded good. Now, you'll have choices." Courtney developed a lump in her throat that she tried to swallow. *I have the best mom*, she knew.

"True statement."

"Courtney-" her mom started in.

"Mom, please, just don't. I can't," she pleaded, her voice wavering.

"You don't have to tell me what happened. I just want you to listen to me, okay?" Courtney didn't respond, which her mom took as agreement. "I need you to know that you're going to be okay, whatever it was that went on last night. You will be, you just have to believe it. I know that your first love is… intense."

"That's not even the word for it."

"Ok then, consuming, exhilarating, mind-blowing… you take your pick of adjective. The point is that you can't lose the person you've become. Since last year, I've seen you change into this amazing young woman," her mom told her, even though that term made Courtney cringe. "And I don't know for sure if that's because of Ethan, but if it's really over with him-"

"I think it is," Courtney choked out.

"Okay. Well, then, even though it is, I don't want to see you go back to being afraid to show people who you are. You've been so open and confident; it's like you've been able to see in yourself what I always saw in you, and it has been amazing to watch. So I need you to promise me that you're not going to let this force you back into hiding or something."

"Mom. I. I don't even know what to do without him. Everything reminds me of him," she explained, as a few tears crossed the threshold. "Like, I can't even look in the mirror because I don't want to see this girl looking back at me who had him but doesn't anymore. I want to be someone else. I don't even know if that makes sense." She took deep breaths and wiped her face, angry that she was letting herself break down in public. "I don't know how to do this."

"It makes perfect sense," her mom assured her as she took out her phone.

"Who could you possibly be calling in the middle of this conversation?" Courtney asked, her annoyance taking precedence over her tears.

"Just trust me." Her mom waved her hand dismissively. "Yeah, hi, Roxanne, it's Julie Ross… good, how are you? I am hoping you have an opening today for a cut and color for Courtney… It's sort of an existential hair crisis, so it needs to be ASAP… okay, perfect. You're the best, see you soon." Her mom hung up her phone. "You better start looking at pictures for how you want your hair to look. You have an appointment in an hour." Courtney got up from her chair and threw her arms around her mother.

"Yes. Thank you. That is exactly what I need." Courtney's appetite made a resurgence and she ate a horrifying amount of the food they ordered. She took to Google on her phone to save pictures she liked for her hair. Having something else to focus on besides the implosion of her relationship was helping. She didn't know how long it would work, but she was willing to hold on to the distraction while she could. As it turned out, it wasn't long at all because she got a text from Ethan in the middle of her perfect hair search.

> E: I'm trying to give you space. I didn't sleep at all…please tell me if you're ok. Are you never going to speak to me again? I don't understand how this fell apart so quickly, just please text me back.

Courtney's mind couldn't land on a course of action. She felt like she needed to talk to him, but wasn't sure what was left to be said. She told her mom she'd wait for her in the car so that she could think about what to do, knowing that given enough time, he could probably convince her of anything, and she needed to remember why this happened in the first place. *He said it was too hard and he couldn't do it. That hasn't changed.*

> C: I'm not ok, but I'm ok. I don't know what there is to talk about right now. Maybe someday? I can't just start being your "friend," coming from where we were 24 hours ago. You do know how we got here, so please don't pretend like you had nothing to do with it. It's really hard for me to hear from you, so unless something has changed from the way you felt when you called me yesterday, I can't… Just, when I look down at my phone and see your name, my heart gets happy for a second, until I remember that there's nothing for it to be happy about right now. You

can't be the person breaking my heart and worrying if I'm okay at the same time.

As soon as she sent it, she wished she hadn't. She didn't want him to know how much this was affecting her, that she felt like she was drowning. She shouldn't have put in the part about his feelings changing; it was like allowing a ray of hope through the door when she didn't really think there was one. Her whole body wanted him to write back and tell her he'd made a horrible mistake and he would love her forever if she'd only forgive him. But she knew that message wasn't coming. She could feel it. Her phone buzzed and she allowed herself to read the incoming text.

> E: I'm so sorry. I know it isn't worth much, but I am. I'll try to leave you alone, but if you ever want to talk, I'm here. I'll always love you.

That was the worst thing he could have said. She didn't know how to get over the fact that if she just lived in a different place, none of this would be happening. *How is this fair? How can he tell me he loves me, but can't be with me?* She let her tears fall now that she was alone. The flashbacks started: the feeling of Ethan's lips on hers and his hands in her hair. She could picture his smirk that drove her crazy. She could recall every detail of when he told her he loved her, and that night at his house when he asked her to homecoming. How she wished for just one minute she could get out of her own brain and escape the barrage of memories that were flooding her vision. She tried to breathe. *Shake it off, think about something else. Anything else. Cheerleading, school, ponies, anything.* She started to get herself together. Her mom had finished paying the bill and got in the car.

"Everything okay?"

"No. But yes. Ready for a make-over." Her mom put the car in drive and took her to the salon. Courtney didn't show her the pictures ahead of time so she could see her reaction when they were finished. Roxanne had been doing her hair for years, but she usually just left it long, dark, and curly. Not a whole lot of variety. Today would be different. Hesitantly, she showed her stylist the photos she found, and a huge smile spread across her face. She was grateful that Roxanne had pretended not to notice the splotchy condition of her face when she took off her sunglasses. *She's good people,* Courtney thought to herself. Determined, she tried to relax into the chair as her color was being mixed. She told herself that this new version would be able to get over Ethan and move on. This new person would be okay. She had decided not to look at herself through the process, so she could just turn around at the end and be surprised like they did on those TV shows. Closing her eyes, she listened to the snipping of the scissors and the sound of her long locks hitting the floor. It took a while, but her hair was finally dry and ready to be revealed. Courtney sat up straight in the chair and prepared herself. Roxanne turned her around to the mirror, and she immediately knew she had achieved the effect she'd hoped for. Her hair was short for the first time since she was a kid, but there was nothing kid-like about it now.

Her curls were cut into a stacked bob; shorter in the back and longer in the front, and it screamed carefree and sexy. Roxanne also pulled some bright blond streaks through the dark, highlighting the spirals. Courtney couldn't believe she was looking at herself. She didn't even resemble the girl who had sat there two hours before. She looked older. Playing with her hair, she put her fingers through it. This was exactly what she wanted. Her mom came back into the salon a few minutes later and gasped.

"Oh my GOD, Courtney. You look amazing! Like an adult. I can't even believe it!" Courtney smiled her first real smile of the day, almost forgetting the reason for the drastic change to begin with. Roxanne had a little surprise for her at the end, and brought out one of the salon's aestheticians to do a quick once-over on her with some makeup before she left. She walked out feeling almost human. Courtney thanked her mom a million times on the way home. She knew she had a lot more crying to do, but was determined to enjoy that moment.

She felt her gray leather purse vibrate and had a sinking feeling in her stomach. She couldn't endure another text from Ethan right then; it was too much. When she looked, though, it wasn't Ethan but Ben who had sent the message.

> B: Hey, are you ok? You never miss school, so I thought I'd check in. I'll give you a copy of my notes for English and history when you get back. Also, it's not a big deal, but I just thought I'd ask one more time about homecoming since it's next weekend. Hope you're feeling all right.

Courtney had forgotten about Ben's group invitation to homecoming. She knew it was the wrong thing to do even as she typed it, but she was feeling reckless and impulsive after changing her appearance, and she needed an outlet.

> C: Yeah, I'm ok. Just needed a day. Thanks for the notes. I'll get them from you tomorrow. I think yes to homecoming. I know your plans are to go with a group, but if you wanna go just you and me, that would be fun too. Either way, count me in.

This is mean, she told herself. *Your heart belongs to Ethan… this will not end well.* Her brain was making a lot of sense, but she just didn't care. She needed to feel like someone wanted her, and she knew Ben was safe. He wasn't going to hurt her or take advantage of her. She didn't have the capacity to worry about anything else.

> B: Ok? Like as friends, or… I'm sorry, I'm confused.

Courtney's impulsiveness was backfiring. *This is why you usually keep your mouth shut.* Now she had to explain.

> C: Friends… or not. We can talk about it more later if you want :).

Now you're flirting with emojis? Jesus, Courtney. But her rebellious side was glad. She had no reason to feel guilty. Ethan had pushed her here. She knew and liked Ben, she wasn't with Ethan, and she deserved to go to her homecoming. *So screw everything else,* she thought, including the know-it-all voice in her head.

> B: Ok, yeah. I'll grab tickets today, and we can talk tomorrow. I'm glad I asked again.
>
> C: Me too, see you then.

She silenced her conscience and refocused her attention on her mom.
"Feel like making one more stop before we head home?"
"Sure, why?"
"I need to pick up a new homecoming dress. No marathon shopping this time, I swear. One store and I'm done. I will shop the clearance rack only. You can even wait in the car if you want." Courtney had to admit that her heart broke a little more when she realized she'd never be able to wear the black dress again. She loved everything about it, but it would kill her to put it on. Her mom almost started to form a question, but the same realization seemed to dawn on her and she turned the car towards the mall.

♪ *"Long Day"* – *Matchbox Twenty*

Twenty-Nine

Eventually they made their way home, and Courtney ran out of things with which she could distract herself. Her homework was done, she had made the cheer list for the following night's football game, and she was caught up on all of her reading. She did enjoy catching glimpses of her new self in all of the reflective surfaces in her house while she flitted around, trying to stay busy.

She paced past the door to her room several times without going in, knowing that once she did, she was going to be faced with the decision of what to do with all of the "Ethan things" that had become a part of her world. She twirled the ring on her thumb. It was never off of her hand. It had just become a constant accessory, and she wrestled with what to do with it. Impulsively, she swung open the door to her room and marched in, determined to make choices without crying. Her hands started gathering up loose photos without really looking at them, and stuffing them into an empty shoebox. The irony was not lost on her that the box was covered in brightly colored hearts and stars, but she was not capable of appreciating it in that moment. She took down the letter that had been carefully folded on her dresser since the day she had arrived home that summer. She felt the sting of the promises made on that paper and resisted the urge to open it. Into the shoebox it went. Next came the CD he had recorded for her. It was placed gently into its case. The tracks from her phone would have to be deleted as well. And almost every single song she had ever listened to.

Her emotions threatened to sabotage her mission of creating an Ethan-free space. She would have to deal with the music issue later. Or start listening to only gangster rap. She briefly envisioned herself wearing some very ostentatious gold chains, but quickly returned to the task at hand. Going into her closet, she tucked away the black homecoming dress into its garment bag and shoved it to the back. As she surveyed her wardrobe, she realized most of her summer clothes would have to go: the denim skirt from Vanessa's party, the red sundress, and the white beaded maxi. She pushed the flashbacks attempting to surface down deep into her subconscious. Stuffing the clothes into the now overflowing shoebox, she tried to force on the lid. It kept popping off, mocking her. She was determined to prove she could force all of the memory of Ethan into that dumb space. She practically ran down the stairs, passing her dad in the kitchen.

"Where is the duct tape?" she asked as calmly as possible, though she knew she must look like a hot mess.

"Um, in the garage? Are you okay?" her dad asked tentatively, his hand running through his graying hair.

"Great. Thanks." Continuing with her determination, she made it back to her room with the key to victory. The box was subsequently subdued with an unnecessary amount of silver tape. Her anxiety episode started to subside. She stood on a chair and tucked everything away on the top shelf of her closet.

She wasn't ready to take off the ring just yet. It was stupid, but it was the only part of him she'd had to hold on to, and she couldn't force herself to let go of it. *Maybe tomorrow.* With a look around her room, it became clear that it didn't feel better. It just felt empty. Like all of the emotions that had surrounded her for the past several months still lingered, but like ghosts. She wasn't naïve enough to believe that she could trick herself into being okay just by cleaning up her room, but she had hoped it would help more than it did. Without anything to occupy her, her mind automatically jumped to calling Ethan, as she had done with every spare moment for months. She wanted to know about his day, to see if he was okay, and just to hear his voice. *How are you going to do this?* She sat down in the middle of her room and let everything she'd been holding in all day come out in a mess of saltwater and muted sobs. She missed him so much it physically hurt. She reached for her phone, not caring that she shouldn't, ready to text him. Instead, she saw she had a missed call from Vanessa, which was very rare. She pulled herself together enough to talk on the phone and called back.

"Girl, what is going on?" Vanessa started in immediately.

"Well? There could be several answers to that question, but I assume you mean with Ethan and me."

"Um, yeah, I mean with Ethan and you."

"Well, I guess we broke up. No, I know we broke up. Sorry, that one's hard to get out," she admitted, her voice wavering.

"Oh my god, are you okay? Why didn't you call me?"

"I don't know. I needed to come to terms with it by myself. How did you know something was up, anyway? Did he say anything?" She bit her lip, hating herself for already asking about him, but she had to know how he was.

"Not exactly. I don't know, do you want to know? I mean, what happened? Should I be despising him and carrying out your revenge? I'm not sure what the best friend protocol is here."

"You don't have to hate him. I don't. I get it. This was hard, and he didn't want to do it anymore. So okay. I hate that this is how things turned out. I hate that I can't stop crying. And I hate that everything would be fine if I just lived there instead of here. But I have no control over any of those things. So, yes, tell me."

"Well, he showed up to school high this morning, which is like, *completely* out of character for Ethan. I mean, maybe he was a little reckless when he first moved here, but this year, well, since he met you, he's been all about school and doing really well, so I knew something was up when I saw him." Courtney's stomach tightened. She wanted to call him. No, she wanted to see him and tell him that he didn't need to self-destruct.

"Did he get… like, suspended or something?"

"Thank god, no. I made Luke catch up with him in the parking lot before he made it on campus and take him home. He would have ruined everything he's been working for if he'd gotten caught. Stupid."

Courtney breathed a sigh of relief knowing that at least he hadn't gotten into serious trouble. "Well, I'm glad Luke was there. I wish there was something I could do, I just don't think I can handle…"

"Of course not. We will take care of Ethan. Who is going to take care of you? I'm so sorry, Court. I feel like I shouldn't have set you guys up."

"Don't be silly, nothing is your fault. I had the most amazing summer of my entire life because of you." A thought hit her. "Speaking of which, I'd kind of like to return the favor."

"What do you mean?"

"Well, I've been saving money to come out there for New Year's, but there's just no way I can come that soon, and see him, or, I don't know, whatever. But who's to say I can't buy the ticket for you to come here?"

"Are you serious? That would be freaking awesome! I wouldn't even have to wear a parka over my hot New Year's Eve outfit!"

"Nope! A light jacket, perhaps."

"Let me talk to my mom about it, but as far as I'm concerned, I'm there."

"Yay! That would make me so happy," Courtney confessed.

"Girl, you know I love you. Please call me if you need me. I know you're putting on a good show right now, but I also know what he meant to you. So pick up the phone, I don't care what time, and I will talk to you, okay?"

"Okay. I will," Courtney managed to get out. "Just, um, make sure he's okay, too, all right? I can't be there for him, but I need to know he's…"

"Don't give it another thought. I'm on it. I'll let you know what my mom says. Take care of yourself."

"Thanks, I will," Courtney promised as she hung up. She knew her best friend was the only one who would understand what this was doing to her. None of her friends at home had ever met Ethan; they hadn't seen how happy he made her. They only got to see her missing him and being miserable. She sighed. Typically, talking to Vanessa made her feel better about everything. But this only intensified her previous struggle with whether or not to reach out to Ethan, and she began to type out a message.

> C: So, maybe I retract my previous statement about not talking? I know I shouldn't, but I need to hear your voice.

She didn't send it. Her decision-making skills couldn't be trusted, so she elected to leave it and defer the choice to her future self. At that particular moment, all she could definitely decide upon was to eat a pint of Peanut Butter Cup ice cream and watch *Pretty in Pink*.

Just as she pried the lid off of the ice cream container, her doorbell rang. *Are you kidding me?* She ignored it at first, being that she wasn't expecting anyone, but then the knocking began. She padded down the entryway to the door and opened it haughtily, prepared to be a bitch to whomever was keeping her from her wallowing. Her face dropped, however, when she saw Ashley and Molly on the other side of the threshold.

"Shut. Up. Your hair looks amazing. Is that why you were out today?" Ashley commented, reaching up and touching her hair.

"You're never absent, so we figured we'd swing by. Are you…are you ok?" Molly asked, now looking at her swollen eyes instead of her new style.

"Yeah, fine. Thanks."

"Um, so that's a lie. We're coming in," Ashley declared, moving past her towards the kitchen. Courtney sighed, really not in the mood to rehash the last twenty-four hours just yet. "Yeah, just as I suspected… we're at def-con three. Or five. I really don't know the terminology, but this is a serious situation," her friend continued when she spied the ice cream out on the counter. Molly looked almost apologetic, but allowed Ashley to demand answers.

"I just... he and I. We broke up." The words found their way out, though the end of the phrase was barely above a whisper.

"Why? Last time we talked you sounded so sure..." Molly questioned gently. Courtney let the entire story pour out. She hadn't intended on it, but once she started, she couldn't stop. While she wished the telling-of-the-tale could have been done without crying, she ended up a sobbing soggy mess in the middle of her kitchen.

"Umm, excuse me?" Ashley relayed in her ultra-controlled tone. "Are you trying to tell me that after you've been here running around in 'perfect girlfriend' mode for the past two months, he has the nerve to complain that he can't, what, hit on other girls? Like, is that supposed to be a joke?" Her delicately featured face had lit up with incredulous anger.

"I have to agree on this one. He's sounding like a complete selfish ass. Does he have no comprehension that you're going through all of the same shit? Like, how ridiculous for him to want to complain *to you* about how hard his life it. The entire male gender seriously kills me," Molly chimed in.

"I don't know. I don't think he meant it to be selfish. I think he was trying to-"

"Yeah, no, don't try to defend him while you're sitting here crying in the kitchen. He doesn't deserve that. But you deserve someone who's going to treat you better. This is insanity," Ashley spouted off.

"Have you talked to him since last night?"

"He texted a lot today... I sent back one, but, I don't know... it's hard not talking to him. I just-"

"Under no circumstance should you text him. That's just asking for more heartache. My mom always says 'you have to teach people how to treat you,' so don't teach him that this is okay. It's not," Ashley coached.

"I one hundred percent agree. You need to get out. Go out with us, or better yet, with *Ben*. He's, like, in love with you, and he's a *nice* boy. Not some prick who thinks he's god's gift to women because he can strum a few chords," Molly continued, getting more worked up. The mention of Ben reminded her that she was now going to homecoming with him. *Well, that was a rash decision,* she chided herself. *What were you thinking?* But now their advice started to sink in, and she wondered if they were right. Was he still just "The Fisher," and she couldn't see it? *Do leopards change their spots?* She wanted to believe that everything he said to her was true, that she had changed things for him. But maybe that was incredibly naïve. *Maybe you're just that stupid,* she thought, tears threatening to fall again.

"Can we stay and eat ice cream with you? We will tell you about Mr. K totally calling Leah out on her ass-kissing today. It was like the best class ever, you'll love it," Ashley bribed. Courtney found herself nodding, and she watched her friends get out spoons and bowls to fulfill her calorie-laden pity-fest. They did cheer her up momentarily with their stories, and her almost-sent text message was forgotten.

♪ *"I Want You To Want Me"* – Letters to Cleo
"Kiss Me" –Sixpence None the Richer

Thirty

She made it through that night and the following day with only small, intermittent breakdowns. Everyone at school was focused on her new hair, so it was easy to avoid talking about anything too serious. She even managed to talk to Ben about homecoming without crying or making a fool out of herself.

"Wow. So that's what you were doing yesterday. You look...different. Good different. I like it," he told her when she walked in to third period.

"So you're saying it looked bad before?" she teased him halfheartedly.

"No! I mean, I've always thought you looked, um, pretty. This is just... new." She blushed, not used to him complimenting her so openly.

"Well thank you," she conveyed sincerely.

"I, well, I bought homecoming tickets yesterday, so that's done. Do you have anywhere you want to go for dinner? Or..."

"Wherever your friends are going is fine if you want to go with them. I bought a dress yesterday, speaking of." She forced herself to sound excited and not to envision the black sparkly dress in the back of her closet with memories of Ethan woven into it.

"Ok, I'll find out where they're going. What does it look like?" he asked curiously.

"Well, I went a little 80s and bought a hot pink ensemble. But other than that you'll just have to see it next weekend." Despite her broken heart, or perhaps because of it, it felt good to flirt with someone who was right in front of her.

"All right then, well, no complaints from me." He wore his smile well. "Just to be clear, uh, well, this dance, us going together. It's a…ha, god I sound stupid. I mean, I don't want to pry, I just wasn't sure what happened with…"

"It's done," she said simply.

"Okay, I'm sorry, I didn't mean to…"

"Don't worry about it, you have every right to ask." She forced herself to smile back. She was grateful he let it drop with that. She focused on getting out her notebook for class to start, but didn't fail to notice that he was still grinning minutes later. *Maybe this is what I need. Things with Ben would be easy if I let them happen,* she thought to herself, though she knew she wouldn't ever get back what she had with Ethan. Her chest grew tight thinking about the night that she met him and their "almost kiss" in Vanessa's kitchen. She was relatively certain she wouldn't find that spark again, and it made her feel very lonely. She sighed softly and readied herself for the note-taking extravaganza that was about to begin.

The school day ended much like it started, and the game that night kept her occupied. She picked up a double shift the next day in order to avoid being alone with her thoughts. Exhaustion overwhelmed her by the time she got home, but she appreciated the fact that at least sleep would come easily that night.

* * *

The next week was like being on a merry-go-round from hell. She kept herself so busy she thought she might collapse at any moment. Whenever she did stop, she was overcome with missing Ethan and couldn't keep the hurt from taking over. She hadn't heard from him again, and she didn't know if that was better or worse. Her mind wandered down the rabbit hole time and time again, imagining he had already moved on with someone else. Kim was typically the girl present in that particular conjecture. Vanessa did let her know that Ethan seemed to be doing okay, though still not himself. She promised not to mention him unless he died or got someone pregnant. Courtney thought those were fair circumstances, though the idea of him sleeping with someone else made her physically ill. *Maybe you're a horrible person for feeling worse about that possibility than him being dead.* She decided she could live with that character flaw.

That Friday night was the homecoming game, and Courtney had worked herself ragged in preparing. Their halftime performance was going to be incredible if they actually landed all of the stunts she'd put in it. She ran through the routine a million times in her head, but tried to appear confident in front of her teammates. She finally breathed for the first time all week after the show was over, and they nailed every eight-count. Enjoying the adrenaline of performing, she let herself feel happy for a moment. She appreciated the second half much more thoroughly now that she could relax, and she actually agreed to go out to Desert Ridge with her friends afterward.

It felt good to fluff up her short hair, and she was feeling a little surer of her new image upon her arrival in the courtyard that night. She had thrown on a bright blue top and dark jeans, and even wore a pair of silver wedges, which was rare. She liked the way her new blond highlights played with her appearance, and she made a conscious effort to let herself have fun. The wallowing could wait for when she was alone. She found Ashley and Molly quickly; they were all still giddy from the high of their team's victory. Courtney was starving as usual, and decided to grab burgers and fries for her and her friends. She jumped slightly when she felt a hand on her waist while she stood in line.

"I'm sorry, I didn't mean to scare you," Ben apologized.

"Oh, no, you're fine," she breathed. "I'm just still so wired. How are you?" Her smile was genuine.

"Good, good. You looked great out there tonight." His voice was tentative, sounding a bit uncertain if this type of comment was appropriate.

"I'll assume you mean my carefully constructed halftime routine that you were closely watching for synchronization and difficulty, and not how I looked in my uniform." She winked at him flirtatiously. Her conscience was having trouble deciding whether or not she should feel guilty for how she was acting with Ben as of late. Her head was so messed up she didn't know what she felt anymore. She only knew that flirting with him was easy, and it made her heart feel less like it was disintegrating.

"Oh yeah, absolutely. I hardly even noticed the short skirt," he smiled, his confidence growing. He stood up straighter, highlighting his height and causing his Horizon t-shirt to stretch across his chest. She had a sudden urge to poke him and ensure he wasn't wearing some sort of blow-up pecs under there. *God, you are awkward.* She quickly shoved away that thought and tried to be a normal person. They moved up the line together, bantering easily. He helped her carry the overflowing paper bags back to her table.

"Do you wanna sit? Or do you need to get back to your friends?" she asked, gesturing to his usual crowd across the courtyard.

"Sure, I can hang out for a bit," he agreed, clearly pleased. Ashley and Molly entertained them both with stories from school, and they picked Ben's brain about basketball season and how he thought Horizon would fare. *This is nice. I'm fine, being here with them. Maybe I can be okay*, she told herself, all the while turning the ring around her thumb absentmindedly. She looked down when she realized what she was doing and sighed to herself. *Or maybe not just yet.* She frowned. She refocused on the conversation and added in her two cents about the fate of the basketball team. As she spoke, Ben's hand found hers. Her hand was very small in his large one, and she was acutely aware of how different it felt compared to holding Ethan's. Ben's hands were like bear paws, in the way that they were masculine and protective.

Ethan's fingers were long and thin, and had easily intertwined with hers.

Ben hung out with them for a while longer, until Courtney's whirlwind schedule from that week caught up with her. The fatigue hit all at once, and she knew she needed to sleep if she was going to make it through the festivities the following night. Ben offered to walk her to her car.

"Sure, thanks," she replied. She said goodnight to Ashley and Molly and walked toward the exit. She pretended not to see them exchange smug looks in seeing her hand in Ben's.

"Tonight was cool, your friends are funny. I've never really hung out with them before, but I see why you like them."

"Yeah, they are amusing. It was nice just to take a break after this crazy week, so thanks for putting up with our girliness."

"Anytime." They arrived at her car and she slowly turned to face him. She was trying to think of something to say when he moved in towards her and leaned down. He lightly kissed her cheek, and she let him, but she took a slight step back when he moved towards her lips.

"I'm sorry," he said stepping back as well. "I shouldn't have-"

"No, no you're okay, it's just me. Well, I like you," she blurted out, surprising even herself with the admission. "I think maybe I've always liked you, I just don't think I'm in the right place to, I don't know. I'm sorry. Now I've made things awkward," she finished, flustered. *Please let me crawl into a hole now.*

"Don't apologize. You just said you liked me, so I'm good with that," he smiled, shaking his head. "I know you just got out of a thing, and you don't have to explain. Just, if you wanna let me know when you feel like you *are* in the right place? Because I like you, Courtney." She gave him a smile in spite of her conflicting emotions.

"You're a nice guy, do you know that?"

"That phrase is like the kiss of death, don't say that!" He laughed.

"No! It's a good thing!" she assured him. "I will. Let you know, I mean. Okay?"

"Okay."

"And I will see you tomorrow."

"Yes, you will, bye Court." He walked back up towards the mall, a new assurance in his gait. Courtney took a deep breath and got into her car. *Okay, that wasn't so bad despite the awkwardness. You can do this, and be a normal high school girl with a nice boy who likes you and lives in the same zip code, it's possible.* She tried to convince herself. As soon as he was out of sight and her car doors were locked, she burst into tears. No amount of coaching or manta chanting or meditating was helping her forget the feeling of Ethan's hands on her and the way it made her come alive. She let the sobs run their course until they became hiccups, and she decided that, after the dance the following night, if she still felt the same, she would call him. No matter the outcome, she had to know if she could ever get that feeling back. Exhausted, she drove home, and her tired body could hardly wait to be in bed.

♪ *"Save Me"* –Hanson

Thirty-One

Courtney hastily put on the first pajamas she saw when she got in her room and threw back the covers. Just as she was getting comfy, she heard the buzz on her nightstand. *Ugh. I want sleep.* She picked it up and saw Ethan's picture. Immediately, she sat up in bed as her heart started thumping in her chest. She answered it and tried to sound calm.

"Ethan?"

"Heyyyy babe," he answered. He was drunk. Her mind raced.

"Listen, if you need a ride or something, I can call-"

"Shhhhhhh, no. I don't need a ride. I need *you*. I'm so stupid Courtnee. You're my bear claw, you know? Just shhh. Just *listen* to me."

"Ethan, please don't do this. I can't handle-" He was saying all of the things she desperately wanted him to say. *Why does he have to be wasted?* This was not how things should have been.

"*Courtney!*" he practically shouted, interrupting her. "You are not understanding what I am *saying*. I hooked up with someone else tonight." His voice broke. "It didn't mean anything, I don't want... I just need you, please." She had stopped listening after his confession. All of the air was sucked out of her lungs and her brain couldn't get enough oxygen. After the initial shock wore off, anger surged in its place.

"Why on earth would you call and TELL ME THAT?!" she yelled. She had never yelled at him before. Ever. Not even during their breakup. She had understood his reasoning then, in spite of her hurt. "I was doing okay, I was freaking *coping* without you. What did you want to happen? You call and tell me you slept with someone else and then we get back together? How is that even a-"

"No! I didn't sleep with anyone! I didn't say that, god, this is all turning out so wrong, if you would just *listen*, and if the world would stop spinning, Jesus."

"Whatever, like it even matters now!" she said, crying openly. "We broke up on decent terms, Ethan. I still loved you. In the back of my mind I was holding out hope that maybe, things could be different. I don't know what I thought, but how can I even contemplate that now? You could have hooked up with whomever you wanted, but to call me and, I don't know, gloat about it? Rub my face in the fact that you're out there being "The Fisher" again? Charming other girls and not me? How do I get over that? How do I get past you doing something just for the purpose of hurting me?" she asked, quieter now. She thought her heart couldn't feel anymore pain, but she had been so wrong. She wanted to throw up. Impossibly, she tried to cry as silently as possible, wishing she had more control. This was so different from just worrying that he had moved on. This was a strategic attack of images she couldn't stop.

"That wasn't what I was doing! I just, I realized I don't want this. Us apart, my worthless senior year. It's meaningless without you. I don't want to 'Fish' for anyone, I hate that stupid nickname. Let's just be together. Please. Come for New Year's, let's go back to how things were." She could tell he was working at trying not to slur his words. He was not even remotely successful.

"I didn't have to hook up with anyone else to know that I loved you and I wanted to be with you. Why is it you needed to make me feel like *this* to figure out what you wanted? I don't even think you know what you want. All I wished for, since the moment you said you couldn't do this, was for you to realize I was worth the distance, but you didn't," she said through tears. "You were sad, and now you feel guilty because you did something you regret, whatever it was, and you want me to make you feel better. But I can't. You just slammed the door on whatever still existed between us."

"Courtney, don't say that! I love you, you know I love you." He was crying too.

"I loved you too." She lied in using the past tense. She hoped that hurt him even a fractional amount of how much he'd hurt her. She hung up the phone and threw it on the floor. She pulled a pillow over her head and let out a sob. All she could do was picture him smiling at some other girl; it was Kim in her imagination, with that smirk that she loved. She couldn't stop the slideshow in her brain at that point: his hands around the other girl's waist, his lips on her neck, his whispers in her ear. Her breath escaped her lungs. She had to do something other than lie there, none of her usual techniques were helping her to calm down. She went into the bathroom and turned the shower on as hot as she could stand it. Her pajamas were left on the floor, and she sat in the tub and let the water roll down her back. She would take any sensation to lessen the sting from what had just happened. She hadn't thought he could hurt something that was already broken, but her heart said otherwise.

The shower ran for a long time, long enough that she had to get out when the water turned cold. She shivered and wrapped a towel around herself, stumbling to her room in a combination of grief and exhaustion. Broken, she went to bed with her hair soaking wet and her pillow tear-stained. *How could he do this to me?* she thought, over and over and over.

* * *

Courtney began her day once again with puffy eyes. She wanted to believe the events of the previous night were all in her head, but reality hit her moments after waking up. Her mirror mocked her as she glanced at her reflection after dragging her butt out of bed. *You are going to stop letting him do this to you. No more crying, no more broken heart. This is done.* She came close to believing the voice in her head. Rage was a powerful emotion, almost strong enough to fight off the gut-wrenching heartbreak that was weighing her down. For the first time, she took Ethan's ring off of her thumb. Her hand tossed it up to the top shelf in her closet, near the general area of the shoebox full of his memory. She wished she had the strength to chuck it in the canal, but she didn't. She took an inventory of the situation. *So this is what comes of eating doughnuts with a boy who plays guitar.* She had always known there was the chance that the heat between them would erupt in flames. That much had been clear the first time he'd touched her. *I guess I was right, then.*

♪ *"Heartbeat Song" – Kelly Clarkson*
"Fight Song" –Rachel Platten

Thirty-Two

As she came back into her room, she realized she had work to do if she was going to be a regular human that night for the dance. It was already late morning. She decided to occupy her time by fixing her curls and playing with hair accessories. She tried several she wasn't fond of, but decided on a simple rhinestone bobby pin to hold back some of her shorter strands. The new dress she bought was hot pink, as she'd told Ben. It was actually two pieces; the top was satin with off-the-shoulder sleeves, and it showed a bit of her midriff. The bottom skirt was made up of layers of fluffy pink tulle, and it made her feel slightly like a ballerina. She decided on rhinestone-embellished flats this time around, regardless of Ben's stature. Her feet couldn't take running around in heels all night, and she knew he wouldn't care either way. Courtney laid out everything on her bed for that evening.

Her phone vibrated a while later, and she was afraid to look. She saw she had missed a couple of messages, but the most recent one confirmed her fear.

> E: Courtney, I'm so so sorry about… everything. I have no worthwhile excuses. I wanted to say this to you over the phone, but I imagined you wouldn't pick up, and I don't blame you. I am going to lie low for a while, because I don't ever want to hurt you again. I'm sorry.

She allowed herself ten minutes to exist in the range of emotions that sprang up. She didn't want to forgive him, but she didn't want him to disappear forever either, no matter how hard she tried to convince herself she did. There was no good solution. That seemed to be a common theme throughout their relationship, so she didn't know why it should be surprising now. She again questioned her decision not to fight harder for him. A long twenty minutes later, she shook off thoughts of Ethan. She was going to have fun at her homecoming if it killed her. She looked at the other messages she'd missed.

> A: Hey! If you want me to do your makeup for tonight, come over.

Courtney quickly wrote her back.

> C: On my way in 15.

Ashley was a true artist with makeup. If anyone could do something with her perpetually swollen eyes, it would be her. The other message was from Ben.

> B: Hey Court, just wanted to let you know I'll pick you up at 6 if that's ok. We're gonna meet everyone else at North. I'll see you then :).
> C: Sounds perfect. See you at 6!

Courtney rushed around to get to Ashley's with enough time to get back and dressed before Ben got there. She told her parents where she was going and ran out the door. She thought she'd get her mind off of things being at Ashley's house, but ended up venting about Ethan entire time. *Apparently I needed to get that out.*

"This guy is seriously on my shit list, not even joking," Ashley told her. "Like I want the imprint of his face on the hood of my Volvo." Courtney laughed softly, appreciating the solidarity. Ashley fixed her up, and even she couldn't deny that her face looked glamorous when she left for home.

Ben rang the bell right on time, and Courtney took one last glance in her mirror. She thought she appeared pretty fierce when it came down to it, rocking the pink tulle. She floated down the stairs and smiled when she saw him in a charcoal suit with a hot pink tie. *How sweet is he?*

The look on his face made her blush. He couldn't take his eyes off of her.

"I like the pink, it suits you," she told him, playfully tugging on his tie.

"Somehow I think no one will be looking at this when I'm standing next to you," he remarked, twirling her around to get the full effect of her dress. Her mom took photos of them posed inside and out in her backyard, but there was not the hullaballoo of the first homecoming. She was glad for it. They walked out to Ben's car, a black Jeep Cherokee, and she grabbed his pinky with hers. She was done feeling any remorse about whatever was going on between them. Clearly things were over with Ethan, and she wanted to be happy. Her heart longed for something easy; it was tired of everything being a struggle. She wanted a connection that would make her feel safe, not consumed. Something that wouldn't crush her if it ended.

Ben opened the door for her and helped all of the tulle from her skirt make it into the car.

"You look incredible. I didn't want to say that in front of your mom, but I mean it," he confessed, his warm brown eyes meeting hers.

"Thank you, you look very dapper as well," she assured him, and she meant it. She'd never felt the kind of chemistry she had with Ethan towards Ben, but she'd always liked him. Even when they were in sixth grade and he'd had a dorky bowl cut and mismatched clothes, he was still cute. They talked mostly about school, and a little about their families before they arrived at North. It was a very nice Italian restaurant located in yet another outdoor mall. There were a few people already there, so they went to join them. She knew most everyone else casually, and one of the girls was on her cheer squad. Making a point to stay focused and join in the conversation as the evening began, she relaxed with Ben holding her hand under the table. Happily, she found herself actually enjoying the company at dinner and excited to go to the dance.

She practically skipped from the school parking lot into the courtyard, her pink skirt bouncing with her. Ben just smiled and humored her. It was still nice enough at night to hold the festivities outside under the stars. That was actually the theme. *Super original,* she thought. They had their picture taken and made their way to the dance floor. Courtney couldn't imagine Ben busting out any break dance moves, but he was a good sport and danced to as many songs as she wanted. He was a master of the "white-guy-head-bob," but his effort to make her happy was appreciated. She wasn't sure when she made the decision, but somewhere between "YMCA" and the "Cupid Shuffle," she knew she had to bite the bullet and figure out where her head was. There was no sense in leading Ben on if nothing existed between them.

During one of the slow songs, she pressed herself as close to him as she could. He responded by tightening his arms around her waist and bending over slightly due to her vertically challenged-ness. She looked up at him and knew this was the moment to find out. She pulled gently on his tie to bring him down to her. She stood on her toes to meet his lips with hers, and was surprised by how it felt. It wasn't the electricity she'd felt with Ethan, but there was something there, drawing her in. His lips were soft and the kiss was inviting. He let her navigate and followed her lead, but he never pulled back. He didn't question her motives; he seemed to trust her to do what she wanted, and that was an encouraging feeling. She finally leaned back.

"Well, that works." Ben laughed. He had a nice laugh. It was warm and sincere.

"Yeah, it does. Can we do it again?" he asked, his smile reaching all the way to his eyes. She grinned and brought him back to her. Ashley caught her eye moments later and gave her a very indiscreet thumb up, but she was okay with it. They danced and kissed for the rest of the evening, and she didn't hesitate to agree to go to the after-party at a nearby resort.

* * *

Someone had gotten a suite, and Courtney imagined his father's Amex was to thank. She and Ben mingled for a while, but she ended up on his lap in an oversized white chair, his hands resting on her bare stomach. It was odd trying to get used to having someone else touch her that way, sort of surreal.

"Did I tell you already that I like this dress?" he asked, tickling her sides lightly.

"Maybe once or twice, but I'm not complaining." With her head resting on his shoulder, she marveled at how small she felt with his arms around her. She willed herself to stay awake, but it was getting late. Ben suggested he drive her home. She agreed, cringing at the stab to her heart, thinking about the last time she broke curfew. She tried to wipe away that memory for the time being and held Ben's hand tightly on the way back to the car.

"I think a bunch of people are going to do breakfast at IHOP in the morning, would you wanna go?" he asked her, opening the car door for her.

"Will there be pancakes?"

"I imagine there will, given the name of the restaurant."

"Will you be there?" she asked, feeling confident.

"I will."

"Then yes, I would wanna go." He leaned down and kissed her lightly before closing her door. *You can do this, see?* she told herself. The ease with which the night had played out amazed her. She was quite cognizant of the absence of the intensity she had with Ethan, but maybe that was for the best. *Look where it got you. Maybe this is how relationships are supposed to be. Simple.* Ben drove her home, and while she missed singing along to whatever song came on the radio, she enjoyed his energy. Being a gentleman, he walked her to her door a full ten minutes early. He ruffled his short auburn hair.

"I, uh, I had a really good time tonight," he confessed, uncertain of himself.

"I did too." She swished her skirt playfully. "I'm glad you asked me."

"Honestly? I never thought you'd say yes. But I'm glad I did too."

"And why is that?"

"I don't know, I felt like you always ignored the compliments I gave you, and we always just talked about school. But this year, I guess you seemed different, so I thought maybe I had a shot. But then Ashley said that you had a boyfriend, so…"

Courtney wanted to get off of the "boyfriend" topic as soon as humanly possible, so she stepped forward and put her arms around his neck, standing on her tiptoes. "Well, we're here now, and you've got a shot." He surprised her by picking her up slightly and kissing her plainly on the mouth. She giggled, kicking her feet behind her, kissing him a second time.

"I'll see you in the morning, ok? I think they said around ten."

"I'll see you then." She let herself into her house as he turned to leave. "Drive safe. Thank you for everything tonight." She closed the door and let out a sigh. Her own emotions were a mystery at that point. She went to see if her mom was still awake. She was, sitting in a plush off-white chair in the family room reading, and her dad already in bed.

"Well? How was it?" she asked, yawning.

"It was… good. I had fun, and Ben is nice guy."

"Good, fun, and nice. This, from my daughter, the wordsmith?" her mom asked. Courtney laughed. She guessed that was pretty generic.

"I don't know; it was better than I expected. I think that's all I can put together right now." It gave her something to hold onto. Something that glimmered like hope about moving past this hollow phase she was in. It also spurred her decision on another issue. "But while we're chatting, I think I've made my college decision. Well, Ethan made it pretty easy for me, I guess. I'm going to stay here and go to U of A." Courtney waited for her mom to cheer or cry or give some sort of elated response. Instead, she closed her book and took a deep breath. *What could she possibly be upset about if I'm staying here?*

"I thought you might come to that conclusion. But I can't be happy about it until I know you're doing it for the right reasons. Choosing *not* to go to the *right* school because of Ethan is just as bad as *choosing* to go to the *wrong* school because of him. Does that make sense? You have to make the decision for you, and leave him out of it. I saw your face when you were on the UD campus, and I was there for the U of A tour too. Your reactions were very different, Court. If UD is the right place for you, don't throw it away because of one boy."

"I thought you would be happy for me to stay here," Courtney said, still processing her mom's words.

"I will be ecstatic if that's the decision you make, but make it based on you, not Ethan, not Vanessa, and not Ashley or Molly or Ben. You've worked your butt off your whole life in school, so go where you want to go. If that's UD, then I can visit. Don't worry about me." Courtney was surprised. She hadn't expected this speech; she had expected tears and a hug.

"Okay," she replied slowly. "I will keep thinking about it."

"Good. But I'm glad you had a good, fun, nice time with Ben. I always liked him, you know." She smiled. "I'm going to bed though, I'm getting too old to stay up this late." And she dragged herself up the stairs.

Courtney grabbed a glass of water and did the same. Her head was full of big decisions and a sudden feeling of having no idea what to do. She decided sleep would help and quickly found comfort in her blankets.

♪ *"In This Diary" – The Ataris*

Thirty-Three

Courtney slept without dreaming of Ethan for the first time since they had broken up. Instead, pancakes were calling her name when she awoke, and that prompted her to get ready quickly. She twisted sections of her curls back into bobby pins, trying something new. She threw on a tight fitting white t-shirt and low rise jeans, unsure of what one should wear to a post-homecoming IHOP breakfast.

Ben picked her up just before ten. She hopped down the stairs and out the door to meet him. He bent down and gave her a serious hello kiss, and she must have looked surprised.

"I just had to make sure last night was real, and that I didn't dream the part where I could kiss you," he explained, smiling so that his dimples showed. She kissed him again, returning the sentiment, and they went to meet up with their friends. Surprisingly, she felt okay. Not about everything, but about the exact present moment of going to eat pancakes with a guy who looked at her like he'd won the lottery. She just couldn't keep comparing. If she did, any shot she had with anyone else would be dead in the water before it began. Desperately, she attempted to put some of her feelings for Ethan up in a duct-taped box in her brain. *Just… for now. I need to be able to think clearly without him in my head all the time.*

If Ben was shocked by her ability to consume a ridiculous amount of food, he didn't show it. Courtney liked that about him.

Without really planning it, their new whatever-it-was became public knowledge that morning when she pecked his cheek for letting her steal bacon off of his plate. She really hadn't contemplated that they were at breakfast with half the basketball team and cheer squad. His friends let out a slow clap, making her blush, but she couldn't help but laugh too.

***

Her relationship with Ben evolved freely. She didn't really have to think about it; it just happened. They eventually talked more about Ethan, and things went slowly in the beginning at Courtney's request. He didn't fault her for crying when she relayed the whole drawn-out story, even though shedding tears over one boy to another made her feel embarrassed. Ben never pushed her, but he also never questioned her judgment when she decided she *was* ready to move forward. They both had crazy schedules with work and sports, but they made time for each other. It was what she always pictured a high school romance to look like. He even charmed Vanessa when she came to visit for New Year's two months later.

"Oh he's *adorable*, Court," she gushed. "Like, I want to just put the two of you in my pocket, you're so cute together."

"Oh my god, stop it."

"No, I'm totally serious. And you seem really happy," she told her sincerely. "I'm glad."

"Me too," Courtney agreed. She and Vanessa had five days of Scottsdale fun before the trip was over, and Courtney couldn't have imagined a better use of her money. She'd needed to be with her best friend.

"So, what's the verdict?" Vanessa asked before she left. "UD or U of A? Don't you have to send your stuff in, like, next week?"

"That I do." Courtney sighed. "But I just don't know. I guess I'll figure it out before then." They said a happy goodbye this time rather than a tearful one. She knew their friendship could survive whatever the distance between them, and Courtney was just glad she got to see her and share her Phoenix universe. There was, of course, the constant twinge of "what if" the whole time Vanessa was there, but Courtney had gotten really good at burying it.

* * *

The last day of winter break, Courtney sat down with a mission. She had to pick a school and mail out her money and dorm request within forty-eight hours. Ben had gotten a partial scholarship to UC Irvine, so regardless of her feelings for him; he wasn't a factor in this particular decision. They had an agreement to just enjoy their time together and figure the rest out later. She sat at her computer for hours, making pro-con lists, re-taking the virtual tours, reading past issues of each school's newspapers, and researching everything from dining choices to crime rates. By the end, her brain was fried and she had no clear winner. She lay on her bed and thought back to her visit on each campus.

She remembered liking the U of A. The campus was pretty, it was far enough away from home to be an adventure, but close enough to drive home quickly if she wanted. Molly would be going there, as well as several other people she knew from school. It seemed the easiest choice. When she thought about her trip to UD with Vanessa and her mom the previous summer, it was completely different. She remembered feeling at home, like she could see herself being a part of something there. She wished she could be sure that those feelings weren't influenced by the ones she'd had for Ethan at the time. Moving away by herself was a terrifying yet exhilarating thought. She pushed the decision off for one more day, giving herself time to sit with both possibilities.

When the following morning arrived, Courtney sat down with her parents and delivered her decision. They were both supportive of her, and even though it was the biggest choice she'd had to make in her eighteen years of life, she was slowly starting to trust that it was the right one. Once plans were in motion, she wished time would slow down. It became very important for her to soak up every moment of her last semester of high school and her time with Ben and her friends.

She finally felt comfortable in her own skin, and she wasn't ready for it all to end.

🎵 *"When You Were Young"* – The Killers
"Drops of Jupiter" –Train

Thirty-Four

It took Courtney a minute to realize where she was. Light was streaming into the room through an unfamiliar window, and she was surrounded by boxes. Her lungs breathed in the moist morning air, and she remembered happily that she was in her room at her new house. The wood floors creaked as she slinked down the stairs in search of coffee. She found Vanessa already in the kitchen, looking as tired as she felt, her blond hair hanging limp in her face. She had not anticipated moving being this exhausting.

"Share," Courtney demanded, pointing to the coffee pot. She soon started to feel more awake, and her disposition improved. The kitchen was little, but bright and airy. She couldn't wait to see what Vanessa was able to do with the house. Unbeknownst to anyone but Luke, her friend had submitted a portfolio to a local design college earlier that year. She claimed she didn't want to be embarrassed when she didn't get in, but that had never come to pass. Courtney was so proud of Vanessa for finding something she loved, and it didn't hurt that her school was less than ten miles from UD, which meant they could live together.

Courtney had been prepared to live in the dorms, but her mom had other plans. Her parents surprised her at graduation with photos of a house just off campus. Her mom claimed she needed a place to stay when she came to visit, and she wasn't sleeping on a futon in a dorm room. Her dad simply stated it was a sound investment property. Courtney had been in shock. She couldn't believe she was getting her little Victorian house and was going to live with Vanessa. It was like everything she had pictured the year before was coming to fruition. She had elected to move out a month before school started, so she could look for a job and work on projects around the house.

Her phone buzzed. She saw that Ben had arrived at Irvine and was headed to a basketball clinic. She missed him painfully. They had parted as friends that summer, and agreed to stay in touch, but she knew all too well that was going to get harder the longer they were apart. He had been the model boyfriend, and she wasn't sure she would ever find someone else who treated her as well.

"What time is your orientation?" Vanessa asked, breaking into her thoughts.

"Ummmm, in like an hour."

"Do you want to shop for house stuff afterward? I have a couple of ideas for in here, and I wanna see what we can find."

"That sounds awesome. Then maybe we actually unpack the rest of these boxes. I don't think they're adding to the décor." She gestured around them.

"Minor details." Vanessa smirked, her blond hair falling in her face. Courtney made her way back to her room to unearth a suitable outfit for her first official day as a student. She knew she had to get her ID photo taken and wanted to look collegiate- if there was such a thing. Her hair had grown out some, but she elected to keep it shorter and liked the blond. She put on a dark pair of boyfriend style jeans and an airy yellow tank top that floated around her. A pair of gold flats completed her look, and she put in the diamond studs Ben had given her at graduation. She tried not to let her missing him interfere with her excitement about orientation.

"Bye, V, I'm walking to campus!"

"Have fun!"

Courtney slipped out the front door and admired her new little porch on her way to school. She had tried to memorize the map of where to go, so she didn't look like a freshman, but could feel it folded up in her pocket just in case. She breathed in deep, the certainty about her decision returning. She walked along the cobblestone pathways and through one of the main courtyards. She couldn't wait to get her schedule and her books. She knew this made her a nerd, but she couldn't have cared less. Upon reaching the correct building, she grabbed an iced coffee before heading inside to find a seat. The first part of the day was to be in a large lecture hall. Not many people had arrived yet, but she was glad. She wanted a moment to look around and appreciate her surroundings. She sat down and sipped the drink- it was much better than what Vanessa had made. *Maybe we need to invest in some sort of cappuccino machine.* She was vaguely aware that someone took the seat right behind her. *Really? The whole auditorium of empty chairs and you are going to invade my personal space?* she thought, irritated.

"Let me guess, an iced mocha with a double shot and sprinkles on top?" a voice commented behind her. A familiar tightening in her chest crept up. She took a breath before turning around, already knowing what she'd find.

"Good memory," she replied, cocking her head to the side, taking in the sight of her first love. He looked impossibly appealing. His hair was longer, but mostly hidden under a loose gray beanie. He had on a striped charcoal sweater over a white T-shirt and dark jeans. It was like he had just stepped out of a catalog. *Dammit.*

"Only for the important stuff," he commented. "Do you mind?" He pointed to the seat next to hers to see if he could move down. She had fantasized about running into him on more occasions than she'd like to admit. Each imaginary encounter had ended differently, however. She wasn't sure how the real deal would play out. She shrugged her shoulders, but shifted her bag to make room. He stepped gracefully over the seats. "So, it appears you picked UD?" he asked obviously.

"It would appear that way, yes." She knew she was being cold, but she couldn't stop herself. Her brain wasn't prepared for this; she just wanted her school schedule.

He sighed quite audibly. "Okay, if I'm being honest, I knew you decided to come here, but I swear it wasn't until after I had sent in my deposits. Luke let it slip when I told him about my acceptance. If you want me to sit somewhere else, I can. I, uh, well? I wasn't even sure if it was you when I walked in, your hair looks good, I like it. I just... I'm happy to see you, I guess," he confessed, his tone turning serious. She shook her head slightly- seeing him act that uncertain, almost vulnerable, was surreal to her. He took all of the fun out of her being aloof when he called her out on it.

"No, it's fine, stay. How are you? I assume those SAT scores did the trick, since you're here? Your mom must be happy." She wracked her brain for more small talk topics as he answered. She wasn't even sure what he'd said.

"Are you living on campus?"

"No, uh, my parents actually bought a house just down the street for V and me to rent from them, essentially," she told him, wishing she wasn't volunteering so much information. "You?"

"I'm living at home, just trying to save up some money. Plus I couldn't really envision myself sharing a room with another guy all year. That's cool, though, that you guys have a house. V got into design school, right? We haven't spoken much, since... but I did hear that. You'll have to tell her congrats for me."

"Yeah, she did. I will, she's super excited." Ethan looked at her and reached his hand towards her face. It was such a natural movement she didn't think to pull back, and he ran his thumb along her cheekbone, sending shivers down her spine.

"Sorry, you had an eyelash," he apologized, his face showing the realization that he'd probably just crossed a line. Courtney's heart had sped up the moment he had touched her, electricity pulsing through her just as it had one year before. *No, no, no, no, no, don't do this to yourself*, her brain argued. She looked him in the eyes, holding onto the silence a little longer. She cleared her throat, forcing herself to breathe and slow her heart rate.

"So, what else have you been-"

"Listen, Courtney," he interrupted, "there are so many things I should say to you, and I get that this isn't the time or the place, but just know that I want the opportunity to say them. I don't deserve it, and quite honestly the fact that you're sitting here and talking to me right now is more than I expected, but if there is any chance you would listen to any of it, I would like to try to do that."

"Ethan, you really don't have to explain yourself to me, that's all in the past," she lied, looking down.

"What if it included tickets to the Train concert this weekend?" he asked sheepishly, knowing he was bribing her. She stopped and looked at him suspiciously.

"You're telling me that you just happen to have an extra ticket to Train this weekend?"

"Well, no, not just happen to. My new band won this 'battle of the bands' series a few weeks back, and we're sort of opening for them. So I have tickets and all-access passes. They're yours if you like, you can take Vanessa too, whatever you want."

Courtney knew she should say no and demand an explanation from Vanessa when she got home as to why she was not informed that Ethan was going to UD. She exhaled through clenched teeth. He gave her his most innocent smile. "You get how absolutely unfair this is right? I mean, if we're being honest, you're dangling a proverbial carrot in front of me and you know I can't *not* chase it. You are fully aware I've wanted to see Train live for forever."

"I may have remembered something like that, yes." He still had a hopeful look on his face.

"Fine, I'll go," she said evenly, shaking her head again as her heart fluttered against her chest. *Stupid, stupid girl.* Ethan gave a hint of the smirk she remembered. He knew exactly what he did when he looked at her that way. The carefully constructed wall she had built concerning her feelings for him started to crumble.

"If you wanna go early and meet the band during sound check I can pick you up, or-"

"Don't push it. Vanessa and I will see you there."

He put his hands up in defeat and smiled. "You got it, that's perfect."

How can one person look that beautiful, it's not fair to the rest of the mortals, she found herself thinking. More people started filling up the hall, and Ethan reached down to pull out the desk top from the side of the chair. His fingers brushed against hers, and her whole body responded. The presentation started shortly thereafter, and she used every bit of will power she had to pay attention and take notes, even though she could feel his eyes on her periodically, and see him smiling out of the corner of her eye. No matter how hard she was trying to deny it, she felt alive being that close to him.

She was grateful when the group session was over and it was time to meet with her advisor. He walked out of the auditorium with her.

"It was good to see you, Court. Like, really good."

"It was good to see you too," she managed. She wasn't sure "good" was the right word, but that's what came out. She reluctantly gave him her new address so he could drop off the tickets before the concert, all the while knowing it was a bad idea for him to be in close proximity to her without proper supervision. Before she left for her meeting, he grabbed her hand, giving her a familiar tingle.

"I promise you won't regret coming to the show or hearing me out. Thank you for not throwing your coffee in my face or something this morning. I'm not the same guy I was last year. Can you at least believe that?"

"That would be an extremely poor use of coffee," she retorted. "And I hope you're right," she added seriously. "Congratulations, by the way. I didn't say that before, but yeah, on winning the battle of the bands. Opening for Train has to be huge for you guys. So, good for you."

"Thanks. That means a lot coming from you." She found herself giving him a small smile before walking away.

She moved through the rest of her morning in a daze, unable to slow down her thoughts. Her sanity came into question several times between the bookstore and the bursar's office. *Maybe I won't go. I don't have to go just because he drops off the tickets,* she reasoned, knowing she was full of crap.

She burst through her new front door and started spitting out what had happened before her brain caught up. Vanessa ran out of her room to see what the hell was wrong with her. Courtney finally managed to get out the whole story. "Why did you not tell me he was going here!? I could have been more prepared!"

"Honestly? I wasn't a hundred percent certain it was true, we sort of grew apart after the whole break-up slash phone-call incident, and I thought it'd only make you anxious, and you'd be fretting about campus, wondering when you'd run into him. Now at least it's over. Are you okay?"

"Yes. No." Courtney sighed. "Let's just go shopping. I need to think about something else, like curtains."

"Okay," Vanessa agreed slowly. They went on a marathon-shopping trip, and as always, Courtney was impressed with Vanessa's ability to put things together. They purchased all manner of decoration, from flowing white cotton curtains for the common rooms, to a wide variety of glass containers for the kitchen, with brightly painted landscapes and old wrought iron keys for the walls. Courtney was excited to see how it all came together. This was what she had looked forward to for so long.

When they got back home, Courtney saw a white paper bag sitting on the front porch. She picked it up before unlocking the door, but had recognized it from afar. There was a larger envelope stapled to the front which contained their tickets, passes, and a recorded CD of what she assumed was Ethan's new band with a note that said, "Just in case you want to listen ahead of time. See you this weekend. –E." Vanessa read over her shoulder. "I've said it before, but the boy's got moves," she said, an impressed tone ringing in her voice.

Inside the bag were sprinkle and bear claw doughnuts. Courtney smiled in spite of herself. Her mind wandered to a duct-taped shoebox located somewhere in the mess that was her new room in additional to the metaphorical one in her mind, and her heart gave an involuntary flutter. She took out a sprinkled pastry before heading inside to unpack the pieces of her old life into the new one.

Thank you so much for reading! I would love for you to leave a review and share your thoughts!

Also By Nicole Campbell

Curious what happens between Ethan and Courtney? Check out:

What Comes of Breaking Promises and Guitar Strings

How One Attempts

to Chase Gravity

Visit NicoleCampbellBooks.com for updates!

Excerpt from *How One Attempts to Chase Gravity*:

♪ *"Magic's In The Makeup" – No Doubt*

What Comes of Breaking Promises and Guitar Strings
Prologue

The feeling rolling around in Courtney's stomach as she read the letter for the third time could not decide if it was angry, nostalgic, or really, really sad.

> Court,
>
> I know how you feel about handwritten letters, so I hope this one is legible. Anyway, I wanted you to get something other than bills or junk in your mailbox when you first moved in. I wanted to cheer you up from the last time we talked. Thinking about you being as sad as I am makes me feel even sadder. Sorry I didn't try to use a synonym, sad was all I could think of.
>
> I know we both said we would try not to make this harder on each other, so that's all I will say. I hope you have all of your pens organized and that you and Vanessa are having fun. Tell her I said hi.
>
> Know you can call, Court.
>
> Miss you,

Ben

Well... there's that. Not making things harder at all. A vision of Ben's easy smile floated into her mind, and the guilt sank like a rock from her chest to her stomach when the actual scene set before her was a newly organized desk with Train tickets for that weekend sitting prominently on top. She slid the letter and the tickets into a drawer in order to make the solid adult decision to, well, ignore it, for the time being.

♪ *"Magic's In The Makeup" – No Doubt*

What Comes of Breaking Promises and Guitar Strings
One

After the literal fourteenth outfit she put on, she was near tears and giving up ever walking out the door. Vanessa stormed in moments later after pretend knocking.

"What *happened* in here?" V asked in disbelief at the state of the room.

"This is the product of the universe knowing it is a terrible idea for me to go to this concert." She took a deep breath, fully understanding that she was being ridiculous.

"To go to the concert or to go backstage and hook up with Fisher in some rock star's dressing room?"

"Does that even exist? Like dressing rooms backstage? That seems fictional… But completely beside the point- I'm not hooking up with him, I've informed you of my stance on this."

"Yeah, you sound all sure of yourself in our kitchen. When he's not there."

"Whatever," she retorted, refusing to admit her friend's point. She went back to the closet for yet another try, and picked out a cream-colored lace sundress with a sweetheart neckline. While it was fancier than she'd typically wear to a concert, it made her feel a little bit like a fairy, so it was deemed a winner. She and Vanessa were in the car fifteen minutes later.

"This dress is too much isn't it?"

"Oh.My.God. If you say one more thing about the dress I am going to freaking lose it. You look fierce. Maybe if you'd just admit that you are having some sort of mental breakdown about seeing Fisher, all of your craziness would die down just a little. So try that."

Courtney exhaled. "Ok. I am having an absolutely freaking meltdown about seeing him." She didn't think it was helping. She felt even crazier than before, like she was introducing herself at an AA meeting.

"Because..."

"Because I don't know what will happen. I like knowing what's going to happen."

"That's boring. Can you just embrace it? I love not knowing what's going to happen. Reason three on the list of why I broke up with Luke. Too predictable."

"You think *Luke* is predictable?"

"No, just our relationship was predictable. I want something exciting. And so should you. You're not attached anymore, Ben is in California for Christ's sake. Ethan is... well, you know I hate to admit it, but he's beautiful. So just chill. Hook up, don't hook up, do whatever you gotta do, but for the love of all that is holy will you just.Calm.Down?"

"I'll try," Courtney mumbled, knowing that was a near impossibility. The parking situation only increased her stress. Living and driving in a city she hadn't resided in for six years was nerve wracking. They finally made it to their seats and the energy from the crowd helped to improve her mood. *You're going to freaking see Train,* she reminded herself, and she was going to be able to do it backstage if she wanted. They were there early, and her mind couldn't help but wander to Ethan and how he was faring knowing he was about to perform.

♪ *"Lover of the Light" – Mumford and Sons*
"For Me, It's You" – Train
"We'll Pick Up Where We Left Off" – OAR
"Learning to Love Again" – Mat Kearney

What Comes of Breaking Promises and Guitar Strings
Two

His shoes squeaked on the sealed cement floor of Crawford's apartment while he paced. They were set to leave in less than thirty minutes, and his mind was racing. They were opening for Train. At the Riverbend Music Center. In front of a lot of freaking people. It would be great exposure for them, and he and Brian had been working tirelessly at designing a banner and getting t-shirts and other promos ready to go for weeks. The radio station was taking care of their merch sales as part of the contest win, and the thought of having his music out there for that many new people in one night was making him antsy. In a good way.

"Ok man, I like you and all, but if you don't stop creating that sound, I am going to chuck your shoes out the window."

Ethan squeaked them loudly once more, but agreed to sit down afterward. "Sorry. Just ready." He knew that opening bands had the difficult task of warming up a crowd with songs they didn't really show up to hear; they were going to have to convince them to listen. The short set list had taken what seemed like ages to iron out, and they tried to showcase the range of what they could do. Southbound was on first, followed by The Fray- not his most favorite band, but he had respect for anyone touring and making money doing what they did. He had driven by the venue a few days before and took a fairly embarrassing amount of photos of the band's name on the marquee. Everyone started loading equipment, and he was relieved with having something to do.

When they arrived at the RMC, he was surprised with how structured and organized everything was. The venue manager had her shit together. They made it through sound check without issue, and Ethan was twirling one of his silver rings around his pointer finger while he listened to the rush of the pre-show around him. He checked his phone and lit up seeing his messages.

> C: I tried not to text you, but I wanted to say I'm excited for you guys. You'll be great, and we will see you later with these fancy backstage passes :).
> E: I'm glad you didn't try too hard ;). Knowing you'll be here makes the crowd seem smaller. Thanks for the vote of confidence- you can message me any time.
> C: I'll keep that in mind.

He was feeling like he could conquer the world right about then. There was another text from his mom saying that she and Tay would be in their seats soon, and that made him feel better as well; he didn't really care if that was lame. He checked his appearance last minute- gray-washed jeans and a tight black t-shirt, and maybe he had on more than his usual amount of jewelry. He liked his hair a bit longer, being that he could push it behind his ears when he inevitably had sweat dripping down his face.

"Fisher, we all know you're the fairest in the land, now can we go do what we came here to do?" Crawford teased him. His stomach dropped the way it did at the top of a roller coaster. He took a breath and nodded. Hearing their name announced made his heart pound in rhythm with some scattered applause throughout the arena. Most people were still milling around and securing their beers at this point in the show. *Here it goes then,* he thought, and wished for a moment that the spots weren't so bright and he'd be able to see Courtney or his mom in the audience. His mind cleared when the drums sounded behind him and he played the opening riff. The difference in the sound system of the RMC and their usual haunts was like comparing a Sentra to a Maserati because they were both street legal. The applause got louder after each song, and his energy was through the roof for their closing. They ended with a song he'd written with Courtney in mind, and he hoped she got that it was for her.

"Thank you all so much, we appreciate it more than we can say. Have a great night!" Crawford finished for the crowd, and they made their way back from where they'd come. All of Ethan's nerves seemed to crash once they were off stage, and his hands were shaking.

"That was amazing- the best we've ever sounded, like ever," Brian relayed to the group.

Ethan breathed slowly, coming to terms with the fact that he'd just played the set of his life, several songs of his own creation, for a real audience. "Hell yeah it was," his cockiness returning as he grabbed a bottle of water.

The venue manager walked by on a mission, her headset pressed to her ear behind her short blond hair, but she stopped to tell them congratulations. "Great set guys, honestly. You're free to hang out here for the rest of the show or the radio station has a suite, Number two twenty-seven, if you wanna head up there with your passes- totally up to you." She walked away, her heels clicking on the floor.

"Yeah, I'm going up to the suite- I'm pretty sure this is the life I was meant for," Brian joked. Chase and Jeremy went with him, but he and Crawford stayed behind. Being backstage with a tour like this one wasn't likely something he'd be able to repeat in the near future. They listened to The Fray and scarfed down some sandwiches.

"I think I should probably thank you," Ethan said to his friend.

"Why?" Crawford questioned.

"I never would have gotten here if you hadn't called that day. Like I'm one-hundred percent sure of that. I mean, I would have kept playing, but nothing of this magnitude. It was a pipe dream, playing on a stage like this."

"If we're handing out some honest gratitude? We wouldn't have gotten here either."

"Nah, you guys were great before me."

"We were good. Now we're better, so at least appreciate that. Your songs killed out there, enjoy it." Crawford got up to talk to some of the label guys who were wandering around- the guy never quit. Ethan elected to relax instead.

"So, I'm pretty sure I've been missing out my whole life by not having all-access passes to everything. The treatment is amazing- like, I want VIP access to the grocery store now. This whole experience has corrupted me, I hope you know." A grin spread across Ethan's face before he turned around, knowing Vanessa was behind the semi-compliment. She stood there looking entitled in four inch heels and painted on jeans, a royal blue top baring her midriff.

"Hi to you too, V. It's been a while." He stood up to greet her and held his arms out for a hug.

"Yeah, you're like *really* sweaty, so I'm going to just stay right here." He rolled his eyes, but started to lose his excitement when he looked around for Courtney. "Stop with the puppy dog face, she's here. She went to find water. You're so obvious," she declared, looking at him pointedly. "A word of advice though? Don't overstep tonight- she's in super-anxiety mode." He nodded his understanding as he saw her come around the corner, water in hand. Vanessa made herself scarce, and he sent her a silent wave of appreciation.

She looked...beautiful. She had ditched her usual jeans and a tank top ensemble for a cream colored strapless number and heels. Before she saw him, her hands worked at repositioning the beaded headband across her forehead, her eyes unsure. "Hey sprin... Courtney," he tried to recover awkwardly. He didn't know how she would feel about his former term of endearment. She covered a laugh at his expense.

"Hey there rock star. Do you want me to tell you how amazing you were out there?" she asked, fluffing her short curls. His nerves were already overworked from being on stage, but they rose to the occasion when he thought about kissing her exposed neck.

"Of course I do, have you met me?" he responded lightly.

She smiled. "Well you were. Honestly- you guys were incredible. Very different than the last time I saw you play. This... well, it suits you better."

"Agreed, I'm a lot happier... I get to play a lot of my own stuff, and the guys are amazing, I'll introduce you to Crawford in a minute, he's around here somewhere. The rest of the guys are up in the radio station suite. You'll like them though, really."

"Well look at you living the high life. I'm proud of you, you seem... steady." *If only you knew how long it took me to get here,* he thought, knowing she would not be as proud if she could have seen him six months earlier.

"Do you wanna hang out for a bit? Or we could go up to the suite..." He was trying so hard not to "overstep" as Vanessa had put it.

"Yeah, I'm down to hang out backstage at a Train concert, you know, no big deal," she grinned, showing her excitement. She practically skipped out of the lounge area so they could get an actual view of the stage. She was nervous, though she played it pretty cool. He caught glimpses of her glancing at him from under her lashes and biting her lip when she thought he wasn't looking. He wanted to fix it- the awkwardness of them not knowing how to act towards each other. They had never been just friends, not really, and he couldn't take the space between them. When Train took the stage and opened with one of her absolute favorite songs, he couldn't overthink his actions anymore.

Leaning over, he pressed his lips to her ear. "Dance with me," he told her, hoping she wasn't going to shut him down.

"Ethan..." she replied warily, looking up at him.

Ignoring her hesitation, he held out his hand. She took it slowly and he twirled her around before bringing her in closer. She laughed softly, and god how he had missed that sound. Her hair smelled the same, and when her fingers traveled up the back of his neck, he could have been right back at the river, falling in love with her the first time. She ran her nails along his shoulder blades lightly, and he tried to keep his hands at a respectable position on her back.

"Have I told you I like your hair this way?"

"Not today." He pushed a stray curl behind her ear that had escaped from the headband, and tipped her face up towards him. Resting his forehead on hers, he tried to think of good reasons not to kiss her. Vanessa's words rang in his head, and he knew he had already left the territory of just pretending to be friendly. The song ended before he made a decision one way or the other, and she let go without making eye contact. Groaning silently, he looked toward the sky, kicking himself internally for not just going for it when he had the chance. She had walked a few paces ahead and he moved to follow her.

"Are you coming?" she asked plainly, holding out her hand.

"Of course," he answered, taking it without hesitation and intertwining their fingers. She led him through a few smaller clumps of people until they came to stop at a metal partition just off the side of the stage. He couldn't deny that it was a great view. She didn't drop the connection once they made it to their destination, and he squeezed slightly. She squeezed back. Two songs later when he moved over to let someone slide by them, she didn't try to stop him from wrapping his arms around her waist from behind. Instead, she ran her fingers across his forearm and pulled him around her tighter. He let his lips brush her neck, and was satisfied when she shivered. *Never underestimate the nostalgia-inducing power of a great song,* he thought, admitting to himself that one of her favorite bands playing live in front of them was probably contributing to her openness at the moment.

Courtney's phone vibrated in her purse and she pulled it out. She held it up for him to see that it was from Vanessa.

V: I'm tired of flirting, come find me.

He took it that she and Luke were in a separation period- it wasn't the first time- and followed Courtney back towards the main backstage area. She stopped abruptly before they walked through the gate and were still largely alone.

"Ok, so I didn't... I don't know what I thought, coming here tonight. You didn't lie... you're different, but it feels the same too. It's kind of messing with my head, and I don't know what you're thinking-"

Before he really thought it through, his hands were in her hair and his lips pressed against hers. Her fingers found their way hastily to his belt loops and she closed the gap still between them. He didn't pull back this time, like he had always done before; he kissed her with the magnitude of a year's worth of mistakes and wishing things were different until she stepped back for air, her hands on his chest.

"I'm sorry," he got out, catching his breath as well. Words began to rush out of his mouth now that it was no longer occupied. "I don't want to mess with your head. You just said you didn't know what I was thinking, and that's what I was thinking... all night. I didn't mean to push." He couldn't stop the stream of jumbled up thoughts finding their way into words. "Can I apologize? For everything? I will make you a list of every stupid thing I did last year if you want, just let me make it up to you. You're-"

"Shhhh." She finally stopped him.

"Ok?"

"Just, let's leave tonight alone. You opened for *Train*, we danced backstage, and that kiss was... well, I think it answered my question," she acknowledged. "Let's just go hang out with V. We will talk. I promise. Just not right now, ok?"

"Ok, yeah, of course. Whatever you want." He brushed her lips with his once more and grabbed her hand to walk through the gates. They found Vanessa chatting it up with Crawford on a sofa in the lounge. It did not escape his notice that Courtney dropped his hand when they crossed into their eye line.

"And where have you two been?" Vanessa asked knowingly as Courtney wiggled in next to her on the couch.

"Watching the band, obviously," Courtney replied evenly. Crawford walked up behind him and clapped him on the shoulder. "You didn't tell me you invited such enchanting ladies to the show tonight, Fisher. I had to come across this one all by myself when I overhead her talking about our band."

"Seriously Ethan, your manners need work. You could have introduced us," Vanessa replied. Crawford handed Vanessa a beer and sat down across from her. He tried to control the surprised look on his face; never in a million years would he have thought the two of them would hit it off.

"I am so sorry, I have been remiss. Courtney, this is Crawford, Crawford, Courtney... clearly you already know Vanessa."

"Nice to meet you, you guys were seriously amazing tonight, congratulations on the contest and this and everything," Courtney relayed sincerely, shaking his friend's hand.

"Nice to meet you too, and thank you- it wouldn't have happened without this guy," he replied, gesturing to Ethan. "So are you guys coming out with us then?"

"Out..." Vanessa questioned.

"There's a party at this hotel, the radio station is running it. Not sure if those guys will be there," referencing the headliners, "but it should be a pretty good time."

"Um, yes," Vanessa replied without hesitating. Courtney cleared her throat.

"Hey there V. Can I talk to you for just a sec?" Vanessa rolled her eyes slightly and let Courtney pull her around the corner. He couldn't help it. He had to try to overhear them. Shooting Crawford a look, he casually made his way closer to where they stood.

"...you know I've been missing Luke, I just wanna go out and blow off some steam. You don't have to come if you don't want, I'm sure I can ride with this hottie out here."

"Ugh. I am not doing a very good job of keeping my distance. You know he gets to me, I just don't think that going out and drinking, at a hotel no less, is the smartest thing I could do," Courtney admitted.

"So then don't be smart. You're always smart. I knew as soon as you were alone with him you'd turn into a pile of mush. Just have *fun*.

You're in college and we're getting invited to a rad party and literally one of your favorite bands of all time could show up at said fiesta. Come on." Courtney took a breath, and he thought she was going to give in.

"Will you hate me if I just go home? Like you can go, and I'll even come back and pick you up if you need a ride at four a.m., I just don't think I can do it." Vanessa gave an exasperated sigh.

"All right girl, whatever makes you happy." Ethan quickly made his way back over to the couch and waited expectantly. The gears were already turning in his mind.

The girls walked back up, and before they could say anything, he interjected. "Hey, I think I'm gonna get a cab home or something, I don't know if I'm in the mood for a crowd tonight, but there'll be room in Crawford's car if you guys wanna go with him. You should, I'm sure it'll be a killer event." He tried to give off the most innocent vibe possible in that moment, and counted on Vanessa to carry his plan to fruition.

"Works for me, I'm gonna take you up on the ride if that's okay with you, Crawford. Courtney's not gonna come because she's allergic to fun," Vanessa admonished, "but she should be able to give you a ride home then," she concluded with a devilish look. Courtney's eyes widened and she shot daggers at her best friend. Vanessa promptly ignored her and slid into the seat next to Crawford, leaning into him flirtatiously.

"Yeah, absolutely. Are you sure, Fisher?" Crawford replied, putting his arm around Vanessa in response.

"Yeah, I'm sure. You guys have fun though." He took a few steps toward a back room where their gear was stashed, and he felt Courtney's eyes on him. "Come with me, you can carry my guitar," he joked.

"There will be no carrying of anything in these shoes," she shot back at him, her face still holding a pissed off look from the unspoken argument with Vanessa.

"Fine, I'll carry it, you keep me company." He knew he was pushing her, but he didn't care. She hesitated, but finally followed behind him.

"You don't have to drive me home. I'm fine taking a cab, honestly," he lied. He wanted more than anything to be alone with her. It was the only way he could picture ending this night.

"Stop, it's fine. I never pass up a chance to drive through Gem anyway. How come you didn't wanna go to the party?" she asked. *Because you didn't wanna go,* he thought.

"I don't know. This whole thing was kind of surreal, so I'm sort of in the mood to appreciate it where it's quiet. I'd also like to keep myself out of whatever's going on between V and Luke, so witnessing her make out with my band mate is not on my to-do list." He grabbed his guitar and made a mental note to apologize to his friends later for not helping load the rest of their stuff. They headed down the corridor towards the parking lot.

"Don't even get me started. You know they'll be back together by next weekend. I think she just wants to prove she can be on her own."

"It's happened before, and history would suggest that you're spot on with that prediction." He held the door open and slid his hand into hers as she walked by. She shot him a sideways glance but did nothing. It took some time, not that he was complaining, but she finally found her little silver Mustang in the still-crowded parking lot. There were a couple of people who recognized him thanks to the telltale sign that he was carrying his instrument, and complimented their performance. He even signed an autograph on one of the 7-11 Southbound t-shirts that had been for sale that night.

"So, how much are you loving all of the girly attention, then?" Courtney asked, amused.

He grinned at her, hoping it was a hint of jealousy he heard in her voice. "It's not terrible, but to tell the truth? I'd really prefer the attention from just one girl," he said carefully, nudging her with his elbow not subtly at all. He placed his guitar in the trunk.

Her eyes rolled, but he had made her smile. "You think you're so smooth." When she turned on the car, his band's music came through the speakers. She quickly reached to turn it down.

"So you listened to the CD then?" he smirked.

"Don't do that."

"Do what?"

"You know what. Don't look like that."

"I literally don't know what you're talking about, but I will try to stop looking however I was looking." He wasn't being entirely truthful. She had mentioned more than once when they were together what it did to her when he carried that expression. He wanted to pretend he didn't know why she was fighting so hard when the pull between them was overwhelming, but he knew exactly why. He felt a familiar sting in his chest when he thought about hurting her.

"Sure you don't," she called him out. Soon an old playlist was resounding through the car, and they were cruising up the highway with the windows down. They fell into the old habit of singing along with one another, and that performance felt just as important as winning the battle of the bands. *You cannot screw this up.*

She pulled up in front of his house, and he was ready to convince her why coming in was the best possible idea. "I can't tell you what it meant for you to be there tonight. I, well… I know you said we would talk another time, but really, when have I ever listened to your timelines? So, will you come in? We can sit on the deck and drink decaf. I get your hesitation, I-"

"Yes, I'll come in. I was going to ask to anyway, but good job selling it," she smiled. He breathed. Originally, he had hoped they'd be alone at her house, because he wanted her out of that dress in the worst way, but being at home with his mom and sister sleeping upstairs was much safer. Memories of the last time she had stood in his kitchen were hard to ignore, but he washed them away with all of the words he'd practiced saying in in head a million times. A pot of coffee brewed while she sat on the porch, and he grabbed her a sweatshirt from his closet.

"Here, it's chilly," he told her, handing it over.

"Oh, thanks, yeah it's so crazy that this is summer. In Phoenix I'd still be sweating in 100 degree heat at night."

"Yeah, but then there's the 70 degree Christmases to enjoy," he smiled.

"True, I can't argue there." There was an expectant pause on both sides as he struggled with exactly what to say.

"Yeah, so...I don't really know how to start, but I'm so sorry for how things ended between us. I don't have any excuses for you, that's not why I wanted you to hear me out- I should have done a lot of things differently. I should have told you how I was feeling along the way instead of always acting like I was fine. It was stupid of me to think things were going to be easy, but I let it get to a point where I couldn't take it anymore, the distance."

"Ethan, I was heartbroken, when we broke up, but I didn't begrudge you that decision. It *was* hard. Like so hard. Just..."

"I know. The phone call. I can't. I don't have words. I was, I don't know, in a downward spiral of poor decisions, and I thought if you would just take me back everything would be fine, and that wasn't fair either. I am so sorry." His voice broke in delivering the last apology. Having her sitting in front of him and seeing the residual hurt in her eyes as she recalled that night was almost too much, but he knew it's what had to happen. "Can you at least believe that me calling you that night had everything to do with my own bullshit and nothing to do with wanting to cause you pain?"

She took a moment and he held his breath. "I can believe that, yeah. I didn't know how much I needed you to say it until right now. I sort of thought I had just put it behind me or risen above it or something, but being with you tonight? Put me right back into last year, and well, I needed it, I guess is the shortest explanation I can give."

He wanted to hold her, but knew she had to be the one to initiate it, and he got the feeling she wasn't quite finished yet. "Can we just be real for a minute?"

"As many minutes as you want, yeah, of course." He was afraid what she'd say next, and that she'd start channeling Vanessa and yelling.

"Tonight felt good," she admitted, surprising him.

"Yeah, it did."

"And Vanessa was being a bitch because she's mad about Luke, but she said a couple of things that hit home for me, and I feel like we just need to get it all out on the table before I go home, or I won't be able to sleep tonight."

"Well? Lay it out there then." She hesitated, but pressed on.

"I just got out of a relationship. It was a good relationship, and leaving Phoenix to come here was… difficult." His stomach tightened at listening to her talk about Ben. "But in the interest of full disclosure, I don't think it was as hard as leaving you after homecoming." He nodded in acknowledgement, not wanting to interrupt her. "Seeing you, and well, kissing you felt… right, like it's how it was supposed to be all along, but in a lot of ways that seems like cheating." He sat back slightly, wondering what she meant. "Not like cheating on him, I mean, I'm single, don't like take that the wrong way. It feels like cheating in a universal sense. Like it shouldn't be this easy to fall back into what we had. It can't be that easy, because if it is, then it seems like my relationship for the past seven months was a placeholder, and I need you to know that it wasn't. I'm not saying that to try to hurt you or to emphasize that I was with someone else, I just need to be clear, I guess, before we… I don't know what we're going to do. There have to be some rules or something."

He had forgotten how much she talked. "I knew that you were with someone else. Vanessa and I sort of had a, well, I wouldn't call it a confrontation because she's the only one who did the confronting, but the point is that I knew. I don't expect-"

"She yelled at you?"

"Yeah, but I had it coming. Really, it's fine."

"No, I just sort of wish I could have seen it, that's all. Sorry, you were saying?"

He gave her a half-smile and laughed slightly at the memory. "I, uh, yeah. I was saying that I don't expect to like… pick up where we left off like nothing happened. I know that I missed the last seven months of your life, and I know that I'm very different now than I was then. Better, I hope, but different. Still, I can't lie and tell you I don't want to do this. I want you. You know that I do."

"And we can agree that there should be... rules? On how exactly to do this?"

"Yes, anything," though he sincerely wondered what possible "ground rules" she had in mind. In the grand scheme of things, it just didn't matter. She stood up and stepped towards the chair where he sat.

"Then I guess we can discuss those tomorrow," she smiled and climbed onto his lap. Her eyes searched his and her expression betrayed her seemingly cool exterior. This moment, with the stars barely visible overhead in the cloudy night sky, it was important. With that her lips pressed into his tentatively, and he reacquainted himself with the way his hands felt on her skin. Heat spread across his chest when her fingertips found their way there. He had never been more thankful for the invention of sundresses in all his life; her legs were so much better in person than in memory. He didn't ask for anything more, and let her show him what she needed. They continued their reunion tour for almost an hour. He finally stopped distracting her when she said she had to leave for the 47th time and his lips were near swollen from their intensity. Dizzily, he walked her out to her car.

"When can I see you again?" he asked. He was not ashamed of his eagerness.

"When do you wanna see me again?" she responded coyly.

"Right now," he assured her and kissed her playfully. She laughed against his lips and stepped back.

"I don't have anything going on tomorrow unless I have to go pick up Vanessa somewhere."

"Nah, Crawford will make sure she gets home, he's a good guy. Can I take you somewhere? Like somewhere good. I canceled all of my lessons and got someone to cover my shift at the pool because I wasn't sure how late I'd be out tonight. Let's go to King's Island and ride roller coasters and eat funnel cake."

Her eyes lit up and she agreed even before he'd said "funnel cake." He kissed her again, his hands unable to stay out of her hair, and let her drive away. *You are the luckiest idiot ever,* he thought, not believing the good fortune that had finally shown up that night. He ran this thumb over his bottom lip and appreciated the fact that he thought he'd never get to feel that way again.

Acknowledgements

The writing of this novel has been one of the greatest experiences of my life. I love this story and these characters, and they make me wish I were 17 again (and also sort of glad I'm not). There are so many people who made publishing this book this possible:

My amazing husband and son for sharing me with my MacBook every night and never complaining. My incredibly talented sister, Taylor, for having a vision of the images for this book, and for calling me out on every plot hole in the original version. Some of my oldest friends, Micah, Zac, and Melissa, for answering emails and phone calls when we hadn't really spoken in 10 years, and on top of that actually agreeing to help me without hesitation. One of my newest friends, Jessica, who jumped at the chance to sit down and talk playlists and marketing over coffee. My fearless test readers, Tamara and Gisele, who overlooked the roughness of the draft and came to love the characters anyway. This book would not be finished without all of you. Last, but not least, all of my friends and family for never once questioning my sanity, but only offering words of encouragement and support. I am lucky to be surrounded by such individuals.

Thank you, and I hope you enjoy the final product knowing that it could not have been accomplished without you.

Visit NicoleCampbellBooks.com for updates.

About the Author

Writing a book was sort of one of those things that I thought about and never actually intended on doing. I spoke to a seventh grader in my English class about the idea for the book one day while I was teaching a creative writing unit, and she *insisted* that I at least write it as a short story. I took that as a challenge more than anything, and I sat down that afternoon and outlined the plot in some random spiral notebook. Exactly four weeks later I had completed the draft. It became a complete obsession for me, I couldn't stop. At this point I have a hard time remembering what life was like before I started writing, and I am so thankful for that initial conversation with one of my (now favorite) students. *Gravity* is the end of Courtney and Ethan's story, but I will publish one more book in the Gem City collection from Vanessa's point of view (it will be a prequel released sometime next spring), and I'm maybe embarrassingly excited to be in her head for that long, AND to get to write more of Luke. He's the best. All in all, I can't imagine *not* writing, and I am eager to get into my next series as well to move a little bit away from just straight Contemporary/Romance. I love chatting with readers, so please comment on my blog or social media, I will totally respond!

  Facebook: https://www.facebook.com/NicoleCampbellBooks/
  Instagram: @NicoleCampbellBooks
  Website: NicoleCampbellBooks.com

Printed in Poland
by Amazon Fulfillment
Poland Sp. z o.o., Wrocław